W9-CHO-659

SPELLSPAM

Also by Alma Alexander
Worldweavers: Gift of the Unmage

WORLDWEAVERS

SPELLSPAM

◆ BOOK 2 ◆

ALMA ALEXANDER

An Imprint of HarperCollins*Publishers*

Eos is an imprint of HarperCollins Publishers.

LIBRARY OF CONGRESS
CATALOGING-IN-PUBLICATION DATA
Alexander, Alma.
    Spellspam / Alma Alexander. —1st ed.
        p.   cm.—(Worldweavers ; bk. 2)
    Summary: Thea and her friends try to stop an outbreak of
a new brand of magic that is attacking students at Wandless
Academy, a school supposedly shielded from spells, that
works through computers, which should be impervious to
magic.
    ISBN 978-0-06-083958-1 (trade bdg.)—ISBN 978-0-06-
083959-8 (lib. bdg.)
    [1. Magic—Fiction. 2. Email—Fiction. 3. Computers
Fiction. 4. Schools—Fiction. 5. Fantasy.] I. Title.
PZ7.A3762Spe 2008   2007008618
[Fic]—dc22   CIP
                                                   AC

Typography by Dave Caplan
1 2 3 4 5 6 7 8 9 10

First Edition

The second book for Sonja, the second sister

1.

T HE FIRST HINT of serious trouble came, as trouble always does, unlooked for, stealthily, catching everyone by surprise. It was the day that LaTasha Jackson suddenly turned into an Anatomy teacher's aid.

Things came to a head during a free-study hour in the comfortable, plush silence of the school library, each student to his or her own cubicle, some finishing homework, others reading. Still others sat furtively hunched over their desks, loose hair covering contraband earphones, trying to hide a music-player-shaped bulge in their pocket. One or two, bored, drew cartoons or wrote snatches of deathless prose that they imagined would turn into a novel someday. The incorrigible chatterboxes whispered and giggled softly to one another from adjoining cubicles. But, on the whole, everything was quiet, and Thea liked it that way. She wasn't doing anything particularly scholastic, but that wasn't because she was goofing off—she usually managed to have most of her work done in reasonable time, and hardly ever needed to resort to trying to write an essay five minutes before it was due. What she used her free study periods for was simply reading. She would meander down the library stacks at the beginning of the hour, pulling out a book here and there to check it out as a title caught her eye, and finally settle on something that interested her.

She was engrossed in a book about the social customs of chimpanzees when a bloodcurdling scream rent the air from the north corner of the library, where the computers slated for student use were situated. Thea jumped, dropping her book on the desk with a thump and losing her place, pushing her chair back on its castors to peer around the edges of her cubicle.

Dozens of other heads were popping out from other cubicles, watching in appalled horror as something ghastly leaped back from a computer screen, overturning a chair and sending it flying, and raced down the length of the library and out through the double doors at the far end.

The only reason Thea even remotely recognized this apparition was LaTasha's trademark hairstyle, dozens of tiny braids finished off with trade beads in garish shades of pink and mustard yellow. The face beneath those braids, however, was something else indeed.

She looks like she's been skinned! was the first thought that came swimming into Thea's astonished mind. And then she shuddered as she realized that this was precisely what LaTasha was. *Skinned.* Or at least looking like a reasonably good imitation of it. *But there was no blood*, Thea thought, frowning. *Surely there should have been . . . but no . . . there was just . . .*

That was it, in a nutshell. Instead of LaTasha's skin, which typically was the color of coffee lightened with a touch of cream, her face was a complicated mass of red muscle, striated bands coming down from her temples to wrap around her mouth, neat folds across her nose and cupping her chin, round orbs around her alarmingly protruding eyeballs, with startling and somewhat unnerving glimpses of stark bone structure underneath it all. Her hands, held out in front of her, looked the same way—a naked, tangled mass of tendon and sinew. But no blood. It was like her skin had just gone see-through, somehow, revealing the building blocks of the body that lay beneath.

There was a swelling of noise in the library as students surged out of their chairs, clustered in tight little knots, the librarian on duty frantically whispering something into a telephone, her hand cupped protectively around the mouthpiece.

For some reason it was only Thea who backed away from the pandemonium and edged almost furtively toward the computer LaTasha had been using.

An e-mail was open on the screen, an e-mail that LaTasha should have known better than to open— anything addressed to person@thisaddress.com should have been immediately suspect, at the very least as an advertisement, unwanted junk mail, spam. But what followed was not merely spam:

Having trouble keeping your skin blemish-free?
Troubled by zits, lines, old scars? Try our incredible

product for 30 days for FREE! We guarantee that we will leave your skin clearer than you could ever have dreamed of. . . .

LaTasha was fourteen years old, and painfully self-conscious of the imperfections of her skin, which was cursed with large pores and periodic zit infestations that made her look like she was coming down with the measles—and that was in addition to an unfortunate scar left behind by her brush with the real measles, which she had had as a toddler. It sat, a small but (to LaTasha) eye-wateringly obvious pit, underneath and to the outside of her left eye.

"It makes my eye droop," she had often complained to friends. "Look, it makes me look like a Saint Bernard puppy, all mournful and woebegone. Who'd want to date *that*? They probably all think I'm going to bore them silly with family tragedies. Like I'd had a twin who was stolen by the Faele or something and never came home. Oh, it's hopeless!"

Perfect skin. The thing had offered perfect skin. That would have been irresistible to someone like LaTasha, who blamed hers for all the injustices in her life—if she could only get perfect skin, she'd be happy, she knew she'd be happy.

Something surfaced briefly in Thea's mind, and then submerged again before she'd had a chance to grab at it. Instead, she sighed and reached out instinctively to clear the screen, as though that e-mail could be used as some sort of evidence against poor LaTasha. Her hand hovered above the red X that would close the e-mail screen; then she hesitated.

The word was *clear*. Not *perfect*.

"Clearer than you could ever have dreamed of," Thea whispered as she hastily clicked on the red X. "Oh, my fur and whiskers . . ."

Clear.

Transparent.

"But that is a spell," Thea muttered to herself, frowning.

She lifted her head to look back across the library, where a couple of staff members were restoring order to the chaos of milling students. The librarian herself, still cradling the telephone receiver, was staring straight back at Thea and at the now-blank computer on the desk beside her. With a sinking feeling that she was still unable to properly articulate, Thea bent her head to hide the sudden color in her cheeks and inched away from the computer desk toward the sanctuary of the stacks.

Everyone knew, of course, that computers were impervious to magic. Computers were where magic was *stored*, because it could do no harm there, and besides, this was the Wandless Academy, which was both magicless and shielded. There could not have been a spell that broke those two defenses—there could not have possibly been such a spell. And yet, Thea had seen the evidence streak out of the library before her very eyes. And *other* people's eyes. And obviously LaTasha herself had been affected. Thea paused for a moment to consider how *she* would have reacted if she had happened to glance at her hands on the computer keyboard and had seen something that looked more like it belonged on a butcher's block or an anatomy dissection board than the familiar limbs she was used to.

It had to have been a very effective illusion spell . . . and it had been transmitted by computer.

Which, of course, was impossible.

Computers couldn't do magic.

They had talked about this a lot, Thea and her friends, since they had returned to the Academy for the new semester. Terry, the computer genius, had naturally asked questions that were practical and to the point.

"Are you saying we can all do this tripping-between-the-worlds thing?" he had asked Thea one day in September, tapping his fingers on a desk. "By ourselves? That first time, we all seemed to be involved. . . ."

"Well, you all came after me into the Whale Hunt, when we were after the Nothing, and I wasn't there to start it," Thea said.

"Yeah, but that time I found the thing on the computer screen and just hit ENTER again, so it *was* you who started it; we just followed."

"Do you think *anyone* could have followed?" Magpie said, sounding frightened. "I would hate for people who don't care or understand to be able to blunder around in a world like that—it was the sea of my own ancestors. . . ."

"We could try it again," Tess began.

"They locked up the computer room," Ben said, shaking his head.

"We have my laptop," Terry said.

"And anyway, we would just get into real trouble," said Ben, scowling at the interruption.

"Besides, they made Thea promise . . ."

"Yeah," Thea said morosely, "they made me promise."

"That can't last," Terry said. "*They* want to know, they'll come and rope you back in—maybe all of us, for all I know—before too long. This whole thing is too big for just a handful of people. Sooner or later it'll come to the attention of the politicians. And then it's anybody's game."

"You think the Federal Bureau of Magic will get involved?" Ben asked.

"Principal Harris said something about shifting the balance of trade," Thea muttered. "If the Alphiri get wind of this . . ."

"I've always thought," Magpie said, turning to stare at her roommate, "that you were a bit obsessed with the Alphiri."

"Oh, yeah?" Thea said, rounding on Magpie with some asperity. "I'm telling you, they're everywhere. Every time I turn around outside the school, I see them—they're all over the place—in the banks, in the coffee shops, in the streets. They're just waiting for something to happen, to confirm whatever it is that they think they already know, and the moment they think they've done that . . ."

"You really think they're going to *snatch* you?" Magpie asked, chastened.

"I have no idea what they're going to do," Thea muttered. "But I'm afraid of them."

"The Alphiri have *always* been everywhere," Terry said. "Ever since they turned up. But all that aside, Thea's right. If any of this comes to threaten our relationship with the Alphiri or any of the other polities, you bet the Feds will come in. And if they can't use you, Thea, they will probably—"

"*Terry*," Tess said sharply, "you are starting to sound awfully like Dad at his most pompously pessimistic."

"Caught between the government and the Alphiri," Thea muttered. "Terrific."

Terry shrugged. "Someday I'd like another stab at it," he said, "see if I can't figure out what's going on. But until then—just do what they want, and lie low, and stay out of people's way."

"Double Seventh at last?" Ben said, with a curious little smile. "Coming into your own?"

Thea tossed her head. "Sometimes," she said trenchantly, "I wish I'd never figured out how to do any of this. I wonder if I shouldn't have just shut up about everything and been content to keep Frankie company."

"Hiding a light under a barrel doesn't put it out," Magpie said.

"You are starting to sound like Cheveyo," Thea said, with a wry grin.

"It's big," Tess said, "and yeah, it's unusual, but there's all kinds of weird and unusual talents amongst those of our kind—this thing you can do might turn out to be no more than an aberration, after all. An accident of magic. We all know that computers are inert; all that you might have done, when they get around to finding out what's behind it all, is discover how to use one to focus what's already inside *you*. The fact that you were anywhere near a computer might have been a complete accident. . . ."

"Still," Terry said doggedly, "watch yourself."

"Computers *can't*!" Tess said. "We all *know* that!"

That was the foundation of it all, of course—the truth that their world was built upon. Computers were impervious to magic and safe from it. It was what all five of them had still believed, despite evidence to the contrary, until that day in the library when a spell transferred by computer had turned LaTasha transparent.

* * *

On the day of LaTasha's transformation, none of the others had been in the library. When Thea rounded up her friends less than an hour later and told them what she had observed, it was hard for everyone to accept the obvious.

"It *must* have been something else, something you missed," Tess insisted.

"Tess, she ran out of there screaming, looking *skinned*. I saw it, the librarian saw it, a whole bunch of other kids saw it, and we all saw *the same thing*. The only person they know of who can do anything with magic on a computer is me—and they will know I was in the library at the time."

Terry gave her a startled look. "You think they'll blame you?"

"But you weren't *at* a computer," Tess said.

Thea looked up. "Oh, yeah, I was," she said, a little desperately. "I should have known better than to meddle, but she ran from the computer . . . and I . . . wanted to see . . . I turned off the computer. I have no idea why I did it, but I did it, and the librarian saw me."

"She couldn't possibly have known what you were doing, or even that you hadn't been there all the time," said Ben.

Thea threw him a grateful but exasperated glance. "That just makes it *worse*," she said. "The librarian might not have known anything, but she will tell them that she remembers seeing me at that computer. And then everyone else will jump to their own obvious conclusions. It's all tied in." She looked at all of them with pleading eyes. "I need to talk to my parents. . . . I need your help. . . ."

"Thea," Terry said, understanding immediately. "*No.*"

"What?" Ben said, bewildered.

"She wants to go back, go home . . . go back *that* way. Thea, you promised them you wouldn't."

"That was before any of this happened. Whatever happened to LaTasha . . . it's going to get out. I want to talk to my father in person. . . . I need a safe place. . . ."

"The computer lab?" Tess said pragmatically, leaving out the ethics of technically breaking and entering, never mind broken promises.

"Do you think Twitterpat knew something?" Terry said sharply, looking up. "That there's a trace of an answer in there somewhere? Is his own computer still there?"

"Probably not," Tess said. "They probably took it when he . . . after he was gone."

"They might not have," Magpie said. "They locked up the whole place—they may not have bothered taking the computer out."

"But it's locked by a security keypad, and we don't have the code, not anymore," said Ben.

"We can open a window," said Magpie brightly.

"Not necessary. Keypads are easy to crack," said Terry.

"Besides, even if Twitterpat's machine is still there, it's probably password-protected—and they probably made sure that the rest of the computers aren't . . . ," began Ben, who obviously thought the whole thing was a really bad idea.

"You can always use my laptop," said Terry. "But now that you mention it . . . I think I'd still like to take a look at the network in the computer lab. They took the library computers off, but the computer lab ones might still be okay. And I can be there to watch your back."

"No," Thea said, "you're coming with me to my parents'. If I just pop in babbling about this, they won't take me seriously. Tess and Ben and Magpie will have to stand guard in the lab."

14

"Tonight?"

"Now," Thea said. "I may not have until tonight. They'll figure this one out fast, if they haven't already."

Terry was already on his feet. "We'll need the laptop to get inside," he said over his shoulder. "I'll get it. Meet you outside the lab."

Computer classes had been suspended since Twitterpat's death, and the computer lab had been declared out of bounds, but it had not occurred to the school authorities that anyone would go so far as to circumvent that ban. The lab was deliberately isolated; no other regular classes were scheduled in that corridor, but it was not guarded, other than by the keypad lock. Terry detailed Ben and Magpie to stand guard at either end of the corridor outside the computer lab and, his laptop open on his knee, calmly hacked the code for the lock. Ben's head snapped around at the sound of the door opening, and then he abandoned his post, trotting back to Terry's side, shaking his head.

"Remind me not to make you mad at me," he muttered at Terry as he slipped past into the dark and silent computer room.

Terry merely smiled and cast a last look up and

down the corridor before clicking the door shut behind him.

"That was easy enough," he said to the others, "but it may well have triggered an alarm somewhere. We may not have all *that* much time. Thea, is the laptop all right, or would you rather fire up one of the desktops?"

"I'd rather not leave anything on those machines," Thea said.

Terry pushed the laptop over to her. "Go for it."

"Tess," Terry said as Thea began typing furiously at the laptop's keyboard, "stay on the door. If you hear anything . . . yank us back. Fast."

"How?" Tess said, staring at the computers. "Don't look at me like that, the last time I was in there with you . . ."

"Just hit ESCAPE," Thea said without taking her eyes off the screen.

"And hit DELETE the moment you see us return," Terry added. "I'll deal with erasing the whole thing properly later, but I don't want it on screen if anyone blunders in here."

"Okay," said Ben, straddling a chair beside Thea's, leaning his crossed arms across the back of the chair and resting his chin on them. He had not been happy with this whole idea, but he was someone who could be trusted to deal with any emergency.

Thea paused for a moment, looking over the few terse sentences she had typed in. She had not bothered to make her passage grammatical or even coherent—just fragments of sentences, glimpses of details, woven into one perfect image of home. Not just the reddish cedar wood of her father's bookshelves and the usual desk accessory of Paul's favorite mug half full of cold and forgotten coffee, but also the soft, worn, chocolate-brown leather of the two small armchairs on the patterned burgundy rug, the musty smell of books, a faint cinnamon smell of concentration, and the lemon-zest whiff given off by active electronics, the familiar softness of the upholstered computer chair. Thea had put her aunt Zoë in that chair first, and then smartly backspaced until she erased her aunt's name, putting in her father's instead, then erased that and put Zoë back in. She wasn't *certain*—she wanted her father, but she wanted the buffer of her aunt's presence, too—but she did not have the luxury of spending too much time on this. She hesitated and then reached a hand out behind her, without turning around.

"Terry."

"Ready," Terry said instantly, slipping his hand over hers.

Their fingers touched, and the computer lab winked out.

2.

TERRY BLINKED, HIS fingers curled around Thea's hand, staring at his new surroundings. Paul's study was perfectly rendered, but it was empty.

"Damn," Thea muttered.

"Is something wrong?" Terry said.

"Yeah. No . . . just wait a moment. Damn, I knew I should have made up my mind before I . . ."

The study door began to open even as Thea spoke. Aunt Zoë stuck her head into the room, glancing around, and then froze as she noticed Thea and Terry in the middle of the room. She threw a quick, careful glance behind her and stepped into the room, closing the door behind her.

"*Thea?*" Zoë asked incredulously.

"Is Dad here?" Thea asked.

Zoë nodded her chin toward the closed door. "I just called him. What are you doing here?"

"I don't know what's going on, but something is happening and I'm not sure what to do. All I know is that it wasn't me, but they'll never . . ."

"Thea," Zoë said, "you're babbling. What's the matter?"

"Spellspam," Thea said.

"What?"

"Spellspam," Thea enunciated. "Tell Daddy to check his e-mail. And tell him to be careful. . . ."

The door opened again, admitting Paul Winthrop into his sanctum. "It's a fine thing," he was muttering, "when you're summoned to your own study by . . . Thea . . . ? What are you doing here? Who's your friend?"

"Sorry, Paul," Zoë said, glancing at him. "It just felt . . . strange in here. I thought something smelled dangerous."

"I'm Terry Dane, sir," Terry said. "I think we're in trouble. We can't stay long, but something happened. . . . Thea will explain."

Paul and Zoë listened without interruption to Thea's account of the events in the library, but when she had finished, Paul shook his head.

"Can't be done," he said. "It *can't be done*. Let me see. . . ."

He crossed the room and slipped into his computer chair, tapping on his keyboard. Even as he began typing, Zoë suddenly subsided into one of the armchairs.

"Oh, boy," she said softly.

Paul turned his head marginally, his hands hovering above the keyboard. "What, Zoë?"

"I thought it was just some sort of bizarre coincidence, but now . . ."

"*What*, Zoë?" Paul said, swiveling in his chair to stare at his sister-in-law, who had gone very white.

"There was an e-mail," Zoë said, "that I got a couple of weeks ago—and deleted, because it was spam. It offered me 'a free gift,' just for looking at the message. Well, I thought I had deleted it, without looking at the message, but obviously they meant it literally. And I just got this weird thing . . ."

"What?"

"Well . . . a gift subscription. To a Chinese magazine. In Mandarin. I got my first two issues yesterday. I thought someone was playing a prank on me. I never connected it to the e-mail, not until now. But what if . . ."

There was an awful silence. "I'll look into it," Paul said, his voice very low. His hands had dropped from the keyboard and were gripping the arms of his computer chair, hard. "Even so—it shouldn't have touched the Academy—"

"The students can access webmail on the school network," Zoë said. "That's an open forum, it's not like a dedicated e-mail program—webmail is nearly impossible to set up filters for, impossible to regulate—anything that pops into your inbox just sits there, ready to make mischief. And it looks as if that might be more than enough. The Academy might have done better to have allowed e-mail contact with the students' own accounts and software, if they allowed it at all. This way, there's no control over any of it."

"This would probably be the worst possible moment for Patrick Wittering not to be in charge," Paul muttered.

"What should I . . . ," Thea began, and then flinched, startled, looking behind her.

"Yes," Terry said, "I felt it. There must be someone coming. We have to go."

"Thea, be careful," Paul began, even as his daughter winked out of his study and thin air closed behind her. "Tell Principal Harris that I will send help—"

22

His voice broke off, as though a door had been slammed on him.

"What is it?" demanded Terry, turning to his laptop as he and Thea found themselves back in the computer lab.

"Sorry," Tess said. "I thought there was someone coming. I told Ben to call you back."

Ben was pushing back from the computer even as she spoke, looking sheepish. "Sorry," he said. "You said to hit DELETE."

"Okay. It's okay. Let me just get rid of this. . . ."

"It was weird to watch it from the outside," Magpie said. "You were kind of . . . there, but see-through."

"Transparent." Tess giggled, suddenly light-headed. "Like LaTasha's skin."

"That's not funny," Thea said, the only one of them who had actually seen the results of that particular spellspam. "I wonder how she's doing—I should have gone to see her."

"You were so intent on doing *this*," Magpie said. "Are you sure she's even in sickbay?"

"They can't exactly let her run around like that, not looking like . . ."

"Terry," Tess said softly, ignoring the other girls.

"That's done. They won't find a trace of it on the hard drive," Terry said, looking up from the laptop. "What, Tess?"

"Look. The office."

The room that had been Patrick Wittering's office led off the computer lab, and its door had been left ajar. Thea glimpsed a desk, now clear of Twitterpat's usual untidy mound of paperwork . . . but still bearing a computer monitor.

Terry and Tess exchanged a swift glance.

"Might not mean the computer is still there," Terry murmured.

"Why would they take the computer and leave the monitor behind?"

"You think it's worth it?"

"What on earth are you hoping to find?" Ben demanded.

"Answers, maybe," Terry said. But still he hung back, hesitating.

"Terry," Magpie said in her most practical voice, "when Twitterpat left, none of this computer stuff was even a question. What kind of answers could you hope to find?"

"They wouldn't have sent an unarmed man to fight the Nothing," Tess said.

24

"And he was good, he was *really* good," said Terry. "If anyone knew what was going on, he would have. The man lived half a step into the future."

"And you really think he would have left it all just lying around like this . . . ? Or that the school would have allowed it?" Ben said.

"Anything could happen," Terry said. "But I wish I felt less like a cat burglar."

"He might have wanted you to know," Tess said. "Someone else might *need* to know."

"Cracking the door code was one thing," Magpie said. "What makes you think you could crack Twitterpat's computer?"

"And Terry"—Thea had subsided into one of the chairs and was now staring up at Terry—"if you thought he might have rigged the door, what might he have done to booby-trap the computer?"

"There are ways," Terry said. "There are always ways. Look, nobody else might have known where to look. . . ."

"Like for instance in a computer left sitting in the middle of an empty office?" Ben said, a little sharply. "Don't you think it's far more likely that, if they left that computer dumped there like that, there might have been nothing of value on it for anyone to find?"

"Ben," Terry said, "I'm probably better than anyone else they have on staff right now. They haven't even made an attempt to replace Twitterpat. Everyone else still treats computers as no more than glorified electronic filing cabinets. But now there's Thea . . . and then this new thing. . . ." He paused. There were things that he could not utter. "What you called it, back in your father's study," he said, glancing at Thea.

"Spellspam," Thea said, shrugging. "It was the first thing that came to mind."

Magpie giggled. "*Spellspam.* Thea, that's brilliant."

"What did your parents say?" Ben asked.

"My aunt thinks she might have received one of them herself," Thea said. "My dad said he'd check it out."

"What if it's worse than we thought?" Terry said. "One might be a joke—two, a coincidence—but what if we just haven't heard of any more as yet, isolated out here as we are? What if this was just the first symptom in a full-scale cyber-epidemic? I don't think they have the first idea about how to deal with something like that."

"They dealt with it when the libraries went feral,"

Thea said. "Spells escaped from grimoires in the stacks and everything suddenly turned to mush and chaos. I know the stories—my father used to do that for a living."

Terry shot a desperate look at Tess, unable to articulate what he was thinking—the conversation was straying into what were, for him, dangerous waters. Tess thought for a moment, and then began speaking, keeping her eyes on her brother's face.

"Feral libraries were localized," Tess said. "They could isolate the afflicted buildings, shut everything down, shield it all tightly, and then deal with it at their leisure. This is something else altogether. They have no concept of what cyberspace really is. If they think the old methods are going to work, they are going to find themselves making a bad situation worse. You can't just constrain a rampant piece of, well, of spellspam if you like, not in the same way that they could shut the doors on a stray spell in the library stacks."

"Trouble," said Thea and Magpie, in unison.

"Trouble," agreed Terry.

"But you're missing something," Tess said slowly.

They all turned toward her expectantly.

"Thea, you can do this thing with the computers,"

Tess said. "It's new. It's *unique*. But we all know you didn't do this." She paused, swallowed hard. "Thea . . . *you are not alone*. At least one other person has figured out how to make computers do magic on command. The answers may not be in Twitterpat's computer—you might be the only one who can figure out how to stop this. From the inside, somehow."

There was a moment of appalled silence as everyone tried to absorb this, and then Thea shook her head violently.

"But I can't do this. I have no idea what's happening, or how it's happening. It isn't the same thing at all."

"You might have no choice except to try to find out," Tess said.

"I may be putting my neck in a noose for nothing," Terry said abruptly, "but I'm here, and Twitterpat's computer is still here. I might as well try. If you guys don't want to get in trouble . . . it's my own funeral."

"You had my back," Thea said, without missing a beat. "I'll watch yours."

"You're all insane!" Ben wailed, but made no move to leave.

Magpie merely stood there grinning.

Tess squared her shoulders and tossed back her hair.

"All right then," Terry said softly.

It had been a while since anybody had been in the office. The door squeaked softly as Terry pushed it all the way open, and their footsteps seemed oddly quiet and muffled.

Twitterpat's computer was on the floor under his desk. Someone had thought to put a plastic cover on the monitor and the keyboard, but the computer tower itself was furred with a thick layer of dust.

"Will it even start up?" Ben said morosely as Terry reached for the switch.

The computer hummed to life. Underneath the dustcover, a blinking light indicated that the monitor was waking up.

"I'm not sure how much time we have," Terry said, pulling off the dustcover with one hand and freeing up the keyboard with the other. "And it might take me half an hour just to figure out a way in."

"That's what I was afraid of," muttered Ben.

A dialogue box appeared on the screen, demanding a password. Terry thought for a few minutes, fingers poised above the keyboard, eyes narrowed in furious thought, and then tapped in a word. The screen froze, and then cleared; a desktop screen full of tiny software icons popped into existence.

"*That* easy?" muttered Terry. "No way."

The screen suddenly changed abruptly, the background changing into a lurid poisonous tree-frog green, the software icons morphing into tiny faces with cartoon grins which, despite the crudeness of their rendition, managed to convey a sense of sardonic amusement. Terry snatched his hands from the keyboard, but it was already too late.

"Great," he growled. "That must have rung every alarm bell in the building."

"What did you do?" Tess said, a tinge of panic in her voice.

"Wrong password. I thought I had it figured out, but obviously . . ."

"Should we leave?" Ben demanded.

"Too late now. Wait a moment, here it comes again. . . ."

The dialogue box popped back onto the screen, demanding a password.

"Blast," Terry said. "If I get it wrong this time . . ."

"Would it self-destruct?" Magpie asked, in all seriousness.

Terry actually laughed. "In a manner of speaking, perhaps," he said.

"You'd think he would have little need of a password," Thea said. "If he were here, he would not have let anyone get this far. And if he were hoarding secrets, let's face it, Terry, Ben is right—he probably wouldn't have kept them in *this* hard drive. Not in an office right next to a bunch of kids who could do damage without even meaning to."

"Great, now you think of that," Terry said. And then straightened. "Wait a minute. You may have something there."

He typed something in, and four asterisks appeared on the screen. Everyone held their breath for a moment, and then Terry let his out with a hiss.

"Well, I'll be," he said, sounding almost ludicrously surprised. "Thea, you're a genius."

The screen cleared, and computer wallpaper appeared, something that looked like a close-up photograph of a spiderweb. Then the software icons started popping into place, and this time it was obvious that they were going to stay put. There seemed to be a great many of them.

"What? What did I say?" Thea said, leaning in over Terry's shoulder.

"It asked for a password. I typed in 'None.' You're right, the password was not important. Not for this computer . . . what's this?"

The cursor was hovering over a tiny silver spider-web in a black circle. The caption underneath said simply "Nex."

"Typo for 'Net'? 'Terranet'?" Tess suggested.

"No, that's over here, I know the icon for that. And besides, Twitterpat would not have kept an obvious misspelling on his screen. It would drive him nuts."

Thea was staring at the icon, frowning. "It looks . . . like a dreamcatcher."

Magpie shot her a startled look, but Terry was concentrating too hard to pay attention, opening directories as though he were pursuing prey.

"It's some sort of internal network," Terry said. "It shows up in the network menu. But no details."

"Can you get in?"

"*That* is probably what you need the real password for," Terry said.

"Terry, why would anyone have left anything of value here?" Ben said. There was a real edge in his voice, close to panic. "You don't even know what you're looking for."

"Oh, yes I do," Terry said softly. "Something called the Nex, which doesn't exist outside the local school network. Bring me the laptop case, would you, Mag? There's a cable in there. . . ."

Magpie obediently scurried off to fetch the case, her eyes alight with interest. Terry dug around in a side pocket until he came up with a tangled cable and dropped to his knees, heedless of the dust on the floor, peering at the back of Twitterpat's machine. He found the socket he needed, plugged in his cable with a grunt, and surfaced again, wiping his hands on his dusty jeans.

"I'll find out," he said. "Give me just a few more minutes . . ."

"What's that?" Magpie hissed suddenly.

"Lock," said Tess, at the same time as Terry whispered,

"Office door! Shut the office door!"

Ben reached out and pushed the office door shut with the lightest of clicks.

"Busted," he said mournfully.

"Damn! Just a few more minutes!" Terry said, frustrated, the other end of the cable plugged into his laptop, fingers flying on his keyboard.

"You're all out of minutes," said Magpie.

The office door opened as she spoke, and Assistant Principal Chen stood framed in the doorway. She stood looking at them for a moment, shaking her head. Terry was the first one to actually move, closing his eyes and letting his head fall back in frustrated defeat.

"Not good," Mrs. Chen said. "The principal will see you now. All of you."

It was rare to have so many students at once in the principal's office—a couple of extra folding chairs had to be brought in. Tess sat staring at her hands; Magpie was looking thoughtful; Ben's face hinted at a dull and persistent toothache. Terry was sitting bolt upright in one of the principal's three comfortable guest chairs, his hands gripping the armrests, his eyes glinting with a guarded defiance; and Thea sat in a second chair, suddenly very calm, her eyes resting with a steady dignity on the two adults in the room.

Principal Harris sat hunched in his own chair, elbows on his desk, his chin balanced on his hands, staring at the miscreants; Margaret Chen stood beside the principal's desk, one hand resting on the polished oak, looking grave.

"You do realize that this is very serious?" Mrs. Chen said.

34

"Under ordinary circumstances, grounds for expulsion," John Harris said. "That classroom was out of bounds, something that should have been obvious to you by the simple fact of its being locked against student entry. Thea, you broke your word to me. Terry, I am astonished that you would hack into a school computer, let alone one that belonged to a teacher you claim to admire and respect."

"Those are the very reasons I believed that he might have an answer for the current situation, sir," Terry said.

"You hacked into a staff member's computer," Principal Harris said. "What could you have been hoping to find?"

"I needed to talk to my father," Thea said, at almost the same moment.

The principal favored Terry with a long glare, and turned to Thea. "Did it not occur to you to come to me first, Thea?" he asked. "Or even to try telephoning your father?"

"There was no time," Thea said, "and the phone . . . I couldn't do that. It might not have been safe."

The principal and Mrs. Chen exchanged a glance.

"Very well," said the principal. "You may explain.

I take it this is all connected with what happened earlier to LaTasha Jackson?"

"I was there," Thea said. "I saw what happened. And I saw the message on her computer. . . ."

She was watching both the principal and Mrs. Chen as she related the events she had witnessed in the library, and although both paid attention to what she was saying and both wore expressions of concern, neither appeared particularly surprised. Thea had expected surprise, even shock. But they were reacting as though—

"But you already knew all this," Thea suddenly said, breaking off her account, and staring at the principal. "Did you . . . did you think it was *me*?"

"And your aunt said that she thinks she had received some of this . . . this spellspam . . . herself?" the principal said, giving no indication that the sudden shift had in any way disconcerted him.

"The 'free gift' thing. Yes."

"Margaret," the principal said after a brief pause, turning to Mrs. Chen in a way that briefly excluded the five students, "our perimeter has been breached."

"I know," Mrs. Chen said in a low voice. "I have already spoken to the nurse, but all she could do was to give LaTasha a sedative until the effect wears off."

The principal paused for a moment. "Have we isolated what was involved?"

"All I know right now is that it's a very simple spell. It will wear off," Mrs. Chen said. "From what I can tell, it's likely a twenty-four-hour thing. Like the flu. It's already starting to fade. The worst aspect of this is that there were so many witnesses. That will be a problem."

"It's a symptom," the principal said. "But we have a far larger problem on our hands."

Terry looked up sharply, opened his mouth, shut it, and glanced over at his sister.

As before, she completed his thought, and said it out loud for him—because he couldn't. It was a word with magic in it. It would have choked him.

"*You* got a spellspam?" Tess said slowly, with Terry watching the principal's expression through narrowed eyes.

Thea couldn't help a startled look at the twins. That offhand word of hers had certainly gathered currency in a hurry.

"That's a symptom too—but for the record, yes, I did," the principal said. "But that isn't even the worst of it. . . ."

He crossed the room again and stood at the

window, staring out at the rainy afternoon, his right hand closed around his left wrist on his back, the fingers on his left hand drumming the air in a manner which suddenly reminded Thea painfully of Twitterpat.

"I've shut down the Nexus," the principal said at last.

Thea suddenly looked up and caught Terry's eye. Nexus. *Nex*. The strange icon on Twitterpat's computer.

Terry dropped his eyes, his fingers clenching over his knees. "You reacted to it. You shut down the computer; you've just let them know that they got a hit," he said faintly. "You've opened a vulnerability—if you'd realized what was happening, if you'd set up a filter in time . . ."

The principal was staring at Terry, his expression slowly changing from astonishment to something very different.

"John, *no*!" Margaret Chen whispered. "They are *children*! You can't . . . !"

1.

THE PRINCIPAL DID not show them the Nexus. Not then. He muttered something about too much curiosity and impatience having gotten the five of them into trouble in the first place, and abruptly dismissed them.

Thea hesitated at the door of the principal's office as they all filed out. "Just before we left . . . I couldn't hear it all, but my father said something about sending help," she said.

"He might, and I will make contact with him on my own terms," the principal said sternly. "But, Thea, this must stop. You have an extraordinary and hard-to-control gift, and until things settle down, I would very much like to trust you out of my sight. There is far more riding on this than any of you can possibly realize."

Thea flushed, hanging her head. "Yes, sir."

"Don't forget what I said. I am actually giving you *permission* to lie about what went on in this office. Use the privilege well. Terry . . . and Tess . . . I would like a word with you, please. The rest of you may go. Margaret, would you make sure that the situation in the halls is under control?"

Margaret Chen knew that she was being dismissed along with the students, and her eyes flashed with something that was suddenly dangerous, a light that changed her face and made Thea see the mage that Margaret had once been. Before she came to the Academy. Before she "retired."

She shook her head, once, decisively, and turned to Thea, Magpie, and Ben. "You three . . . you heard the principal," she said, and her voice was brittle and hard-edged, like broken glass. "Stay quiet and stay out of trouble. I will check in on you later. John . . . if you insist on doing this, I stay."

"Very well," said the principal.

Thea, Magpie, and Ben knew better than to ask questions, given the expression on Mrs. Chen's face. They filed out of the office, with the door closing softly but firmly behind them, and then out of the administrative building, pausing on the top of the five shallow stairs that led down to the graveled path.

"Well," Ben breathed. "Who knew what a hornet's nest we'd kick over?"

"You did," Magpie said. "Or at least you kept on saying so, back in the computer lab. Well, you were right about the hornet's nest—but *we* didn't kick it over. It's this whole spellspam thing." She snorted, pushing her hair back behind her ears, glancing back into the building. "What do you suppose he wants with Terry and Tess? And what's this Nex—"

Thea flung out a hand. "Walls. Ears."

"Oh," said Magpie. "Right."

"The skunk hospital. Tonight," Thea said.

"You think they'll let us wander around at night, with all this going on?" Ben said, sounding genuinely appalled. "And what's a skunk hospital, anyway? I wouldn't be surprised if they locked down the—"

"Doing your laundry late at night means there aren't any crowds," Thea said innocently, and was rewarded by a sudden irrepressible grin from Magpie and a stubbornly skeptical look from Ben. "We'd better go," she said, glancing around, "or they *will* be coming after us."

"But he said not to talk . . ."

"Not to other *people*," Thea said, tossing the

words over her shoulder as she skipped down the stone steps, followed by Magpie. A couple of passing students had stopped to stare, and Thea paused to turn her head briefly, glancing back at Ben. "You'd better get moving," she said, "before the audience gets any bigger."

"You're impossible," Ben muttered.

"So they all seem to think," Thea said agreeably. "See you later, then."

"Ben was right, you know," Magpie whispered to Thea. The halls of the residence were quiet and deserted; once they froze at a sudden muffled noise before realizing it was only someone listening to music after lights-out. "Chen will come checking. Particularly you and me."

"They might be fooled," Thea said. They had left rolls of sweaters and spare blankets tucked under their bedclothes, with the fringe of a black silk shawl spread upon Magpie's pillow to impersonate her hair.

"Not for long," Magpie said. "Thea, couldn't we have talked about this tomorrow . . . ? Like . . . in daylight? Somewhere *warm*?"

"Where? A place where we can't be overheard . . . ?"

42

"We could always break into a classroom again," Magpie said, her teeth flashing white in the shadowed stairwell.

"Quiet!" Thea said, flattening them both against the wall. They held their breath, but there was silence, and Magpie finally turned her head a fraction.

"*What?*" she demanded.

"Nothing. Thought I heard a noise. Come on."

At first, the back door leading out of the laundry area would not open. It gave suddenly with a muffled crack that made both Thea and Magpie jump. But nobody came to investigate, and they slipped outside onto the small concrete porch.

"Ew," Magpie said. "It's raining."

They both uttered small, smothered shrieks as another shivering figure stepped out of the shadows and joined them on the concrete.

"Where *were* you?" Tess demanded waspishly. "I had to actually bribe my roommate to shut up, and then you guys show up *late*—"

"We're not late," Thea said. "Do the guys know exactly where . . . ?"

"I told Terry," Tess said. "He'll bring Ben. Now come *on*, already."

They all wore hooded parkas, and on Tess's word, they pulled the hoods low over their eyes and raced off across the lawn into the wooded area beside the residence hall. They reached the gardening shed without incident.

Magpie inched open the door, and they slipped inside; Thea brought up the rear and pulled the door shut behind her.

In the darkness, someone sneezed loudly.

"Ow! Watch it!" said someone else.

"Hey, that wasn't me," Tess said, flicking on her light.

"That was me," Ben said, sniffling, his nose wrinkled up in anticipation of another sneeze.

"Do you smell something interesting?" Thea asked, remembering Ben's predilection to sneeze in the presence of magic.

"Not that I can tell," Ben said. "My hair is wet," he added after a moment, as though further explanation was required. "I catch cold easily when my head gets wet."

"Terry?" Tess said. "You there?"

A shadow detached itself from the far wall. "All present and accounted for, I think," Terry said, his hands stuffed deep into the pockets of his parka.

"The war council can begin."

"You guys first," Thea said. "What did the principal want with you?"

"I'll talk," Tess said. "Thea, this is far more dangerous for Terry than you realize."

"I know," Thea whispered. "The allergy . . . Terry can't actually say anything, can he? Even that *spellspam* word I just made up. It's got magic in it, and it would stick in Terry's throat like a fish bone. If the principal wanted to talk to Terry about spellspam, then he had to talk to *you*, Tess."

"He could have written things down . . . couldn't he?" Magpie said.

"That could get old real fast," Ben said. "The thing is, he *can* talk about the computer stuff, and that's what the principal really wanted to talk about."

"But it's risky," Thea said slowly. "That's why Mrs. Chen insisted on staying. If anything happened, she could at least try and reverse it, right there. Mage First Class."

"Retired," Magpie said. "So she keeps on saying."

"I'm not so sure about that," Thea said. "I'm not sure about a lot of things anymore. So—then— what's this Nexus thing?"

"That's what he wanted to talk to me about," Terry said. "That's what this whole place is about. *Really* about."

"The school?" Magpie said. "I thought the idea was to educate magidims like us for somehow making a living in a magic-run world."

"Except that it turns out we aren't all 'dims," Tess said, "and that the teachers are far more than meets the eye."

"They did take rather a lot of them from here, when the Nothing came," Ben said. "I thought that was odd. Nobody said anything other than that it was a magical threat, and yet the people they kept on sending to face it were all from a school without magic. . . ."

"Firewalls within firewalls," Thea murmured.

"What?" Terry said, his head whipping around to face her.

"I had to come clean to my parents, after the Nothing," Thea said. "I was afraid they'd never let me back here—the Academy was supposedly the one place where magic was not supposed to be able to enter—and there I was . . . but Mrs. Chen said something odd . . ."

"About this place?" Magpie asked.

Thea nodded. "Protection always has two sides, she said. What is warded against a thing may also be warded to keep that same thing safe. She said . . . that the safest place to hide anything is right behind a mirror." She grinned suddenly, and shot Magpie a quicksilver grin. "She knows all about your animal hospital, by the way, Mag."

"What?" Magpie roused, distracted. "I was *so* careful. She couldn't—"

"She said it was her hall, and she knew about everything that went on in there," Thea said.

"Hey," Ben said, sounding a little aggrieved, "we didn't come here to talk about Magpie's skunks."

"Firewalls," Terry murmured. "They were hiding the truth behind that mirror all the time. *We*, the students, are a firewall. The 'dims. Who would look for the heart of magic in a place where magic is forbidden by decree . . . ?"

It appeared as though he had simply petered out, but Tess turned with sudden, frightened speed. *"Dammit!"* she said. "I knew this would happen!"

"What?" Ben said, startled, as Tess reached for the collar on her brother's shirt, scrabbling desperately for something underneath.

"What can we do to help?" Thea said, stepping

closer, helpless, watching Terry's mouth open and close and realizing that no air was getting through at all.

"He has the emergency antidote," Tess said, fishing out a small vial and unstopping it with frantic speed. "Terry, swallow, *now*!"

The vial contained no more than a mouthful of liquid. For a ghastly moment they all thought that it had come too late, but Terry suddenly drew a gasping breath and sagged against his sister, gulping down air, his eyes streaming.

"I'm sorry," Thea said. "I should have woven us a safety net . . . I should have *thought*—"

"You could have woven us a safe place where nobody would overhear, tomorrow, in the daylight, too," Magpie said. "And we would have had someone to call if he needed help."

"You okay?" Tess said, her arm around her brother's shoulders.

He straightened, his breathing still a little ragged. "Fine," he said, his voice oddly hoarse. "I'm fine. Thanks, Tess. You can let go now. Really. I won't keel over. What were we talking about . . . ?"

"Probably not something we should go back to discussing," Ben murmured.

"So what *did* the principal want?" Magpie asked.

"If you can talk about it . . . ?"

"I can, it's indirect," Terry said. "You heard him mention this Nexus. . . ."

"I'd better," Tess said, not looking entirely convinced that Terry was back to normal. "We don't have another dose of the antidote handy. We'd better make sure you have more than the usual emergency supply, Terry. Under the circumstances. But about the Nexus . . . you know what computers are to the users of magic. Storage. Archives. The Nexus is a level above that, a supercomputer. It's hidden right here, at the school. Twitterpat maintained it. After he was gone, it was the principal himself who worked on it, pending the authorities sending him a replacement for Twitterpat. The principal said he's rejected at least two candidates since Twitterpat was lost. And it gets harder and harder for him to do it himself because he doesn't have the training to do it long-term."

"They should offer you the job, Terry," Magpie said with a grin.

"They . . . kind of . . . did," Terry said faintly.

Thea, now perched uncomfortably on the other side of the wheelbarrow from Ben, sat up sharply. "They what?"

"I'm a natural," Terry said. It was said with no smugness, very matter-of-factly. "I'm already here, so they can stop looking for someone with a good cover story; I would have no teaching obligations to distract me. . . ."

"Just graduating high school," Thea said. "Piece of cake."

"It *is*," Terry said, flashing her a quick grin. "And then there's the other beneficial side effect."

"Such as?" Magpie said.

"We're a political family," Tess said. "Mom works at the Federal Bureau of Magic, and Uncle Kevin *runs* it, and apparently their stamp of approval is required on any candidate who the principal decides is good enough to consider for this job. And besides, they wouldn't even have to administer an oath of confidentiality—he can't talk about this to anybody, not in any meaningful way, not without endangering his life. It turns out that this wretched allergy of his is extremely convenient, didn't it?"

"And besides . . . ," Terry said.

They all turned to him.

"It would seem that Twitterpat had me in mind all along," Terry said. "Apparently he spoke to the principal about me. About this."

"But what happens during summer holidays? When you graduate? When you leave here? If you go to college . . . if you get a job somewhere?" Ben said.

"Logistics," Terry said. "Besides, I'll already *have* a job."

"But Terry . . ." Thea hadn't taken her eyes off Terry's face. "How useful are you if someone always has to be there as backup, just in case you forget yourself and start saying some word that has a magical underlay? What would happen if you were alone and you did that?"

"I told you it was dangerous," Tess said. "I'm scared."

"Are you supposed to be with him whenever he's working on this Nexus thing?" Thea asked. "Because then it's *both* of you who are bound by it. Is it that essential, that it needs to swallow two lives?"

"Has he shown you the actual Nexus?" Ben asked.

"No," Terry said. "And you're right, Thea. It would mean supervisory duty for someone, constantly, all the time. It'll always be a sword hanging over my head."

"Terry, do you actually *want* to do this?" Thea asked softly.

Terry shrugged. "Yes, of course I do," he said. "And at the same time . . . it all sounds great, but I sure wish I had someone like Twitterpat to talk this over with. I really wish he were here right now. . . ."

2.

THE AIR IN the shed stirred as though a breath of wind had found its way through a crack and gusted inside. Tess instinctively turned around to close the shed door—and found that it was already closed.

Outside, the whisper of the rain on the roof abruptly ceased, and another sound came in its wake—a sort of distant creak, like a tree bending in high wind.

A sense of *wrongness* settled into the small dark shed, heavy and clammy, hard to breathe through. Ben reacted first, standing up with such speed and force that he almost sent Thea headfirst into the dirt floor. Heedless of obstructions, he launched himself at Terry.

"Take it back! Take it back right now! *Unwish it!*"

"What?" Tess said, slowly, too slowly, as though

she were talking through molasses.

"The e-mail! That e-mail you got this evening, in the library, Terry! You laughed at it, but it was *spellspam*! It gave you three wishes, and you just used one—and Twitterpat's been dead for months . . ."

"I wish he'd go away," Terry said, his eyes wide. "I wish . . ."

"*Shut up!* Not another word!" Ben said sharply, lifting his head to listen.

The rain had returned, the solidity of the air dissipated slowly, almost reluctantly. Thea drew in a ragged breath.

"You have one more wish," Ben said. "You'd better use it. Otherwise you'll be looking over your shoulder constantly, until it slips out at the worst possible moment, giving you precisely the thing you don't want. They stole this one from the Faele; it isn't a human trick."

"But a human wrought it into a spell," Thea said slowly.

"A spell," Magpie said. "How come you didn't . . . you know . . . choke on it again . . . ?"

"It was just 'I wish,'" Ben said. "The magic was in intent, not the words. He got off lucky that time."

"What if he just . . . said . . . that he wanted

everything to be okay?" Magpie said hopefully.

Ben shook his head. "It doesn't work that way. It has to be specific, very specific. Look what you just said—you wanted 'someone like Twitterpat,' and Twitterpat himself has been dead, buried, and decomposing these last few months—who knows what would have walked in here just now if you hadn't, uh, *wussshed* it away?"

"What if I asked for . . . for the ability to . . . for the allergy to go away?" Terry said.

"Knowing the Faele, it would probably let you talk *only* about the things you had been unable to utter beforehand and nothing else—and you've already used two of your wishes. Don't waste the third on something you wouldn't be able to undo. But use it, use it on something, because we humans are wishing machines, and the Faele knew that about us long before our paths officially crossed in the history books. We can't *help* wishing, and it gets us into trouble without even trying."

"I wish . . . ," Terry began abruptly, and nodded as Ben mouthed at him, *Specific! Be specific!* "I wish we all get back to our beds safely tonight without anyone seeing us and that nobody other than the five of us ever knows that we were here tonight."

"Will that do?" Magpie said, weighing each word to see if it was specific enough.

"It should be pretty safe," said Ben slowly, "although it is usually safer not to wish for anything that involves other people. You never know how things play out, and the other people in question may not be very pleased at the results."

"But what could possibly go wrong with . . . ," Tess began.

"If you saw it too, Ben," Thea said, interrupting with sudden concern, "that e-mail, I mean—aren't you also at risk? What are *your* three wishes? Shouldn't you do the same thing—get them out of the way?"

"I will," Ben said. "Don't worry about me."

"Be careful with those wishes," Thea said.

Ben nodded mutely, stuffing his hands into his pockets.

"Pity you didn't just . . . er . . . ask for this Nexus thing to just take care of itself, Terry," Magpie said.

"No!" said Terry, Thea, and Ben in unison.

Magpie blinked. "It was just an idea."

"That's what I mean about humans being W-I-S-H generators," Ben said, spelling the word out. "It's a very bad idea. Think about what the Faele could do with that wish."

"It could make the thing come alive and turn to some agenda of its own," Tess said.

"I didn't say I *liked* the idea," Magpie said, raising her hands in protest. "I was just saying—"

"And it's a good thing *you* didn't get that particular spellspam," Ben said, with a crooked little grin.

Magpie bristled at that. "And what is that supposed to mean?" she demanded.

"Nothing! Nothing!" Ben ducked his head in self-defense. "It's just that . . . you're the perfect mark for the Faele. You'd try to bend it all to the good, and be sweeping, and you'd wind up creating a bigger mess than you could possibly imagine."

"Well, I look forward to seeing what you pick, Mister Broomstick," Magpie said, still in a huff.

Ben winced. The nickname that Mr. Siffer had hung on him had stuck, and he was having a hard time living with it. "How I wish everyone could forget that stupid na—"

"Ben!" everybody except Magpie squawked.

"Forget what?" Magpie said, after a beat.

Ben looked around at the others, and shook his head. "I knew that would happen. Look, I need to go away right now and deal with this thing, before I waste the last two wishes."

"Ben, wait . . . ," Thea began, but he had already pulled up the hood of his parka and slipped out of the shed into the drizzle.

"We'd better all get back," Tess said, glancing at her watch.

"Before we go . . . ," Thea said hurriedly, as everyone got to their feet, "Terry . . . where did you leave it? With the principal?"

"I'm supposed to go back and talk to him—in a couple of days, when the furor with LaTasha dies down."

"Is there any way I can help?" Thea asked. "I know I can't do anything that's technical, but maybe I can spell Tess."

"Under the circumstances," Tess said, "that's hardly the word to use. We really should all just go back to bed."

"I'm for that," Terry said. "We can figure out what to do later."

"What if we can't find a place to talk?" Magpie said.

"There's always e-mail," Terry said.

"Uh-huh," said Tess, hunching her shoulders. "After what happened with LaTasha, they might put the lid on that."

"They can filter and firewall and screen—but even if they shut down the library computer bank, too many of us have our own laptops," Terry said.

"But if they shut down the server . . ."

"That's the trouble—they can't, for long—not the main trunk of it. Too much is computer-run these days. Especially here, where—" Terry stopped abruptly, biting off the sentence, apparently tasting something sour in his mouth. "I hate this," he said. "Let's just say that they won't be able to keep the lid on e-mail forever . . . but Thea, we have to figure out what else is going on here."

"You mean the whole spellspam thing," Magpie said.

"But I have no idea . . . ," Thea said, her voice ending on a squeak of helpless indignation.

"We'd all better get an idea, and fast," Tess said.

"You think we might get more from the Free Gift menu?" Magpie said. "That could actually be rather fun. If anything so far has been harmless, that one has. People just get weird stuff . . ."

"I phoned my parents earlier and asked just casu-ally about that gifts thing," Tess said. "It wouldn't be so funny, Magpie, if you had been on the receiving end of a pair of Emperor penguins, or a truckful of an obscure out-of-print novel from the 1930s, or a metric ton of paper clips—or a snowplow delivered to your Florida condo, all of which apparently happened to people my family knows. Terry's right, it's a cyber-epidemic—and you can't return something that has no return address on it. So you're stuck with the stuff." She tried very hard to suppress a giggle, but failed, and she lowered her head to hide her face, shaking her hair down over her mirth. "Although," she said, "I have to admit, I would rather have liked being a fly on the wall when Grandma MacAllister received her penguins," she said.

They spilled carefully out into the drizzle, letting just enough light from their flashlights play between their fingers to light a safe path back. Terry quickly melted away into the rainy night and the three girls pulled up their hoods and raced back to the residence hall across the wet grass and under dripping trees.

They made it to the back door of the hall and stood for a moment on the concrete porch, shaking the rain off their parkas, and then Thea nudged open the door to the laundry room.

"Come on," she began, "quick, before anyone . . ."

They were all inside before they fully realized that one of the washing machines had a red pilot light on, and emitted a businesslike hum and a faint scent of suds and steam. The room was dark, but even as the three froze, a light switch was thrown and the room was awash in bright, neon-white light.

Tess moaned softly.

But the woman who had come into the laundry room, one of the junior housemistresses, was apparently oblivious of their unsanctioned presence. She crossed over to another machine, opened the lid, and started hauling laundry out without showing the least sign of awareness of the wet and shivering girls who stood not three feet from her.

Magpie lifted a hand and waved it experimentally. The woman hauling laundry didn't blink.

"Terry said . . . that nobody was to see us," whispered Magpie, in the same instant as Tess opened her mouth.

Thea nodded. "I remember this," she said softly. "I *remember* this, when I was little, when they were reading me fairy tales from before the contact with the Faele, from the times when we thought it was all made up. There was a cantrip—*Before me day, behind me night so I may pass out of sight* . . . It's an invisibility spell. Come on, before it quits."

"But magic isn't supposed to *work* here," Magpie said helplessly.

"Nobody ever actually said that," Thea said slowly as they made their way up the stairs, squelching ever so softly with each step and leaving wet footprints on the carpet. "Not in so many words. All that was ever claimed was that magic was not *allowed* at the Academy."

"They might not see us," Magpie said practically, "but someone will be stepping on soggy carpet tomorrow."

Tess rolled her eyes. "Good *night*," she said.

"We'd better get out of sight," muttered Thea. "Who knows how long this invisibility thing will last?"

"Until we get into bed, if I remember Terry's precise wording right," Magpie said. "Bed is actually starting to sound awfully good, spell or no spell. I don't think I can feel my feet."

Magpie had always been blessed with the ability to live in the moment, discarding both memory and dream, past and future, when she crawled into her bed at night. She was asleep in moments. It was Thea who lay awake for a long time, staring up at the shadowed ceiling.

After everything that had happened, one image simply wouldn't leave Thea's mind; her first glimpse of the Nexus icon on Twitterpat's computer screen, and the thing that it had reminded her of.

A dreamcatcher.

Grandmother Spider.

One of Grandmother Spider's silvery, gleaming dreamcatchers spun in Thea's mind's eye, hypnotic, catching the light, weaving it all into a softness that was night and rain and love and accomplishment.

Grandmother Spider . . . the words formed in Thea's mind, unlooked for, unexpected, but heartfelt. *You know how to live in a world that changes around you faster than you can see. I wish you'd come and remind me. . . .*

1.

*O*PEN THE WINDOW.

The voice was soft and familiar, and hard to pin down—it seemed to come from inside Thea's own head, from the room behind her in which Magpie was peacefully sleeping, and from out in the rainy night somewhere. But Thea knew it, and trusted it, and obeyed it without question.

The window latch resisted for a moment, but even as it gave, and the wings of the window opened into the room, Thea knew that she was no longer in quite the same space as the sleeping presence of her room-mate. There was an odd moment where what she saw—a rainy night in the Pacific Northwest—clashed violently with the scent that came drifting in through the open window, a scent of warm, dry air and desert sage and red dust. She could see that other world dimly through a fading curtain of rain. Then the rain and the wet firs were scent and memory, and then she was looking straight into

64

the comfortable room that she had once been invited to enter by a tiny spider in the palm of her hand.

That spider, in its human form, sat curled elegantly on the pile of furs by her hearth, her hair once again snow-white and bobbed at the jawline. There was a disconcerting wrench, a moment of dizziness—Grandmother Spider looked exactly like she had looked when Thea had first set eyes on her, and she had the feeling that if a hundred years passed, or a thousand, it would make no difference at all. Grandmother Spider would look the same.

She looked up at Thea and smiled.

"Come in," she said, as though she had been expecting Thea, as though Thea's presence in this room was not yet another tiny miracle that Grandmother Spider seemed to be almost unaware that she was performing, something that came as naturally to her as breathing did to Thea.

"I thought . . . I couldn't just *do* this," Thea whispered. What had been her window had elongated into a door at Grandmother Spider's words of welcome, and Thea stepped through and into that other world. "This passing back and forth between your space and mine. It took the Alphiri, that first time, and after that it was the computers. . . ."

She remembered the words that had shaped themselves in her mind, that had brought her here. *I wish*, she had said. She was suddenly unsure if everyone in that shed had been afflicted by the three-wishes spellspam, whether they'd seen it or not.

But Grandmother Spider didn't appear worried.

"Child," she said, "perhaps you have forgotten that the first thing that you raised with the touch of your own hand, back when you walked under the skies of the First World with me, was a portal. Built from your own memory, your own music, your own dreams."

"But that was back there. And everything is possible there," Thea said.

Grandmother Spider raised one eyebrow. "You think everyone just weaves their own doorways into a different world, just like that? No, you are a worldweaver, whether you're in the First World or in your own sphere—and if you have a different way of weaving there, that is part of the way that you choose to use your gift. However, this time I came to *you*. I heard you calling my name."

Thea smiled as she settled down on the guest furs beside Grandmother Spider. "But I didn't even say anything out loud. . . ."

Grandmother Spider reached out with one long-fingered hand to cup Thea's cheek. "You are troubled, child of my spirit."

Thea opened her mouth to start explaining and stopped, wondering just how much of what she had to say would make any sense in this room—where the technology that her own world was so proud of was not only absent, but felt entirely superfluous. She felt as though she were about to start explaining algebra to a cat who was indifferent to the theory of it all but already knew how to bend dimensions of space and time and teleport through solid walls if the need arose.

"It's all right," Grandmother Spider said, her hair suddenly an impish shade of carrot-red, her eyes a sort of bright emerald green. "It may surprise you to know that I've actually heard of computers. What you have, I gather, is a trickster storm—and those are not confined to the computer world. Tricksters have always been with us. What is it?"

"Corey and I crossed paths," Thea said. The memory of the wayward raven feathers that had been driving Corey crazy during her last encounter with him, back on the Puget Sound ferry last summer, was still vivid in her mind's eye. "After I left here, I mean. He was . . . in some little trouble."

"He always is," Grandmother Spider said. "It is his nature."

"You think he has something to do with what's been going on?" Thea asked, sitting up straighter. Corey could be extremely charming or amusing, but he was no less dangerous for all that.

"If he does, then it's with assistance—he, like all of his kin, has little use for computers. But he could have provided material and inspiration. He was always good at that."

"My friend Ben said that one of the spellspams they used—the three wishes one—um, it *is* okay to talk about it out loud here? It won't mess things up . . . ?"

"It's fine. Nothing that's said in this room can cause harm unless I will it so."

"There is a spellspam going around right now; it asks what you would do if you got three wishes, and people could really get into trouble with that."

"Yes," Grandmother Spider murmured. "Wishes and hopes—your greatest strength, and your greatest weakness. Your people, of all my children, can be most lethally wounded by the best in you."

"Ben said whoever sent that one out stole the idea from the Faele," Thea said.

"They always knew how to exploit vulnerabilities, the Faele," Grandmother Spider said. "Yours is the only race they have ever used the weapon of the three wishes against. You'd be surprised at what works with folk like, for instance, the Alphiri."

It was hard to keep a thread of thought going. Grandmother Spider was apparently able to keep it all in her head, to flutter from idea to idea with the ease of a butterfly. But Thea found herself easily distracted when in Grandmother Spider's presence, if only because she came out with the most incredible things in very matter-of-fact ways. Thea tried to wrestle the conversation back to the topic of spellspam and its fallout.

"You said if it's Corey, he'd need human help . . . ?"

Grandmother Spider nodded, choosing to remain silent, letting Thea navigate her thoughts until she could ask the questions she needed to ask.

"He's kind of . . . hard to find if he doesn't want to be, isn't he?" Thea said. "But does his influence . . . leave a mark? Is there any way of finding that human point of contact? The person to whom the spellspam is being suggested?"

"Just trace the headers," said Grandmother Spider tranquilly.

Thea did a double take. "What?"

"The headers," Grandmother Spider said helpfully. "You know, the bits attached to the e-mail that tell you where it came from, who sent it, the pathways it followed from origin to destination—trace them back, from the receiving computer to the originating one."

"I wouldn't have the first idea how to go about that," Thea said, astonished.

"But you have friends who do," Grandmother Spider said. "And yes, I know, a good hacker could disguise and channel things in a different way every time—but you wouldn't be looking for the originating server so much as for an identifying mark."

"How do you even *know* about headers?" Thea demanded, sitting up straight.

"I told you, I know all sorts of things," Grandmother Spider said.

"But spam is so common," Thea said, "and we've all been trained that just *looking* at an e-mail isn't dangerous. Or wasn't, until the spellspam started. It seems it doesn't carry viruses or any other kind of attachments or even send you to a website to look at something. It's even been funny. The names that it comes under!"

"Trickster, all over," Grandmother Spider said, nodding. "Never doubt that they can be dangerous, even while you're laughing. Especially if you are laughing. But there are ways of telling the merely irritating from the potentially dangerous."

"I do have . . . a friend," Thea said. "I know it sounds strange, but he has an allergy. He can't talk about magic without literally choking on it. And he's the best computer mind they've got at the school. He could probably track headers in his sleep." Grandmother Spider chuckled but did not interrupt. "And the school has this huge computer called the Nexus. It used to be maintained by one of the teachers, but he was killed last year fighting the Nothing, and they haven't had anyone else to do it ever since, and now they're asking Terry. I know he can do it. But there's the other aspect, the spellspam, and he's already been caught by it once. If he's alone with it, it might destroy him without anyone knowing, especially if it gets any worse than just jokes and teasing. If he isn't alone, he can't tell anyone that he's caught on it because that would kill him anyway. Other than having one of us—one of us other four, who

71

originally did the computer crossing, back when we lured the Nothing into the sea world—with Terry constantly, I don't know what to tell him, how to help him. . . . Does any of this make any sense at all?"

"Well," Grandmother Spider said with a smile, "I get the idea."

"I thought of you," Thea said, "when Terry first found the icon for the Nexus on a computer—and it looked . . . it looked just like one of your dream-catchers."

Grandmother Spider raised an eyebrow. "Precisely what I was going to suggest."

"A dreamcatcher?" Thea said.

"A dreamcatcher. But a special one."

"One of yours . . . ?"

Grandmother Spider shook her head. "Ah, no. Those don't leave this room—and if one of them did make it to your world, you'd have the Alphiri down on you so fast that you wouldn't have the time to worry about anything as trivial as spellspam. Don't ever get between an Alphiri and something they really want, not without a very good reason . . . and perhaps not even then. But I *can* give you one that will be just as useful to you. You could call it . . . a *spell*checker."

Thea actually laughed out loud. "How would that work?"

"It's a very innocuous thing," Grandmother Spider said. "You hang it on the monitor, and it's a pretty toy—but if you get e-mail, you look at it through the spellchecker. If there's something dangerous there, you can see that it's present—and you can flag the e-mail, or quarantine it, or delete it before you have to look at it with the unaided eye."

"Would that work? In our world?" Thea asked, sitting up eagerly.

"Your world is one that Tawaha and I made," Grandmother Spider said. "What I decree works in it. You will have the thing before sundown tomorrow. But have you considered something else? A different solution?"

"Like what?"

"You're a weaver of worlds. You can pass through a world lightly; you don't always have to ring the front doorbell to announce your arrival. Sometimes you just need to open a window into another room in your mind."

Thea's eyes were wide. "I thought about that. I didn't know if I could sustain it. If I can duplicate the Nexus control room and make it exist in a world in which his allergy *doesn't*—so he's safe, then he could work on *that* Nexus, and it would be echoed on the primary one in our world. When he's done, he returns to our world, the real world."

"You really have to learn," Grandmother Spider said with an amused shake of her head, "not to cling so hard to what is *real*. Or to what you think should be real. Both those Nexus rooms are 'real' in their moment—reality is what you are living, the things important to you. Those are the only things that are real. Everything else is illusions and dreams, trapped in my dreamcatchers."

Thea found herself remembering an exchange on the subject of illusion and reality that she had had with Margaret Chen, who had been delegated to figure out how far Thea's unexpected abilities went. Thea had taken Mrs. Chen to several very different worlds—and the Academy mage was starting to look a little green as they re-emerged into her study after one of these excursions.

"I asked my parents for a laptop for Christmas," Thea had said, unable to hold back a grin.

"Please tell me you didn't get it," Mrs. Chen had said. "Keeping an eye on you in my hall is one thing, but knowing that you can type a sentence into a computer and go heaven knows where, without the remotest possibility that someone could drag you back to reality, is a responsibility I'm not ready for."

"But it *is* reality," Thea. "Those other places—they're just as real."

"I hope not," Mrs. Chen said firmly. "The real you is always still here, in this room, at that computer. Everything else is just mirror play."

"But you said the safest place to hide something is behind a mirror," Thea said. "How do you know that the place I'm in is not more real than the place where only a ghost-me remains?"

"Thea Winthrop, you're almost fifteen," Mrs. Chen said. "I don't feel remotely ready to discuss the nature of reality with you right now, despite the fact that you can apparently create your own. There's still a lot we don't know about this thing you can do, and I prefer to withhold judgment on which reality is more real until I have more information."

Thea blinked, and Mrs. Chen was far away again. In front of her, looking faintly quizzical, Grandmother Spider was looking at her with a tiny smile hovering around the edges of her mouth.

"Thank you," Thea said.

"You're welcome," Grandmother Spider said.

"I'm watching over you. If you need me, all you have to do is call. Rest and save your strength—you will need it. And I will do what I promised. Sleep, now."

Thea woke with a start, blinking. She was in her bed, in her nightgown, her comforter wrapped around her as it always was—an ordinary morning, even down to the small mewling sounds in the next bed that meant that Magpie was waking, too.

Except that Thea could not recall going through the motions of getting ready for bed the night before. Her memory of the clandestine gathering in the garden shed was sharp, right up to the point where she and Magpie returned to their room—and after that, what intruded as memory could not possibly have been anything but dream.

"I'm going crazy," Thea announced to the ceiling.

"Urngh?" Magpie said sleepily, turning her head a little. "What do you mean, *going*?"

Thea glanced at the clock on her bedside table. "We're late," she said. "I didn't hear the alarm."

"It's *Saturday*," Magpie said patiently.

Thea rubbed her eyes. "Crazy," she repeated, and swung her legs out of bed. She froze as her gaze fell on the crack in the drawn curtains, which was letting in a cold gray light.

She got up and padded to the window, flinging the curtains open, heedless of Magpie's squawk of protest. Outside, the weather had worsened, and what had been a gentle drizzle had turned into a full-fledged storm with rain lashing down and trees swaying in the wind.

"Just as well we weren't planning on any expeditions today," Magpie said as she raised herself on one elbow and cast a glance out the window.

Thea shook her head. "Just as well," she muttered. "If I told you just how much farther I went last night than the garden shed, you'd probably tell me I was losing it."

"Anyone else, probably," Magpie said. "You promised you'd do no more solo flights, but it isn't as though I believe you. So, are you going to tell me about it?"

"When I wake up," Thea said. "Talk to me after breakfast. I really hope we have a nice, quiet day. I don't think I could handle much more excitement right now."

"Perhaps we should drop in on LaTasha, if they're letting her have visitors," Magpie said, getting out of her own bed. "It's funny, but there's been very little talk about it. You'd think that anyone who was actually there would—"

"Magpie, people don't particularly want to sound like complete nuts, even to their own best friends. People who saw LaTasha yesterday probably preferred to think they hadn't. But it won't be too long before even the kids in here realize that what happened to LaTasha wasn't an isolated incident."

"Do you think other stuff might get through? More spellspam?" Magpie asked, running her hands through her tangled hair. "Will they shut down Terranet completely in here?"

"They'd probably find it harder to do than they think. Most of us at this school depend far too much on e-mail. And parents will want to know their kids are okay. If they shut down those avenues of communication, they may as well shut down the school."

"There's always telephones," Magpie protested, but without much conviction.

"Sure, until people start getting annoyed that the phone is always busy. Which it will be, if everyone in this school starts phoning home."

"There's always *cell* phones," Magpie said obstinately.

"Okay, you win—there's cell phones! But they can carry only so much—and you *know* how much we all depend on e-mail for real information. The Nexus is the center of operations for Terranet access from the Academy—and if the principal keeps it shut down for much longer . . . Well, I guess we'll find out what happens when chaos breaks loose." She paused. "I need to talk to Terry."

Magpie looked at her beadily. "About what?"

"About how to stay safe," Thea said. "I had an idea."

She actually felt the blood rush to her cheeks at that, the blatant claiming of Grandmother Spider's inspiration, but somewhere deep inside her, she heard Grandmother Spider chuckle softly. *It's quite all right. It was your idea. I just helped you put it all together.*

2.

THE "IDEA" ARRIVED in a manila envelope later that morning.

Mrs. Chen waved Thea down in the entrance hall as she and Magpie raced down the stairs.

"You've got mail," Mrs. Chen called out, diverting Thea into her office. "Who on earth," she added, peering at the return address before handing Thea the envelope, "is Arachne Yiayia?"

"A grandmother," Thea said with a grin, "of sorts. Thanks!"

Mrs. Chen hesitated, and Thea looked up with wide eyes that were pools of innocence. "Do I have to open it now?"

"No-oo, but . . . ,"

"Trust me, Mrs. Chen," Thea said. "What's in here may solve a lot of problems."

"Why is it that sentences that begin with *trust me*

usually wind up being trouble?" Mrs. Chen murmured, relinquishing her hold on the envelope. "I'm not sure I should—"

"I will do absolutely nothing without talking to the principal," Thea said. "I promise."

Shaking her head, Mrs. Chen waved her out of the office.

Magpie craned her head at the envelope across Thea's shoulder.

"'Surprise, AZ,'" she read out loud, scanning the return address. "There's a place called Surprise in Arizona? Somebody made that up!"

"No," Thea said with a slight smile, "Grandmother Spider doesn't make things up. She makes them *real*. Even if there wasn't ever a place called Surprise in Arizona, there is now. You could find it in any atlas. I'd bet money on it."

"Grandmother Spider sent you *mail*?" Magpie squeaked. "What's in there?"

"A spellchecker," Thea said, and burst out laughing at the expression on Magpie's face. "Come on, we need to find Terry, and then the principal—it's complicated enough without me having to explain it more than once. . . ."

They ran out into the deluge, pulling hoods over

their hair. They found and cornered Terry in the library entranceway, pausing to shake excess water off himself.

"Terry," Thea called out as she ran toward him, "have you figured out what you're going to say yet? To the principal?"

Terry looked at her a little strangely. "Well, good morning to you, too. . . . If you're thinking about the job . . . it's a no-brainer," he said. "The big picture is pretty easy to see. It's the details that are going to be messy."

"Not necessarily," Thea said triumphantly, brandishing her envelope. "When do you start? Can you do it this weekend? We can test it out!"

"Thea!" Magpie wailed. "You said you were going to *explain* it!"

"I will. But it will be easiest to show it. It doesn't have to be on the Ne . . . on the you-know-what. . . ." She glanced around a little furtively before ripping open the envelope. "Oh! She sent *five*! You get your own, Magpie!"

"My own what?" Magpie demanded testily.

"One of these," Thea said, brandishing a small but exquisite dreamcatcher, which appeared to be attached to a keyring. *Nice camouflage,* Thea thought.

Terry, to whom she had handed the first dream-catcher, was looking at it skeptically. "Okay," he said, squinting through the web at Thea. "I'll bite. What is it supposed to do?"

"Let's go inside," Thea said, closing the envelope and running inside. Magpie and Terry, exchanging thoroughly baffled glances, followed.

Thea found an empty set of cubicles wedged in a dark corner of the library and posted Magpie as sentry in the nearest aisle, where she could keep an eye out for people who might be paying too much attention to what was going on. It was just as well that nobody was, because Magpie was a terrible perimeter guard—she was far more interested in trying to figure out what Thea and Terry were up to than protecting them from intrusion.

Thea instructed Terry to fire up the laptop.

"I can't get on Terranet anymore, if that's what you're after," Terry warned as the machine hummed into life. "Not until I figure out how to start up the Ne . . . the . . . other thing again. That's the gateway. All of the 'net is down at the Academy right now."

"Just as well, but I can still show you how it's supposed to work," Thea said. "And you can try it for real, after. Maybe you can talk to the principal about starting . . . your project . . . this weekend."

"There, it's up," Terry said, grinning in spite of himself. "What do you want me to do?"

"Open up an e-mail," Thea said.

"But I just told you I can't . . ."

"It doesn't have to be *live*," Thea said impatiently. "Just open up the software, and open up an e-mail. Have you still got the one, you know, that got you into trouble last night?"

"The 3-W one? Not on your life. Some things it's better not to keep as mementos," Terry said, tapping at his keyboard. "There. Now what?"

Thea picked up the dreamcatcher. "You had the right idea before," she said. "Next time you get an e-mail, look at it only through this. If it's . . . problematic . . . you can see that it is without the . . . problem . . . affecting you in any way, and you can kill the thing. Before it gets you." She closed one eye and peered at the sample e-mail Terry had opened through the dreamcatcher web. "Just like that. So that's the first thing. There's something else, but that . . . had better wait until you get into the . . . other place. It's hard to have a conversation when you have to talk in circles around things all the time!"

"Tell me about it," Terry said, with feeling, reaching

for the dreamcatcher. "I've had that particular problem all my life. Things I *can't* talk about, without . . . talking in circles. Don't worry, you've found an expert at it." He squinted at his laptop screen through the circle of the dreamcatcher, and then past it with his naked eye. "I can't see anything different," he said.

"That's because it isn't a you-know-what," Thea said impatiently. "When it matters, you'll see."

"Where did you say you got these?" Terry said, turning the dreamcatcher over in his hand.

"From someone who knows what they're doing," Thea said. "Are you going to talk to the principal? Tell him that I should be there, too. That first time, anyway. There's something we need to do, together."

Terry raised an eyebrow at her. "Just tell him that, eh," he said. "Maybe I should send *you* to talk to him."

"He'll listen," Thea said, grinning. It was all suddenly solvable, exciting, even exhilarating. "Just *go*, already."

Terry shut down the laptop, slipped it into its carrying case, and glanced over at where Magpie stood, riveted, with a book half pulled out of its place on the shelf.

"Watch out," he said conversationally. "Mr. Siffer's right behind you."

Magpie jumped, whipping her head around, and dropped the book, which bounced off her foot and against the stack on the shelf.

"Ow," Magpie said. "You can be such a *dork*, Terry."

But he was already gone, only an echo of his laughter left in between the tall stacks. Magpie bent to pick up the book she had dropped.

"Come on," Thea said, "we'd better follow him."

"What is this *we* you speak of?" Magpie muttered mutinously, her face hidden in the fall of her dark hair. "You haven't told me anything about any-thing—you've been on some secret personal crusade all morning!"

"Next time you get an e-mail, you'll see," Thea said. "Just hang onto your little dreamcatcher."

"Nobody sends me e-mail," Magpie complained. "I get letters. I get phone calls. You computer peo-ple. You think you know everything."

Thea turned around to stare at her friend. "I'm sorry," she said. "It's just . . . I get kind of carried away with it all."

"Yeah. I know. It's your own sick skunk,"

Magpie said, with a helplessly wicked grin. "Lead on, I follow!"

They loitered in the entrance hall of the administration building long enough for the principal to send for them.

Terry, Tess, and Mrs. Chen were waiting in the principal's office. Principal Harris rose from behind his desk as Magpie and Thea came in.

"These . . . gadgets," the principal said, gesturing to the dreamcatcher dangling from Terry's fingers. "I had half a dozen unwanted messages that arrived before I shut down the system, and which I hadn't even looked at—Terry tells me these things can identify them, so we tried it out on my quarantined stash—and it works like a charm." He rolled his eyes at his own choice of words. "Like a charm. Of course it does. The point is, it's a good monitoring system. If I can have one up here to . . ."

"Sorry, sir," Thea said. "She sent me five. One for each of the five of us—Terry and Tess, Magpie, Ben, me. I don't have any more to give away."

"Who sent them?" Mrs. Chen said, with an edge to her voice.

"*Arachne Yiayia* means Grandmother Spider," Thea said.

Mrs. Chen stared at her. "Grandmother Spider," she repeated.

"Grandmother Spider. *The* Grandmother Spider," Thea said helpfully. "According to legend, she helped create the world."

Mrs. Chen looked even more puzzled.

"Thea was sent back to the Anasazi," the principal said, but did not elaborate. "Frankly, Margaret, nothing has the power to surprise me anymore. The point is, these things aren't very useful if only the five of you have access to them."

"Oh, but they are," Thea said. "Only one is really ever needed here—the one used by Terry, on your Nexus. He can channel e-mail through that, kill anything that is dangerous."

"But the spell," began Mrs. Chen stubbornly. "I cannot condone leaving a student alone with the Nexus under the circumstances, particularly Terry, knowing what the side effects could be if he so much as mouthed something with a particle of magic in it. And that would mean round-the-clock surveillance . . ."

"No," Thea said. "I have an idea."

Sometimes you just need to open a window into another room in your mind.

They were all looking at her; the weight of all those eyes sank into Grandmother Spider's gentle words.

"I'd like to show you," Thea said. "I need a computer—any computer—to stand in for your Nexus."

"Be my guest," Terry said, offering his laptop. "What do you need? Just word processing?"

"That will do."

He pulled the computer out of its case, switched it on, tapped a few keys on the keyboard, and pushed it toward Thea on the principal's desk. "Go for it."

"Look," Thea said, and began typing.

Everything stays the same, except Terry can speak freely. What is done here is done in the real world outside this bubble.

She typed the period at the end of the sentence with a small flourish, and then glanced up at her audience. "Hold on to me," she said. "Just a hand on a shoulder. Anything. Okay?" She felt the weight of two hands—Terry's light touch with an encouraging squeeze on her upper arm, Principal Harris's heavier hand on her shoulder—and hit ENTER.

The other two waited a beat.

"Nothing happened," the principal said after a moment.

Thea looked up. "Terry, say 'spellspam.'"

"Thea," the principal began, an urgent warning in his voice, "he could—"

"You know I can't!" Terry said at the same instant.

"Trust me," Thea said. "Just say it."

"Sp . . . spellspam," Terry said, stammering, clutching the edge of the desk with a white-knuckled grip. He swallowed hard as the word left his lips, and then drew a deep breath. Without any trouble at all.

It hit them both, at the same moment. Terry's mouth dropped open, and the principal drew in a sharp breath.

"I said it," Terry said, astonished. "I actually said it . . . and I'm still breathing. . . . Thea, what did you *do*?"

Thea's smile was luminous.

"Someone told me that it is sometimes enough just to open a window into another room," she said. "We're in the same world, Terry. Our world. What-ever you do here will be echoed precisely back into the room that we just left—you can 'switch on' this world, the world in which you are safe, and you can do whatever needs to be done with the Nexus. I'm not sure how long you can stay safely without returning to claim your place in the *other* world, but it doesn't have to be long; you can do it in short snatches. But you're safe, and you can do anything here. Anything. It doesn't matter if it has magic in it; its taste will not kill you. You have the dreamcatcher, and you can deal with things that need to be dealt with here instead of back there, where you can be hurt by them. And when you're done, you go back."

"But how do I get back?" Terry said.

"Like this," Thea said, and added another word to the sentences she had typed on the laptop screen.

"We're back," Terry said.

Mrs. Chen was standing by the principal's desk, clutching at it with both hands. The principal glanced at her and gave her a reassuring nod.

"It's all right, Margaret," he said. "This might actually work."

"John . . ."

"Margaret, it will be all right, really. Next time, you go—you'll understand. Terry, are you officially accepting this responsibility? It's a lot for a young man to take on, but I think Mr. Wittering was not wrong when he told me that the Nexus would be in safe hands if we entrusted it to you."

"I will, sir," Terry said, standing with his back straight and his eyes glowing.

"Then it's time you met the Nexus," the principal said.

He crossed to a floor-to-ceiling bookcase on one of the walls of his study, and pulled a pair of books, apparently at random, out at a forty-five-degree angle. The bookcase clicked, detached from the wall, and then moved slowly, very slowly, on silent runners to reveal a dark doorway beyond.

"Follow me," the principal said, flicking on a light switch on the inside wall of the hidden passage, revealing a set of spiraling stairs leading toward a faint glow that came from somewhere out of sight down below.

Terry went first, followed by Tess, then Thea, and then Magpie, with Mrs. Chen bringing up the rear, still mumbling about how all of this was a bad idea.

It didn't look like much at first sight. The Nexus apparently consisted of little else besides a couple of large monitors on a rather ordinary wooden desk, which also held a headphone set, a keyboard, and a trackball mouse. The monitors were switched off. Everything was dark, except for a single red pilot light on each monitor and a faint opalescent glow coming out of walls that looked half-translucent, barely solid enough to mute a bright light blazing underneath.

"Like an iceberg," the principal said. "You only see the essentials, the things above the waterline. The Nexus is in the walls, in the ceiling, all around you."

"Wow," breathed Terry, the only one who knew enough to be impressed.

"It's been switched off for days," the principal said. "We need this thing back on line. Terry, do you think you're up to this?"

"I can do it, sir," Terry said.

The principal exchanged glances with Mrs. Chen, who stepped back, crossing her arms in front of her in an eloquent gesture of disapproval.

The principal sighed deeply. "The switch on the left monitor. That's the master. It'll turn the whole system on."

Terry reached for the switch, and the principal closed his eyes. Nothing seemed to happen for a moment, and then a series of seemingly less-than-extraordinary things occurred. A familiar hum of a computer, albeit deeper and more resonant than what anybody there was used to, filled the room; first one monitor and then the other woke out of a deep slumber and began going through power-up screens. Then the first monitor blinked, resolved into a complicated array of icons and menu bars; the second one opened several different windows, some showing complex and moving graphs as though on a hospital monitor, others with actual images, or indicating that they were a visual representation of audio or other kinds of signals.

Then the apparently featureless wall suddenly split open to reveal a hidden panel—more monitors, a luminous keypad, what looked like a built-in speaker.

"I'll show you the ropes," the principal said, watching Terry's eyes flick rapidly from one thing to another. "All of these things have meaning, and even a few days' shutdown will have caused a fair amount of chaos—it seems particularly unfair to fling you into that when such turmoil is brewing out there. But I didn't have a choice—I did not know enough about keeping this safe, how to protect it. I only hope I didn't do more harm than good."

"How essential is the Terranet connection?" Terry said. "Perhaps we can see what else needs to be done first, before we . . ."

"Terry," the principal said gently, "this is a gateway. You're already on the 'net, just by virtue of being powered up. We have good filters, but at least one . . . well, but we aren't in the safe place yet, so let us not speak of that in those terms. But one of the first things that you will have to do is check on the filters, protect the gateway, screen out malicious mail."

"Then it looks like I have a lot to do," Terry said, folding himself into the computer chair before the desk and reaching for the keyboard. "Thea, you'd better show me what you did upstairs. I might as well start dealing with things . . . from . . . *other-where*."

Thea stepped up to the desk. Tess, chewing her lip, trailed in her wake. Magpie hung back, standing beside Mrs. Chen, her hand folded tightly around her own dreamcatcher as though it were a talisman against everything. Magpie saw one of Mrs. Chen's hands clench tightly as Thea leaned over Terry's shoulder to type something and he, leaning forward eagerly, began scanning the monitors. Mrs. Chen appeared to have stopped herself from saying something by an act of heroic will, and Magpie glanced up just in time to see Principal Harris lay a reassuring hand on her arm and say, very softly, "It's all right, Margaret. The future has always been theirs."

They had a week of grace, while Terry attended classes during the day and wrestled with the Nexus almost every other waking hour. He caught and destroyed four different spellspams on the first afternoon of his acquaintance with the supercomputer, running on very little sleep and pure adrenaline. The principal spent a lot of time with Terry in the Nexus room and caught the early errors before they got out of hand—and Terry rarely made the same mistake twice. But the spellspam onslaught didn't appear to be letting up, and finally even this doubled vigilance proved not to be enough.

On the following Monday morning, the firestorm broke.

It started out innocently enough. Thea and Magpie passed a group of students in a corridor and happened to overhear a disgruntled-looking senior, someone whose athletic prowess had always exceeded his academic abilities, utter a mouthful of words Thea wouldn't have thought he was even aware of, let alone knew how to use correctly.

"This cessation of telecommunication is especially

vexing," he was complaining.

"It is pretty inconsequential," someone replied. "It is an annoyance, not a calamity. I would think that the systems would have needed an upgrade long before their primitivistic nature was overwhelmed by circumstances . . ."

Thea exchanged a baffled look with Magpie as they passed out of earshot.

"What was *that* about?" Magpie said.

"I have no idea," Thea said. "And I strongly suspect they don't either. Did I miss the class where memorizing the dictionary was handed out as homework?"

The two of them barely made it to their next class on time. It was math, with Mr. Siffer in a particularly unlovely mood.

"Can you explain to me," Mr. Siffer thundered at a cowed student, "just why it is that I have to repeat everything five times before your brain will retain even a quarter of anything I say?"

"It is probably overnervousness, and a disproportionate apprehension of what you are likely to dispense as punishment," the hapless boy blurted, and then sat there with such genuinely slack-jawed astonishment at what had just come out of his mouth that Thea suddenly felt a cold shiver run down her spine.

"Are you trying to be smart with me, boy?" Mr. Siffer said in a dangerously calm voice.

"It isn't my fault! I am just osseocarnisanguineo-viscericartilaginonervomedullary[1]," squeaked the boy, miraculously without even a stutter, and then winced, waiting for Mr. Siffer's inevitable retaliation.

A murmur of voices exploded helplessly in the class as other students stared at one another in complete bewilderment.

"What in blazes does that *mean*? If anything?" Thea hissed at Magpie. "Is it even a word?"

"It's Latin, I *think*," Magpie whispered back.

"You think? You take Latin, you're supposed to *know*—what does it mean?"

But Mr. Siffer was speaking again.

"You will," Mr. Siffer said, still calmly, speaking to the original student and ignoring everyone else, "report to the principal's office immediately after this class, Mister Williams. I will not be mocked."

But Thea was suddenly sitting up, cold shivers

---

[1]*bone, flesh, blood, organs, gristle, nerve, and marrow (derived from Latin)*

running down her spine.

"It's spellspam," she whispered to Magpie. "It's got to be. Those other kids, too, back in the corridor—"

Mr. Siffer began to turn around, to sweep the classroom with a gimlet eye. "I will have silence in this class!" he bellowed. "Or there will be—"

"I apologize, sir, I most profoundly apologize—I have no idea why I am so discombobulated."

Something blinked, passed almost too fast to notice. The classroom settled back into ordinariness, but there was something . . . different. A glitter in the air. A sense of strangeness, and change.

Someone sneezed explosively.

"Cease treating the matter with such floccin- aucinihilipilification![2]" Mr. Siffer shouted, and then stopped, startled at what had just come out of his own mouth. "These are incomprehensibilities!" he roared. "Something is starting to transpire here that I do not comprehend!"

"And isn't that a verisimilitude," Magpie said, and looked just as startled as Mr. Siffer had a moment before.

---

[2]*the categorizing of something as worthless or trivial*

"It's certainly disconcerting . . . ," Thea began, and then slapped herself on the side of the head with an open palm. "Aaargh! Now I am committing the same ridiculousness! And I haven't even seen the pestilential spellspam! How did *I* get afflicted with it?"

Ben, his eyes still watering from his sneeze, bent forward across his desk, catercorner to the two girls. "We *all* are," he said. "Everyone is using hippopotomonstrosesquipedalian[3] words. Right after he said . . . 'discombobulated.'"

It took Thea a moment or two, and then she put her face in her hands, shaking her head.

"Oh, for the love of everything sacred. Those original spellspams . . . the thing that got LaTasha . . . they never seemed to affect more than just the one person, the first person who saw it. But this one— this one is like the old ones, like the ones Dad cleaned up in the feral libraries. It's spread by the spoken word . . . it's *airborne*."

[3] *long*

To: Learn_a_new_language@babel.com
From: Polly Glott < Learn_a_new_language@babel.com>
Subject: Total immersion—speak a new language as though you learned it in the cradle!

Speak a foreign language instantly! You will be amazed at how easy it is to be misunderstood in a dozen exotic languages! Learn the language of your dreams now!

1.

*T*ELL PRINCIPAL HARRIS *that I will send* . . . Paul Winthrop's last words after Thea had taken the spellspam problem to her father had seemed to indicate he would send help.

She didn't know what kind of help she should be expecting—but when someone *did* come, it was not what anyone had expected.

The three visitors arrived almost unnoticed, as the school was frantically trying to cope with the aftermath of the polysyllabic epidemic. Classes had been suspended to avoid further spread of the 'infection'; the library and the cafeteria were declared out of bounds, and students were asked to remain in their rooms until everyone had been cleared. The teachers, with Mrs. Chen at the head of the team, tried to deal with the most affected cases first—a couple of students, including Ben, had had to be removed to the infirmary because exposure to the spellspam had triggered actual physical symptoms. The whole school was in an uproar, but it was the infirmary that was the most urgent center of concern, and it was there that the three visitors presented themselves to the nurse.

"What seems to be the problem?" said one of the trio, a young woman with skin the color of milky coffee and her hair in long dreadlocks down her back.

The nurse, who had been surprised in the act of removing a plastic bucket into which someone had just been sick, looked up in astonishment.

"I've got sick kids," she said. "That would seem to be the problem. Can I help you?"

"Luana," said one of the young woman's companions in a tone of mild rebuke. He was much older than she, a veteran with deep lines on his face and grizzled salt-and-pepper hair. "My name is Keir Adama," he said, looking as though he would have stepped forward to shake the nurse's hand by way of introduction, but thinking better of it. "We're from the Federal Bureau of Magic. We've been sent to help with the situation. May we speak to someone in charge?"

The nurse glanced down into the bucket in her hands and pressed her lips together in disapproval.

"You are. In here, that person would be me. But you probably want Margaret Chen. I," said the nurse firmly, putting out the hand bearing the bucket of vomit to prevent a determined move by Luana, "will go and get her. She is with a sick child right now." Luana raised a hand to remonstrate, and the nurse promptly thrust the bucket into it. Luana accepted the bucket with an instinctive gesture that was already at war with the expression of outraged disgust that was creeping across her face. "If you want to be helpful in the meantime, empty that. The bathroom is just to your right, there. Remember to flush. I'll be right back with Margaret. Please wait here."

Luana stood there for a moment with her hands gingerly folded around the bucket, her face tight-lipped and rebellious, before she uttered a smothered curse and turned to the bathroom. There was a slightly delayed sound of a toilet flushing, then the rush of running water, and then Luana re-emerged, her face thunderous, drying her hands with a paper towel.

"Just who does she think she is?" Luana growled, glaring at the nurse's retreating back.

After another moment, Mrs. Chen emerged and

walked over to the waiting trio.

"I am Margaret Chen," she said. "The nurse tells me you wish to speak with me?"

"We were sent to aid Principal Harris," Luana said. Keir quickly stepped forward, courteously offering his hand.

"Keir Adama, Mage First Class," he said. "These are my colleagues, Luana Lilley and Humphrey May. Paul Winthrop called us in from the Federal Bureau. Apparently you have a situation brewing here."

Mrs. Chen turned her head marginally as a cough from one of the cubicles behind her morphed into a soft moan. "A situation," she echoed, shaking her head and looking faintly dismayed. "If you'll give me a moment, I'll take you to see the principal."

Mrs. Chen escorted the trio to the administration building, directing them up the stairs to the principal's office, and then detouring to the residence hall to snatch up a startled Thea from where she and Magpie were playing Scrabble in their room.

"Your father's cavalry has arrived," Mrs. Chen said. "You'd better come with me."

When Thea and Mrs. Chen walked into the principal's office, a heated discussion was already taking place.

"I *saw* your methods," Luana was saying to Terry. "Quite aside from being old-fashioned and obsolete, you're doing it piecemeal. It's taking up far too much room, energy, and manpower. We need a wider net."

"That would be . . . what?" Mrs. Chen snapped.

"Figure out exactly what the spell was. Figure out a counterspell. Lay it on the entire Academy."

"Thereby breaking every law we have made about the use of magic on this campus," the principal said. "We can't sanction that. We *have* actually done the first part of what you suggest—the spell has been identified, and there is already a counterspell in place—but yes, we are dealing with it piecemeal right now."

"You are fighting symptoms," Luana said. "Not the disease."

"What about the students, the ones who are in real danger from this?" Mrs. Chen said obstinately. "We have quite a few of them, Luana. You've seen the infirmary. Ben Broome had to be sedated; he was sneezing so much he developed a nosebleed that wouldn't stop. Sarah McMurtry keeps threatening to slip into some sort of a coma. These are real kids with real problems—some of them are directly and sometimes radically affected by the backlash of a spell. Some of them, indeed, were sent here to *protect* them against magic and its effects."

"It's a bushfire," said Luana trenchantly. "We need to stamp it out. Now. We can worry about the details later."

Mrs. Chen roused. "Those *details* in this instance are somebody's children," she snapped. "This isn't some political game, Luana."

"It's fighting fire with fire," supplied Keir with a peacemaking smile.

Luana rolled her eyes at that, just a little. "Platitudes won't help, Keir."

"This school was supposed to be a firebreak," Mrs. Chen said. "The whole reason behind this being neutral ground, non-magic territory—"

"Perhaps, when the whole thing was first mooted," said Luana. "Right now, we don't have an option—we didn't introduce the magic to this place, but we have the responsibility to stop whatever's happening. I'm sorry, Principal Harris, but I think drastic action now is far more likely to stop this thing in its tracks than mollycoddling the situation and then trying to fight the aftershocks."

"But the ones who can't handle the direct

magic . . . ," Mrs. Chen began again.

"Like Terry Dane," Luana said, turning her dread-locked head slightly to skewer Terry with a sharp look. "Yes, I *am* aware of special circumstances. Kevin McAllister is my boss, as well as Terry's uncle. And Terry's condition does technically fall under our jurisdiction. What I want to know now is how this stuff got loose here at the Academy in the first place. Terry, I'm told that *you* are in charge of the Nexus here. Are you absolutely sure that you are up to the job?"

"Patrick Wittering thought he was," the principal said. "I have found no reason so far to suspect otherwise."

"Who decided you were up for yours?" Mrs. Chen muttered darkly, glancing at Luana with an angry dislike.

"All right," said Keir soothingly. "What *did* happen, Terry? Any ideas on that score?"

"You aren't going to like it," Terry said, and then hesitated, glancing helplessly at the principal.

"And he can't . . . actually . . . tell you. Not here. Not without endangering himself," Mrs. Chen snapped.

"Not . . . here?" Luana said, her eyes sharp with

suspicion. "If not here, where?"

"Thea," the principal said abruptly, "can you take us all through?"

Thea pushed her hair back behind her ears in a nervous gesture. "I don't know," she said. "I've never done it that way. When it's been other people . . . it's, well, they have to be holding on to me."

Terry opened his mouth, thought better of it, snatched up a loose pen off the principal's desk, ripped a page from a dog-eared notebook that he fished out of his pocket, and handed the piece of paper to Thea.

I'm not sure if I can actually utter this or not without choking on it—that's not true—we all went the first time, and nobody was physically touching you then.

"You can do it," he said, out loud. "You want the laptop?"

"Do what?" Luana said sharply, her gaze flickering from Terry to Thea.

"I can try," Thea said. "Pass it here."

"What is she doing?" Luana demanded as Thea's fingers flew over the keyboard.

Then the room blinked out, and blinked back in.

"What was that?" Luana barked, her hands coming forward instinctively into a position of casting a spell, staring up at the light fixture.

"Power surge?" said Humphrey hopefully.

"No," the principal said. "And no defense is necessary, Luana."

"Does this have anything to do with what's been going on here?" Luana said sharply. "You can't expect us to help if you withhold things—I think you owe me . . . you owe us . . . an explanation!"

Thea shot a desperate look at the principal, and then at Terry. "You can talk now," she said directly to Terry.

Terry drew a deep breath and nodded. "If you say so," he said. He turned back to the adults. "This whole situation shouldn't be possible," he began. "Technically it can't be done, not with computers— not through cyberspace. And then it *was* done, and e-mail took on a whole new dimension, and we just had to accept that we were wrong. This is something that can't be done on a simple level. Not by just anyone, and not from just any computer. Certainly not something that could affect the Nexus. A *lot* of this . . . spellspam . . ." He hesitated. "A lot of it is increasingly copycatted," he continued. "People who see what's floating around out there and like the idea of it then try it. Some of it is quite original, but none of the copycat stuff is good enough to pass through the filters that I've set up. It's all just . . . like . . . shadows of the originals. And I can always tell an original spellspam."

"In what way?" Luana said, frowning.

"They're the only thing that can consistently bypass any countermeasures," Terry said. "They . . . *evolve*. The first ones were really simplistic, but we've had a couple of generations since that and they're getting better, smarter—all the time."

"So are you telling me that the only thing that gets through is the stuff that really *can* hurt us?" Humphrey May asked.

"The bad stuff, or the really good stuff, depending on how you want to look at it." Terry looked back at the principal. "You told me there were two super-computers."

"Two . . . ?" the principal began, and then sat up, his expression stricken. "No. Oh, no, not that. Are you saying that Nexus 2 is the source of the spellspam?"

"Either that, or it's being channeled through it," Terry said.

"There are, or were, in point of fact, three," said Humphrey, almost too quietly to be heard, but the very softness of his voice served to focus everyone's attention. "The very first one . . . was lost. A long time ago."

"Lost how?" the principal said. "Please tell me you mean that it was destroyed and not just mislaid."

"That's ancient history," said Luana. "We have quite enough on our plate as it is. Perhaps I should see this latest spellspam, the one that caused your epidemic."

"Perhaps we all should," murmured Humphrey. "Not that this *particular* one stands out as special."

"It seemed to be . . . airborne," Thea said, remembering the incident in Mr. Siffer's classroom. "That's something none of them have ever been before. With this one . . . if someone said something that had been triggered by the original spellspam, it just seemed to—I don't know—spread, somehow. All you had to do was just hear it."

"It was in all the classes before lunchtime," Terry said quietly. "And that one came in only that morning. And it wasn't just that it was airborne, it was also the first one that required active intervention—

an antidote, as it were. The early ones would just wear off after a day or two."

"You said you had filters . . . ?" Humphrey prodded gently.

Terry glanced back at Thea again. "Some of them are a little . . . unorthodox," he said. "We'd need to go down to the Nexus. That's where the backbone setup is."

"We can't *all* go," said the principal firmly, opening his eyes and sitting up. "That room isn't set up as an auditorium. It will take three people, four maximum, but that's pushing it. Terry, you and I . . . and one of you three. At a time."

Luana stood up without waiting for discussion or consensus. "Fine. Let's go."

Keir was exuding dignified disapproval. "Perhaps I should go first," he said.

"You both go," Humphrey said mildly. "I can go with the second wave. You said four is okay, Principal Harris, so take Keir and Luana, and I'll wait. I have a few ideas of my own, but I think we ought to learn more about the problem before we plan how to fight it."

Thea bent her head, allowing her hair to fall over her face. If it had been up to her, she would have taken Humphrey and left the other two up in the office to continue bickering. Humphrey didn't seem interested in jockeying for position with Luana, or with anyone. His eyes were mild, but sharp with interest and intelligence; as the others disappeared down the stairs, he crossed the room to fold his long, lanky frame into the seat next to Thea's.

"I may be wrong," he murmured in his usual quiet voice, "but I think that something *else* is going on here, something quite separate from the spellspam issue. What do I need to know?"

For a moment Thea saw Cheveyo's dark eyes staring back at her instead of Humphrey's washed-out blue gaze. *Questions. Always questions with you, Catori.*

But when she had asked the question that Humphrey had just asked of her, or something very like it, Cheveyo had judged it a *good* question. Except now she had been cornered into answering, not asking. She shot a small, panicked look at Margaret Chen, who got up from her own chair and came over to pull up another so that she could join the huddle over the laptop computer Thea still balanced on her knees.

"I'll tell you what we know," Mrs. Chen said,

"but it isn't much right now—we were hoping to learn more before involving the FBM."

"I hear you," said Humphrey. "Thea . . . you are Paul and Ysabeau's daughter, the Double Seventh child. Am I to understand that you have found your path . . . ? I know you did something to this room. With a computer in your hands."

Thea bit her lip, and then said quietly, "There *is* a way of getting more than four people into that room. And I could just . . . show you. . . ."

"It would save a lot of explaining," Mrs. Chen murmured.

Humphrey said nothing, but his eyes were vivid with interest.

"But . . . wait a minute," said Mrs. Chen, "you've already transferred once . . . can you go one further from a secondary sphere and not affect the four there below with it?"

"I think so," Thea said. "If I *specify* that. Wait just a second. . . ."

She thought for a moment, chewing on her lower lip, and then typed furiously for a few moments before looking up from her screen.

"This time, you'd better hold on," Thea said.

"Mr. May, put your hand on her shoulder," said

Mrs. Chen after a moment.

Humphrey May obeyed with an economical motion, his fingers resting lightly on Thea's upper arm.

"Okay, here goes," Thea said, and punched ENTER.

2.

"Oy," SAID HUMPHREY, after a beat of silence.

Thea and Humphrey appeared to materialize above and behind the quartet in the Nexus room, looking at them as though through a mirrored one-way window.

The four in the Nexus room seemed to be unaware of the watchers. Terry was seated at the computer, typing something and apparently talking at the same time—or at least Thea and Humphrey could see his mouth moving, but there was no audio to this scene.

"Can we turn up the sound?" Humphrey asked, as both became aware of the barrier of silence.

"I don't know, I never thought to specify *that*, there were too many other things to think of. But let me see," said Thea. "You stay. I'll be right back."

She winked out next to Humphrey, who actually flinched. Mrs. Chen flinched in exactly the same way as Thea popped back into her other self, back into the principal's office.

"What did you do with him?" Mrs. Chen asked, with some consternation, looking around for Humphrey. She may not have liked the presence of the government mages at the Academy, but the loss of one of them, at a student's hands, would probably have been more trouble than it was worth.

"Don't worry, he's fine," Thea said with a grin, typing. "I just needed the computer. There, that's done it. I'll be right back, Mrs. Chen."

She winked out again, back to where Humphrey May was apparently trying to lip-read the conversation through the backs of the heads of the people in the room below. Just as Thea materialized beside him, both their ears seemed to pop in a manner not unlike that in a climbing airplane, and sound flooded in from the room below.

Where, now, there appeared to be *five* people.

Thea blinked and blanched, the color draining from her face as she reached out to clutch the nearest support—which just happened to be Humphrey May's elbow.

"That's *Twitterpat*! . . . I mean . . . that's Mr. Wittering . . . ," she whispered. "How . . . ?"

Humphrey turned to her. "Twitterpat?" he echoed, amused. "But that isn't a ghost—Terry just turned him on. I'm guessing that Twitterpat must be some sort of a holographic projection, left behind as a program in the machine. I think they've been having a chat in there, but the sound . . . only just came back on. Thanks, by the way. Neat trick. Now, *shhh*."

". . . would rephrase your question," the Twitterpat hologram was saying. It was not very good quality, with blurring at the edges and a set of defined expressions that appeared to rotate on its features randomly. "My abilities are limited at this time."

"Again?" Luana said. "What's the point of this, if he can't answer a simple question? If you go to the trouble of leaving behind a virtual copy of yourself as a help file, it isn't very helpful to be constantly told that the help file can't help you."

"I only just found the program," Terry said. "There may be refinements I haven't discovered yet."

"Have you asked it?" Luana said acerbically. "I know, don't tell me, it told you to rephrase the question. Which brings us back to the original track. The gobbledygook spellspam. I can see how that was done."

"I figured that one out myself," Terry said under

his breath, staring at his hands on the keyboard. "As soon as it hit. As soon as I found it."

Luana shot him a look of pure dislike, and continued as if she had not been interrupted.

"I can see exactly how that particular spell was executed—it's a pretty neat embedding," she said. "I know precisely how to counter now. Principal Harris, you simply have to let us handle this one our way. We were sent in to deal with this problem even before you had the emergency—but right now, it's of the utmost importance that we contain this outbreak. And that, while making absolutely *sure* . . ." She glanced at Terry again, briefly enough to be deliberately insulting, and then back at the principal. "We have to firewall this location, apparently far more solidly than has been done so far."

Terry roused, his head coming up sharply, his eyes flicking briefly to Luana's face and then coming back to fasten on the principal's—who was standing back, his arms folded defensively across his chest.

"I'd be grateful if you could rephrase your question. My abilities are limited at this time," said Twitterpat's hologram serenely.

"Shut that thing off!" Luana snapped. "If it isn't helping . . ."

The computer pinged once, sharply, in a "you've got mail" alert.

Luana and Keir both turned instinctively toward the screen even as Terry reached for the dreamcatcher device lying on the desk. The principal unfolded his arms, leaning forward, and then glanced briefly up toward the stairwell. Thea thought she could hear a voice calling down something almost inaudible, but raised, as though posing a question.

Luana, who was on the right side of the desk, reached out and seized the computer mouse at Terry's elbow.

"No, wait . . . *don't touch that*! I need to . . . ," Terry yelped, trying to prevent anyone from looking on it with an unshielded eye.

"*Usme bhi kuch na kuch gadbad hai[4],*" Luana said.

"What?" said the principal, leaning closer.

"*Lako ih je prepoznati kad znaš šta tražiš[5],*" Keir said practically in the same instant, nodding.

"*Kya bola?[6]*" said Luana, turning around to look at him.

---

[4] *That one looks like trouble, too. (Hindustani)*
[5] *It's easy to recognize them when you know what you're looking for. (Serbo-Croat)*
[6] *What? (Hindustani)*

"Meddyliais i buasa hyn yn digwydd[7]," the principal muttered, closing his eyes.

"Molim?[8]" said Keir.

"I'd be grateful if you could rephrase your question. My abilities are limited at this time," said Twitterpat's hologram helpfully.

Luana straightened up, staring at the two men. *"Tum dono kya khel khel rahe ho?[9]"* she demanded.

"Oh, *God*," Thea said, already raising a hand as though she was about to smash it through the "window" that separated her from the others. "I've got to—"

"Wait!" Humphrey said, catching her wrist. "I still don't know how you do what you do, but forcibly breaking a boundary between any two of your spheres can't be a good thing for anyone. Let's get back and we will go and . . ."

"Olin ka ilii an my öhässä sil lä kerrallan[10]," said Terry despairingly.

Humphrey stopped, mid-sentence, mid-motion. "*That* was Alphiri," he said softly. "Now I am really

---

[7] *I was afraid this was going to happen. (Welsh)*
[8] *What? (Serbo-Croat)*
[9] *What are you two playing at? (Hindustani)*
[10] *I think I was too late that time. (adulterated Finnish standing in for Alphiri . . .)*

starting to worry about this. How did they get their fingers into this pie? Take us back, Thea. Now. I need to undo this one, fast."

With a last frightened look at the astonished people talking at one another in four different languages, Thea obeyed.

"Is everything all right?" Mrs. Chen demanded, surging forward as Thea and Humphrey popped back into the principal's office.

"No," said Humphrey, crossing the room in two long strides and launching his lanky frame down the hidden stairwell.

"Thea?" said Mrs. Chen weakly as she subsided onto the edge of the principal's desk, clutching it for support.

"There's been another spellspam," Thea said, typing furiously. "Luana went and opened it, and they all . . . That's what Humphrey's gone down there to try and fix. And I'm trying to . . . take them all back to . . ."

The room blinked again, as it did once before, and then everything seemed to settle down into its proper position once more.

"Hang on," Thea said, dumping the laptop unceremoniously onto the chair next to her and crossing the office in Humphrey's wake to peer down the stairwell. "Everybody okay?" she called out.

There was a murmur of voices from below, and then a sound of footsteps on the stairwell. Thea stepped back, her face white and drawn. Mrs. Chen launched herself from the principal's desk, in time to catch Thea as she swayed and crumpled, her legs folding bonelessly underneath her.

"Is she all right?" the principal demanded, stepping into his office from the Nexus stairwell.

"I think you'd better get the nurse in here," Mrs. Chen murmured. "What just happened?"

"She stretched too far," Terry murmured, from the stairwell doorway.

Humphrey came over as well, knelt beside the principal, took one of Thea's hands in his own, and rubbed at it gently. "By the time I got down there, she'd . . . I don't know . . . wound back time. To just before the spellspam e-mail came in. Just before everyone looked at it. I made sure . . . they didn't. I was going to try a counterspell, but it wasn't needed—Thea had managed to . . . prevent . . ." He shook his head, very slightly. "Time *and* space," he murmured. "Perhaps we should reconvene tomorrow, and before then I'll try to explain to Luana why her approach . . . would not be a good thing right now. But I also have a far bigger problem."

"Bigger than *her*?" Mrs. Chen muttered, with a swift glance of dislike in Luana's direction.

"The Alphiri," Humphrey said. "I'll set Luana on that—it's the sort of crisis that would be far more her thing. And while she's doing that . . . let me take care of the Academy. In the meantime . . ." He bent forward and effortlessly scooped Thea into his arms, unfolding his long legs like a crane and getting up while cradling her against his shoulder. "Terry, would you like to show me the way back to the infirmary?"

To: destinations@travelmate.com
From: Miss D. Wreck-Shunn < destinations@travel-mate.com >
Subject: See all the exotic places of the world!

A magical mystery ride as you explore all the places that you've only heard of—imagine what you might find in these distant and dramatic destinations! Come travel with us and see the things you never believed possible!

1.

THEA WOKE SUDDENLY, with a start. She was in a strange room with a white enamel bedside cabinet on which sat a half-full glass of water. The window was in the wrong place, across the room instead of beside her, and in front of it sat Tess, engrossed in a book.

Thea's mind clicked into gear and started to classify. Infirmary.

The Nexus. People doing strange things . . . speaking in weird languages . . . *Twitterpat*.

Thea laid her palms flat against the mattress and bolted upright into a sitting position.

The sharp movement made Tess lift her head. For a moment it looked like she might content herself with that and go back to her book, but then her eyes lost their soft, slightly unfocused look and her face lit up with a smile of genuine delight. She closed the book with one hand and crossed the room to perch on the edge of Thea's bed.

"Well, hello, Sleeping Beauty," Tess said. "About time you woke up."

"What time is it?" Thea said. "What happened? Where is everyone? Did they really . . ."

Tess laughed, lifting both hands to stem the outburst. "You slept for . . ." She consulted her watch briefly. "Well, it's pretty close to twenty hours," she said. "Another hour or two and Mrs. Chen would have had the nurse declare you to be in a coma and taken to the hospital. But Humphrey May said you'd be okay, and apparently he was right."

"Are they still here?" Thea asked.

"Who?" Tess said. "The hotshot triplets? Yeah. Luana's been prowling the place like a caged tiger. She was supposed to go back to Washington yesterday with Keir, but the car that was supposed to pick them up never arrived—and now apparently the bigwigs are sending a helicopter for them. Or so the rumors have it. It seems that whatever was going on with all of you folks just before you passed out has stirred up a nice little hornet's nest back at headquarters."

"Could you start at the beginning, please?" Thea

asked. Her hair was a tangled mess, hanging over her face and dangling before her eyes, and she lifted one hand to push it back. "I've been *asleep* for nearly a whole day."

"I was hoping you'd tell me the details," Tess said. "All I know is that Terry somehow invoked Twitterpat's ghost, and apparently that was enough to spook everyone—"

"That wasn't what spooked everyone," Thea said slowly, trying to piece together the fragments of her memory. "When Terry suddenly started spouting Alphiri . . ."

Tess sat up sharply. "What?"

"Everyone was jabbering in tongues," Thea said. "I have no idea what any of them actually *were*, even, and I don't know if they did either—and I'm not even sure that any of them were aware that they were talking funny, they all just thought that everyone else was—and then Terry said something and Humphrey said that was Alphiri, and that he needed to find out . . . and then we went back . . . and I went . . ."

Her voice died out altogether as she sat in the infirmary bed, frowning slightly, trying to remember something elusive and yet important, which was nagging at the fringes of her memory. Tess glanced down at her watch again, and then at the door.

"Humphrey made everyone swear that they'd call him the moment you woke up," she said, "but if nobody else knows you're awake, then nobody can call him. . . . Do you want a bit more time to pull yourself together?"

"Are you telling me that someone's been sitting with me nonstop?"

"Yeah," Tess said. "It was mostly Magpie and me, in shifts, and Ben, once—and the nurse has been keeping an eye on you at night. Whatever went down was *big*, apparently, and you made quite an impression on the government folks." She shook her head a little, a gesture full of the regretful knowledge of someone bearing bad news. "I have to tell you, I am not entirely sure of how much of a good thing that is."

"From obscurity straight to center stage," Thea said with a grimace. "Out of the frying pan and into the fire."

"Mrs. Deaver would shoot you for using a cliché," Tess said primly, and then laughed. "But I know what you mean."

"I just wish . . . I could remember what exactly happened back there," Thea said. "I can see stuff, but it doesn't make any real sense. . . ."

"Do you want me to get Humphrey?" Tess said. "Maybe he can explain things to you."

"He'll probably need to haul the other two in here, too," Thea said. "Mrs. Chen doesn't like that Luana woman, and I can't say I do, either."

"She's a political sharklet," Tess said. "I've seen plenty like her—they show up at our house all the time currying favor—young and hungry and just waiting for a chance to make her mark. I think she smells it here. Which is bad, because such people are remarkably good at stirring up trouble where there wasn't any before. But I know how to get word to Humphrey alone." Tess actually smirked as she said that, and Thea was instantly distracted.

"You *know* something," she said.

Tess leaned forward a little in a conspiratorial manner. "He's smitten with our Woodling, apparently, from what I hear," she said.

"Signe? Signe Lovransdottir?"

"Yup. He practically ran our gorgeous environmental science teacher down in a corridor just outside the infirmary after he left you here, and he looked into her eyes and was lost. He's been following her around adoringly ever since. What's more, it's mutual."

"How do you know? You've been in here with me," Thea said.

"Well, I have the first from eyewitness testimony—Terry saw them trip over each other."

"Terry wouldn't know smitten if it bit him on the nose," Thea said succinctly.

Tess laughed. "Not all wrong, but in this case he was just reporting on what he saw, not stating an opinion."

"Ugh, enough, already," Thea said. "Is there anything to eat around here?"

"I'll see what I can do," Tess said with a grin, and slipped out of the room.

About fifteen minutes later, a plate of chicken and mashed potatoes in front of her, Thea was feeling much better—but increasingly frustrated.

"I think you'd better call Humphrey May," she said to Tess through a mouthful of potato. "I need to know what happened back there. I'll be no use to anyone if I just wilt away like a scythed flower every time I try to do anything with . . . you know. I need a vacation. . . ."

"I don't think you can count on having one this summer," Tess said frankly. "You had a reprieve because nobody outside your family and a few trustworthy friends knew what you could do. Now you've done it in public. The Feds know. They'll want a piece of you. Trust me."

"But we can *all* do it," Thea said, rebellious. "With the whale . . . when we hunted the Nothing . . . you guys followed me. . . ."

"You left a trail," Tess said. "*You* led the way there. You left us a message, however cryptic, on the computer—and we knew what it meant, because of what we had all done before. But that was before anyone else knew about it—before you ripped away the curtain, and Luana was there to see it. You're dead meat. They'll cut you up and serve you with relish."

"Thanks a lot," Thea said.

"My uncle will make sure of it," Tess said morosely.

"Knock, knock," said Humphrey May from the door. "Okay if I come in? Your uncle will make sure of what, Tess?"

Tess had looked up, startled, and her look quickly passed from surprise to wariness. "I'm just saying," she said, with a touch of defensiveness in her voice, "Thea is toast. After this. What with the Bureau . . ."

Humphrey raised a hand, palm out, in a gesture of

oath-taking. "I will not let anyone toast Thea," he said solemnly. "That's a promise. Glad you're finally awake. Are you feeling better now?"

"A little," Thea said. It was hard to believe, after having slept for so long, but now that she was safe and fed and warm, she was beginning to feel drowsy again.

Humphrey saw her eyelids fluttering, and smiled.

"I do want to talk to you—no toasting involved— but it can wait until tomorrow. I am going to strongly suggest to Mrs. Chen that you spend tonight here before going back to the residence hall. And I'll keep Luana away from you, at least until you're well enough to run and hide by yourself."

"Is everything . . . all right?" Thea asked carefully.

"Everything is under control," Humphrey said. "Sleep it off. We'll talk in the morning—there's plenty of time for everything."

As it turned out, he was wrong—but Thea happily snuggled back down into her pillow until late the next morning, when she finally woke up feeling much more like herself—ready for yet another day that threatened to dissolve into crisis.

It was a Saturday, and Tess and Magpie both came to spring Thea from the infirmary, walking on either side of her like a pair of human bookends. The three of them ran into Ben and Terry on the steps of the infirmary.

"They're at our heels," Ben said, "and I don't know if I should tell you to stand your ground or turn around and flee back to bed, Thea."

"It's probably just as well you're near the infirmary," Terry said. "Back to bed might not be a bad idea."

"Talk sense!" Tess said. "What are you going on about?"

"Her," said Thea with an economical toss of her head in the direction of Luana Lilley, who was striding toward them with a sense of doom-filled purpose, closely followed by Mrs. Chen and a couple of other people who might have been the principal and Keir Adama.

"Where's Humphrey?" Tess hissed. "He said he would be here to protect you. . . ."

"He's on his way," Terry said. "I swear, I don't ever want to get that guy angry at me. He sent us here, and he was *mad*."

"At whom?" Thea said, just as Luana and Mrs. Chen both arrived at the foot of the steps, flushed and breathless.

"All right, you're awake," Luana snapped. "And I want some answers, now."

"I don't care who you are, I will not have you terrorizing a student in this manner," Mrs. Chen snapped back. "The principal is on his way, and you can be sure that I will make a report directly to Washington if I have to. . . ."

"You don't. I've already done so," said a familiar voice from behind Thea.

Humphrey May, who had just rounded the corner of the infirmary, was coldly and fiercely angry, his blue eyes chips of diamond-edged ice. "She knew better, as always," Humphrey said, and his voice, too, was low and cold. "What were you hoping Thea could tell you, Luana? That she could lead you to Signe?"

"What happened to Signe?" Thea asked. She liked her Environmental Studies teacher, aside from being honestly intrigued by her exotic Faele origins.

"Thea Winthrop should come to Washington with us right now, Humphrey—you know that," Luana said, lifting her chin defiantly. "You have to admit she's been close to every one of these spellspams when they happened. *She* was in the library when the first one hit the school. *She* was there when the long-word spellspam became an aural spell and started spreading by the spoken word. *She* was close by when we were all hit by the language spell at the Nexus—"

"And she was still practically unconscious when *you* opened the one that sent Signe away," Humphrey said. "You're reaching, Luana."

"Thea and Terry both," Luana said obstinately, keeping the focus off Signe and what had happened to her. "We should take them both back with us. I think we all agree that they know more than they are saying. They can help us figure it all out."

"They are *kids*, Luana," Humphrey said. "Your entire case rests on two kids from the Last Ditch School for the Incurably Incompetent?"

They all winced at the deliberate use of those words. It was a name Thea herself had used once, but that seemed a very long time ago. Mrs. Chen looked honestly appalled that the phrase had been uttered out loud, right in the heart of the Academy, within hearing of its students.

But it had not been Humphrey who had used those words first. It was obvious that it had been Luana's snide dismissal of the place, not his own.

"Well," Humphrey said, ignoring everyone else's reaction, "you've learned better, haven't you? We will discuss later, in much more detail, whose competence is in question here."

"What happened . . . ?" whispered Thea.

"There was another," Terry said. "Another of those messages."

Humphrey made a chopping motion with his hand. "Not out here," he said. "Terry is right. Another of those spellspam messages slipped through. Luana didn't go through your gateway, Terry, she used an outside network—from *my* laptop—and one got through. And it was just Signe's bad luck that she happened to be the one to see it first. And Signe's *gone*. I don't know how or where yet. But you"—he turned back to Luana, the ice back in his eyes and voice—"you *are* going straight back to Washington, and I will make an earnest recommendation that you be held fully responsible for all of this. You've always wanted responsibility—I will make sure you get it, in spades. Keir," he said, addressing their recently arrived colleague, "make sure she doesn't get into any more trouble before the helicopter gets here."

"What are you going to do?" Keir asked in a low voice.

"I'll stay here. I have to find her. Fast."

"The branch," Magpie said, suddenly understanding. "Her branch. Her tree. If she was taken without it, and stays without it for too long . . ."

"What?" Thea whispered, her eyes full of tears.

"She could die," Magpie said.

Humphrey turned a bleak look on her, and then turned away.

Keir had shepherded Luana away, and the principal, after a few whispered words to Mrs. Chen and a quick nod to Thea, had followed them.

"Phone your parents from my office, Thea," Mrs. Chen said as she gathered the others and turned toward the residence hall. "I have been keeping them apprised, and Humphrey talked to your father, but I think you should reassure them that you are all right."

A passing teacher hailed Mrs. Chen with a question, and she broke step to answer; while her attention was elsewhere, Thea turned and clutched at Terry's sleeve. "What got through?" she hissed, and then rolled her eyes. "You probably can't even say it. Tess, do you know?"

"No," Tess said, glancing at her brother, who gave the briefest of nods. "But he knows. He can write it down for me. Why do you ask?"

"I need to know what happened," Thea said. "I just want to . . ."

"I'll find out later," Tess whispered, just as Mrs. Chen turned back.

"I need to fetch some notes from Terry, Mrs. Chen," Tess said. "I missed one class when I was sitting with Thea. Can I go do that now?"

"All right," Mrs. Chen said.

Ben stuck his hands into his pockets, looking suddenly awkward. "I'll see you later, then," Ben said, without quite meeting Thea's eyes, and then loped off after Terry and Tess, who had peeled off already and were discussing something in low voices.

"I'll keep you company," Magpie said.

2.

AUNT ZOË ANSWERED the phone at Thea's house. "Your father had to go out, and I persuaded your mother to get some sleep," Zoë said, explaining her presence. "I'll get her to give you a call when she wakes up—she really needs to hear you're okay. And your father wants to know *what happened*. I think they should both just move up there so they can keep tabs on you. Anyway . . . are you sure you're all right? . . . Do *you* know what happened?"

"Not yet, but when I do you will be the first to know," Thea said with a hollow little laugh. "You *can* tell Dad that his friends from Washington are really awful, all of them except Humphrey May, and there's more trouble. . . ."

"What?" Zoë said sharply as Thea's voice died away. "Please stay out of it for once. Go and lock yourself in your room and don't stir until you've talked to your father. If you go flitting off on some adventure again, I will send Anthony over there with instructions not to let you out of his sight," Zoë said, her voice heavy with warning.

"I believe you," Thea replied. "Tell Mom I'm fine. I'll call again later, or she can."

Magpie was in their room when Thea went upstairs, laying out a game of patience. She looked up as Thea came in, and gathered the cards up into an untidy pile.

"So," she said, "tell me. I'm completely weirded out by the whole thing, and I don't really understand this spellspam stuff at all—and what's going on with Signe?"

"I have no idea," Thea said. "I know as little as you do about the latest crisis. Probably less. At least you were awake for it—I slept through everything."

"Spellspam," Magpie prompted. "I know the basics—how it started with LaTasha—but please explain."

"It's junk e-mail. With embedded spells. That cause real damage, apparently," Thea said. She described what she could remember from the scene in the Nexus room and the babbling in foreign languages; Magpie began by having the giggles, but then, thinking it all through, quickly sobered up.

"And Signe? Humphrey said that she's *gone* . . . gone where?"

"It sounds like another spellspam," Thea said. "But the others were more or less practical jokes—if Signe is really gone, disappeared, because she glanced at a piece of e-mail on-screen, then we have a bigger problem than we thought. I should have asked Aunt Zoë if anyone else out there has disappeared. Tess said she'd find out from Terry what the real story was."

"But where could she have gone?" Magpie said, frowning. "Is this anything at all like the sort of thing that you do? You know, slip off into a pocket universe of your own?"

Thea sat up. "It's like Tess said," she whispered. "They think it's me—I'm the only one they've seen do anything like this. Even Humphrey has his suspicions. Luana will tell everyone back in Washington that the only person she's seen do magic stuff with computers is me. But there *is* someone else out there. Someone like me."

Magpie's eyes were wide. "Someone else who can do computer magic?" she echoed.

"These spellspams have to come from somewhere," Thea said.

"So now you think it isn't a Double Seventh thing after all?" Magpie asked carefully.

"I think this gift might be something new. It's not a Double Seventh talent. It could be anybody—and we have no way of knowing who this other person is, the one who is doing all this."

"Thea, where do you think Signe might be?" Magpie murmured. "If she's been taken too far away from even a scrap of her spirit tree, the last connection to her life force . . . I don't know how long she has, but the clock is definitely ticking. Humphrey may not know enough to know where—or even how—to look for her."

Thea turned to her, startled, but anything she might have said was forestalled by a light knock on the door. Tess poked her head into the room.

"Hey," she said. "Terry got a copy of the spellspam." She held out a piece of folded paper.

"Is it okay to read this, just like that?" Thea asked, hesitating.

"Terry says it's okay. He rewrote it. The original spell was in the computer version."

"What does it say?" Magpie said impatiently.

Thea opened up the note. "*A magical mystery ride as you explore all the places you've only heard of— imagine what you might find in these distant and dramatic destinations! Come travel with us and see the things you never believed possible!*" she said, reading out loud.

"Thea," Magpie gasped, "it *is* the same thing . . ."

"No," Thea said slowly, staring at the message. "*I* need to have a clear picture in my own head of where I want to go. This . . . it's different. It has a different feel to it altogether. I *knew* I should have asked Aunt Zoë if anyone else—"

Tess interrupted. "If you wanted to ask if anyone else outside the school has disappeared in this way lately, the answer is yes. Apparently people have been plucked right out of their chairs and found as far away as China and Polynesia. This one's real trouble, Thea."

"Can Terry try and follow them in any way?" Thea asked.

"He looked at the headers, through the Nexus," Tess said. "It's a dead end, like always."

"But Humphrey thinks he can find Signe . . . ?" Magpie said in a small voice.

There was something about the wording of the

143

spellspam that made Thea very uneasy. "This is very vague and broad," she said, staring at the paper in her hand. "If this is all he's got to go on, they're likely to end up in the opposite corners of the known universe . . ."

They didn't see much of Terry over the next two days, and they saw Humphrey only once, looking drawn and haggard.

"He's driving himself too hard," Thea had said.

"Signe is running out of time," Magpie said quietly.

It was only a few hours later when Thea looked up with a sense of déjà vu as Tess flung open the door to Thea and Magpie's room.

"Humphrey's gone, too," she said. "Terry said that he was last seen heading toward his quarters bearing a green-leaf branch in his hand—and then nothing, and he wasn't in his room or anywhere else . . ."

"Signe's branch," Magpie gasped. "Thea, who knows where *he* is now—do you think that the e-mail might have taken him, too? He might have thought, if he allowed himself to be voluntarily taken by the same spellspam . . ."

"Tess . . . those other people that were missing . . .

how long did it take to find them?" Magpie asked.

"Terry didn't say," Tess said slowly. "Why?"

"Signe doesn't have time to wait and be found," Thea said, looking up. "Not without that branch. She could die, in whatever way Woodlings die. She could just . . . wither away. Disappear. And it's been—what—nearly four days now?"

"Thea," Magpie said, "could *you* . . . ?"

"I can't go places I haven't been!" Thea said violently, crossing the room to stand at the window and stare out at the cedars. "I don't know how! And I wouldn't know where to start looking!"

"That isn't exactly true," Tess said slowly.

Thea turned her head to look at her friend, her eyes sparkling with tears. "Yes, it is," she said. "What do you mean?"

"When we went to hunt the Nothing," Tess said, "was that ocean a place you've been before?"

"Not really," Thea said. "It was something I *made up* . . . not a real place, just a place that was *right* for what we needed . . . and besides . . ." Grandmother Spider had helped her cross into that world, but the world had been her own, had sparkled in a miniature vision in one of Grandmother Spider's dreamcatchers before anything else had happened. It was her own world, a place she had never been before.

A true weaver.

"Thea," Magpie said, "what are you going to do?"

"I need a computer," Thea whispered. "Can you get me Terry's laptop?"

"If Mrs. Chen saw me coming in here with a computer, she'd blow a gasket," Tess said.

"Please," Thea said. "It'll be safest from right here. You two can keep an eye on things. You know how to bring me back . . . if it all goes wrong."

"Thea . . . ," Tess began.

"I'll get it," Magpie said quietly. "Mrs. Chen would not even think about suspecting *me*. Are you sure, Thea . . . ?"

"What are you going to do?" Tess asked.

"If I knew," Thea said, "I would tell you."

A few minutes later, Magpie slipped back into the room with the contraband laptop. Thea sat down cross-legged on her bed with it on her lap, hands poised over the keyboard. And then, suddenly, Cheveyo's voice was in her head again.

The Road goes to where it needs to take you. Where do you choose to let the Road take you now?

"The Barefoot Road," she murmured.

"Huh?" Tess said, leaning closer.

Thea twisted slightly to rummage briefly in a drawer of her bureau, coming back out with a length of leather thong wrapped around her knuckles. Three feathers dangled from between the fingers of one hand as she hunched her shoulders and began to type.

"No, wait," Magpie said. "Leave her alone. She needs . . ."

A rush of white noise whipped the words away from the fringes of Thea's hearing, and her surroundings—her room, her friends' anxious faces—shimmered briefly and were gone.

3.

THEA REACHED UP slowly to draw the thong necklace over her head and smoothed the three feathers down as they came to rest on her chest. The
clear light of the high desert surrounded her, red
mesas rising around her, and a wide, straight road
unfolding from where she stood upon it with her
feet bare to the earth before it vanished beyond the
horizon.

"Well done," said a familiar voice, and Thea
turned her head slightly, already smiling. Cheveyo
stood just a step away from the Road, but not on it.

"I was hoping I would find you here," Thea said.
"You told me once that I could choose to have this
Road take me to where I want to go."

"I did," Cheveyo said serenely. "Are you ready to
make that choice?"

"But Cheveyo . . . how do I make it take me

somewhere if I don't know where I am supposed to be going?"

"The Road," Cheveyo said, "cuts across many worlds. Weave the place you need to find as you walk. You know how to do this. You have done it before."

"I wove light," Thea said.

"And space," Cheveyo said. "And even time. Grandmother Spider has told me of your achievements."

"Time?" Thea murmured.

"You may not have been ready for that," Cheveyo said, inclining his head a little. "It drained you. But what you do now, that is not nearly as taxing for you. Everything else stays the same, Catori—the only thing you need to do is to weave a world with a hole shaped like whatever that thing that you are seeking needs to be. Its very absence will lead you to where it is to be found."

Thea hesitated, considering this new angle. "There are *two* things," she said at length. "They probably aren't together."

"Then you have two choices," Cheveyo said.

Thea stared at him, but it became obvious that this was all she was going to get from Cheveyo.

"I'd better get going, then," she said, reaching up

to close her hand around her feathers.

Cheveyo inclined his head, stepped back. "When you are done," he murmured, "perhaps you can come back and tell me of it some day. Now go, and may the Road take you true."

And then she was alone. Alone with the choices Cheveyo had laid before her.

Signe . . . or Humphrey? Her vulnerable teacher, or the government mage more than capable of taking care of himself?

But Humphrey held Signe's lifeline, the branch of her spirit tree. If she found Signe first and she was in any kind of trouble, and then took too long to find Humphrey with the branch, it could all be for nothing. Her first instinct was to find the Woodling, but she quickly realized that it would be far more practical to search out Humphrey May first.

Thea reached out impulsively and grabbed a handful of the dusty red shadow pooling below a mesa she was passing, weaving it in and out with a narrow ribbon of the intense blue she had picked from the sky. The simple weaving of light had been the first piece of true magic that she had touched—a rope of light and shadow, a small miracle. Now, faced with something far greater than she understood, it gave her courage.

It also brought to mind the precise shade of Humphrey May's eyes; and then Thea hunted around for something that would remind her of his hair, of his stature, weaving these hints around a central gap which, under her hands, began to assume a certain kind of pattern, a certain kind of shape. She hesitated for a moment as a scent of something *green* drifted by her, a glimpse of trees and a mountain and a sky that was somehow very different from the one that arched above the mesas . . . and then houses, unfamiliar ones, nothing like she had ever seen before. And then she stepped onto something hard, a texture very different from the Barefoot Road, and it was cold and wet, and she realized that she stood on the edge of a platform that dropped down into a narrow concrete canyon, at the bottom of which lay a set of railway tracks, glistening in a drizzly rain.

A railway station.

With a sudden and sure instinct, Thea reached back through a hole in the air, and hung on to a thread of light from the world in which the Barefoot Road lay; that piece of sunshine now lay beside her feet, a golden filament, out of place with her new surroundings. It was much cooler here than it had been in that other sunlit world, and Thea shivered where she stood, bare feet on damp concrete, wrapping her arms around herself to preserve what body warmth she could.

She had stepped off of the Road precisely in front of a sign bearing the name of the place where she had emerged:

Llanfairpwllgwyngyllgogerychwyrndrobllllantysiliogogogoch.

Why on earth would Humphrey show up here? Would anyone here actually speak English, enough of it for Thea to ask if anyone had seen a blue-eyed mage wandering around clutching a piece of green-leaved wood . . .

"Thea?"

It was Humphrey May's voice, and the rest of him followed his incredulous question as he unfolded himself from a bench beside the apparently abandoned station house, and took a step toward her.

"What are *you* doing here?" he said, and there was something wary in his voice, as though he could not believe that Thea's arrival in this place was pure coincidence. But when he spoke again, there was an edge to his voice that made Thea shiver with far more than cold—something wild, very close to panic. "Thank God you found me," he said. "I hope that you haven't trapped yourself in this place, too. How did you get here?"

"I followed you," Thea said. "I found you, and I followed you. I wove . . ." She realized that whatever she said would make no sense, not without a great deal of explanation, and they had no time for that. "How long have you been here?" she asked instead.

"There's a clock over there, but it hasn't moved since I've been here," Humphrey said. "It could have been days, for all I know. The spellspam that took Signe . . . I found another copy, thought I could follow. But when I first found myself in this place—it was up on the hills, I was flat on my back in a field full of sheep, and I spent some time hunting around because I thought that Signe might be somewhere close . . . but she wasn't, *nobody* was, there seems to be no living thing here except the sheep. I finally came down and found the tracks, and then followed them back to this place."

"Llanfair . . . *what*?" Thea asked.

"It's a place in Wales. With the longest known name in geography, I believe. I've been here before." Humphrey looked around slowly, searching the empty shadows of the station's platforms. "But this is different. Thea, *there is nobody else here.*"

"I can see that," she said. "Perhaps the next train . . ."

"No. There is no next train. There is no train, there will never be a train here. All of this . . ." Humphrey waved his hand at the station behind him, the empty platform. "All of it, it's stage setting. There is nobody here except me . . . us. This is an empty world. It is a place something . . . somebody . . . created out of my own fears, and the spell in that e-mail took me there. The last time I came here, back in our own world, it was thronged with people—with tourists, locals. . . . The idea that such a place could be emptied of people—that it's possible to be this alone . . . It terrifies me to see it like this, to know that my secret fears, the things that I am most afraid of, can be made this real for me. This is powerful stuff, this virtual magic you are dabbling in."

For a moment he looked troubled again, as though he were trying to put together an equation in his mind, trying to figure out what really connected Thea with this eerie, empty place.

"Places you never believed possible," Thea murmured, making her own connections.

"What was that?" Humphrey said.

"That was in the spellspam. That was the spell—places you never believed possible. Places you dreamed about, or want to go, or fear. That's where it takes you." *And what did that mean for poor Signe? Where did she wind up?*

"I tried the phone in the station, tried to call my office, to get someone who could come and get me home . . . but it just rang and rang and rang," Humphrey said. "That's when I knew that something was really wrong. It just isn't possible that there would be no reply on the other end. Not in the real world. Not in *our* world. The station might have just been between trains, but this . . ." His expression suddenly changed, and the eyes that he turned to Thea became pleading. "Thea . . . do you know where Signe is?"

"No, but I can find her, like I found you," Thea said, with far more confidence than she felt.

"Can you get us out of this place?" Humphrey asked. Thea could feel the weight of his anxiety in his voice.

She turned around and picked up the thread of sunshine that lay coiled at her feet. "With this," she said, "yes. Come over here."

Humphrey, pausing only to carefully gather up Signe's branch from a bench behind him, vaulted down onto the rails even before she had finished speaking, and then up onto her side of the platform.

"Are you ready?" Thea said as he scrambled up.

He drew a deep, ragged sigh. "Never more ready to leave anyplace in my life," he said.

Thea wrapped her fingers more securely around the thread of light, and pulled. The air opened before them; she took Humphrey's elbow with her free hand and pushed him forward; he staggered for a moment, and then stood, astonished, as the rain-drenched little railway station dissolved around him into the warm dry heat of the high desert. Thea looked down.

"You've got shoes on," she said.

He followed her gaze. "Yes," he agreed. "That would seem to be the case."

"Then don't move," Thea said, "or we'll lose it." She reached up and lifted her feather necklace over her head. "Here," she said, "this will bring me straight back to you. Stay absolutely still—I'll try to be back as soon as I can."

"Back from where?" Humphrey said, staring at the red mesas around him with unbelieving eyes.

"What is this place? How on earth did you *get* here?"

"Later," Thea said. "Signe."

His face changed. "Go."

It was harder to weave Signe out here—she was the stuff of Faele, and that was slipperier by far than Thea's own kind. By very virtue of her identity, Signe was a sort of shape-shifter and it was hard to "weave" a Signe-shaped hole when that hole wavered between being a delicately boned woman and an elegant silver birch. Thea thought she had failed completely when the pattern in her hand began to assume a shape that was far too familiar— but not that which she was seeking.

And then she picked up one last shadow, one last thread of light, one last piece of understanding, and it all fell into place for her.

The things most feared.

An exiled Faele-kin.

The pattern in Thea's hand was beginning to show her the thing she herself feared—the Alphiri. She had been ignoring it, willing it to go away, because part of her was sure it was her own fears that she was weaving into the pattern, but it all made sense—the Alphiri were of a similar kindred to the Faele, but a higher caste, ones that might have judged, ones that might have had a hand in an exile . . . ones that might choose to hold on to some condemned soul delivered to them until such time as a ransom could be paid. The Alphiri, after all, did nothing for free.

And once she realized all this, Thea could suddenly sense Signe's presence, a weakening light, almost at the end of her endurance . . . in the glittering tower of the Alphiri capital city.

I can't do this!

It was a moment of pure panic, and she reached for her feather necklace . . . *courage . . . wisdom . . . patience . . .* even as Alphiri minds became aware of this intruding, seeking presence and reached out tendrils to capture, to hold.

She was back at Humphrey's side in an instant, shivering violently. He reached out instinctively to steady her, and she flung out a restraining hand.

"Don't move!" she said. "I know where she is. The Alphiri have her. Signe is in a crystal city somewhere. You will know. It should be easy to find her now that you know where to look."

To: student@anyschool.com
From: Dr. Nowitt Alle
<Headmaster@HouseOfDiplomas.com>
Subject: You've already got a diploma!

There's a diploma waiting for YOU—and it's already on
its way! Perfect for framing!

1.

THEA HAD NOT been able to take Humphrey May
into the Alphiri city itself, so she deposited him,
after he gave her a few essential details, in his Bureau
office before using her Road tendril to get back to
her own room at the Academy.

Humphrey had pulled every string at his disposal,
slashing through protocol and red tape and charging
into the Alphiri heartland demanding Signe
Lovransdottir's instant repatriation. The Alphiri had
tried to bargain, seeing the possibility of turning the
situation to their profit, and their own version of the
story had emphasized that Signe was of Woodling
blood, and thus Faele, therefore she belonged far
more in the nonhuman polities than in the human
world. That version of events collapsed when it
turned out that it had been a high court of the
Alphiri themselves who had exiled Signe from her
own home, destroyed her spirit tree, and sent her

away with a single branch of it to cling to for survival. Without the tree, Signe could not live very long in any polity, and in fact she had already been very weak when she was found. When Humphrey threatened to take the matter to an emergency session of inter-polity court and invoke possible trade sanctions, the Alphiri handed over Signe without any further spin.

Humphrey brought Signe back to the shielded grounds of the Academy, where she could safely retreat into her spirit branch and spend time healing and regenerating. Before leaving again for Washington, he sought out Thea.

"Signe was almost transparent by the time we got her back—but once she's had a chance to recover a bit, I'm sure that she will very much want to thank you herself for your part in all of this," Humphrey said.

"You didn't tell anyone else . . . ?" Thea said. That was the one thing she had made him promise—that he would tell no one about her own role in the whole affair. "If the Alphiri found out . . ."

"No, and I have no intention of doing so," Humphrey said. "I keep my promises. I don't know why you are so afraid of the Alphiri—they cannot do anything to harm you, not while we are watching over you, and we *are*, Thea—but quite aside from any of that, telling anybody would mean telling them about that awful, awful place I got myself trapped in, and the fact that it took a *kid* to spring a high-powered government mage from there. I still don't even understand *what* you did, let alone how you did any of it."

"I'm figuring it out as I go," Thea murmured.

Humphrey grinned.

"*However*," he said, "I do think the time for concealment is over, Thea. If you think Luana will keep her mouth shut, you're sorely mistaken. If she cannot find a way to pin any of this directly on you, at the very least she'll manage to make your inability to fully understand or control your own gift a part of the plot to regain her own standing in the Bureau. Much of this Alphiri mess was Luana's own doing, and she'll try very, very hard to focus everyone's attention elsewhere right now because she herself would collapse under too much scrutiny."

"So they'll still think that I did it all," Thea said.

"I seriously doubt that a case could be made for that anymore," said Humphrey.

"*Anymore?*" Thea echoed.

"You did some pretty strange things back in the principal's office the first time I saw you work," Humphrey said gently. "I had no explanation for any of it."

Thea simply stared at him.

Humphrey sighed. "You seem to have been riding to everyone's rescue from the sidelines, but it's high time that someone came riding to yours—and now I think it's time we let a real expert do a little digging."

"Who?" Thea asked. And then, hopefully, looking up at him, "You?"

"I don't have the credentials," Humphrey said. "Even if I thought I had, you taught me different when you hauled me out of that appalling trap I had managed to get myself into. Let me discuss this with the principal, and I think I'll call in your parents, too. I do have someone in mind. There's only one man I can think of who knows enough on the background of this. Trust me."

It was left at that. Shortly after that conversation, Humphrey had made himself scarce again, leaving Thea alone to try to pick up the unraveled threads of her academic responsibilities. But he returned to the

Academy before the end of the month, took Thea and, somewhat unexpectedly, Terry aside for a private chat.

"You know the Nexus has been placed at the Academy because it can be well concealed here," Humphrey said. "All of our people here were effectively undercover agents, acting as instructors at the Academy—there were others before Patrick Wittering. You might say this school was built around the Nexus. But there are *two* Nexus sites. And the second Nexus is notable not for its location . . . but for its keeper. You've heard of him, no doubt—he is one of that rare breed of mage, of which Patrick was also one, who actually understands the working innards of a computer."

"Professor de los Reyes," Terry said faintly.

Humphrey nodded. "He has been known to take in students for the summer, especially since he's supposedly retired from Amford. So I figured, we could send him both of our young stars. It will seem, to any prying eyes, to be no more than the professor taking on an interesting summer project with a couple of promising apprentices. Proximity to the other Nexus will give Terry valuable experience. And the professor can concentrate on figuring out the puzzle that is Thea . . . and perhaps all of you can find the answer to this spellspam problem, while you're at it. I can't think of a better man for the job than Sebastian de los Reyes."

"How long are we supposed to be there for?" Terry asked.

"Four weeks, at the outset," Humphrey said. "If that needs to be adjusted, it can be."

But Thea was thinking about what Tess had told her recently—*you can forget your summer*. She became conscious of a profound sense of growing up too fast—of missing her family, or even just missing a summer vacation.

"*After* you've both had a chance to catch up with your lives," Humphrey said gently. "Your summer internship doesn't start until July."

Naturally Magpie, Ben, and Tess were all waiting impatiently to hear what the meeting with Humphrey had been about.

"Well?" Tess said. "What did he say?"

"We're both being sent off to summer school," Thea said.

Ben blinked at her. "Why? Your grade average is better than mine."

"Not remedial, silly," Tess said. "Where?"

"They're sending us to Sebastian de los Reyes. The

professor," Terry said. "*God*. Do you think Isabella will be there?"

"Was she the one who applied to be Uncle Kevin's intern last year? The one whose résumé you saw and drooled all over her photo?" Tess said. But Terry didn't laugh, and Tess gave her brother a beady look. "I don't believe it," she said. "You've never even seen her in the flesh, Terry. All you know about her is that she's a brain, and she's *hot*."

"Don't be ridiculous!" Terry said, snapping his head back as if Tess had struck him.

"Oh, yes, you are soft on her!" Tess crowed glee-fully. "She won't give you the time of day, you know—you might be a prodigy, but she's a sopho-more at Amford and gorgeous and probably can't even remember being fifteen."

Terry stuffed his hands into his pockets, his eyes slid-ing away from his sister's. "I wonder if they'll let me take along the palmtop link to the Academy N . . . ," he began, and then halted, as Ben drew breath to interrupt. He looked around with deliberately exag-gerated care, and then said loftily, "Well, we can't talk about it here. I'd better talk to Humphrey about it later. In the meantime, I have some think-ing to do."

"Whatever the original idea was, sending *you* there will prove to be a total waste of time if Isabella is in residence," Tess said.

Terry gathered up what shreds of dignity remained and sauntered off, head held high, trying to look very casual—but his sister stared after him with an expression that eloquently conveyed that she, at least, was not fooled.

"Smitten," Tess said as Terry rounded the corner of the building out of earshot.

"Sophomore at Amford, eh?" Thea said thoughtfully.

"She's blond, aristocratic, and by all accounts she was a child prodigy at whatever she put her hand on," Tess said. "Don't know much more than that."

"I have brothers who will," Thea said. "I knew I'd find an actual use for Anthony someday."

"You'd do better to pump your father for information on the professor," Tess said, suddenly serious. "I've never met him, but by reputation he's a crotchety, moody old medieval Spanish grandee transplanted into a modern world, and he isn't supposed to like it here much."

Thea shrugged. "Then being under Mr. Siffer's thumb all these months will have been good training."

* * *

The worst of the epidemic was over. Over the next few weeks, one or two pieces of spellspam popped up like poisonous mushrooms, but people were being careful and Terry's filters seemed to be holding the spellspam at bay—at least in the protected environment of the Academy.

The rest of the school year flew by with startling speed, and then the summer break was upon them.

"You *will* write and tell us what's going on, won't you?" Magpie said as they were all saying their good-byes.

"E-mail?" Thea said with a grin.

"That would be just fine. I have the spellspam dreamcatcher with me," Magpie said, "but I have no e-mail access at home, and I don't think you'll want this floating around the rec center computers . . . so that settles that."

"I have the filter," Ben said, clearing his throat. "You can e-mail me."

He was sounding very awkward, even for Ben, and Thea gave him a startled look. "Okay, if you like, I'll try—but I'm not the greatest correspondent."

"Well, I just wanted to say . . . ," he began and

then stopped. "Have a good summer. Hope they don't keep you too busy. . . ."

"See you in the fall," Thea said.

Ben just smiled, raised a hand in a half-wave, let it drop, and turned away.

"What's the matter with him?" Thea muttered, staring after his departing back.

"He only wanted to ask you to the Harvest Ball, when we get back in September, that's all," Magpie said.

"Well, why didn't he?"

Magpie shook her head. "Figure it out, doofus. I think he's jealous, actually—there you'll be, cooped up all summer in some exotic household with Terry—even if Terry *is* interested in someone else altogether—but there you two will be. Please do write, by the way. Promise?"

She was curious, naturally, as was everybody.

By the time Thea got home, her brothers all knew about her summer internship. They all thought that her spending the summer with Amford's most famous academic in his own private retreat in San Francisco was, in their terms, *awesome*. Frankie was openly jealous, and sulked for three days before the curiosity overwhelmed him and he joined the others as they questioned Thea as to the details of the trip. Anthony was the only brother who wasn't home, and that frustrated Thea's own original intention to pump him for information on the fabulous Isabella, but at the mention of Isabella de los Reyes's name, her second-oldest brother, Ben, himself a student at Amford, merely laughed.

"Anthony would not have told you a thing about her. He rarely boasts about his failures," Ben said.

"Did he try dating her?"

"She turned up her nose at him," Ben said. "She turns up her nose at pretty much everyone. The last I heard she was seen out on the town with a member of European royalty. Anthony's pedigree just wasn't up to scratch."

Thea snorted. "I didn't *think* I would like her," she said.

But the best news came when Aunt Zoë bounced into Thea's room a couple of days before she was due to depart.

"Could you use company?" Zoë said.

"Huh? Right now?"

"I have some vacation coming," Zoë said. "I thought I'd spend it in San Francisco. You and I could go down together, and then I'd be doing the tourist thing—for a week or so at least. When you have some free time, I could take you and your friend Terry out to see the Golden Gate Bridge, or into Napa, maybe. . . . What do you say?"

No words were necessary, as Thea wrapped herself around her aunt in a tight hug.

"That's settled, then, I take it?" Zoë said, amused. "I'll go and make arrangements. Go pack!"

They flew down to San Francisco from Seattle, and then Zoë rented a tiny hatchback at the airport and handed Thea a map.

"Presidio Terrace," she said. "The swanky part of town, by all accounts. You're the navigator."

Swanky was an understatement.

"Can't I just stay at a hotel with you and come up here if I need to see him?" Thea asked as they swept onto the tree-lined entrance of the Presidio Terrace estate. "What do I call him, anyway? Professor de los Reyes is such a mouthful."

"I think 'sir' would do," Zoë murmured. "As for the rest . . . Thea, the idea was that you spend some time with the man. Terry will be around, too. It isn't like you'd be entirely alone—"

She swung the car into a wide, brick-paved circular

drive outside a white-washed house of palatial size, with a huge carved double door that wouldn't have looked out of place in a medieval castle, and windows adorned by elaborate wrought-iron grilles in the manner of an old Spanish hacienda. On the island in the middle of the drive, a fountain played quietly over smooth stones.

Zoë pulled up in front of the three stone steps that led to the carved door, and turned to her niece. "Well, I'll get you checked in and then I'm off," she said. "You have my cell number. Just call if you need me, anytime."

"Thanks for coming with me, Aunt Zoë," Thea said. "I wish you could stay here. . . ."

"That would defeat the object of the exercise," Zoë said. "Now go on, ring the doorbell. I'll get the luggage out."

Thea got out of the car and dragged her feet up the stairs; finding no doorbell, she picked up the enormous brass knocker and brought it down hard on the door.

2.

BEFORE ZOË HAD a chance to wrestle Thea's two suitcases out of the trunk, the door swung soundlessly open to reveal a middle-aged woman with her hair swept back into a loose chignon and wearing a tidy ensemble of blouse and knee-length skirt.

"You must be Galathea Winthrop," the woman said, glancing at Thea, and then at Zoë, who slammed the trunk lid shut.

"I'm Zoë," she said. "I'm Thea's aunt. I'll be staying down in the city for a week or so while she's . . . studying here, and I'll probably be in and out, taking her for an occasional lunch or something. Are you Señora de los Reyes?" Zoë spoke Spanish, and she gave the name the correct lilt and pronunciation, but the woman she was addressing responded with a tight little smile that implied a grievous error of some kind.

"I am Madeline Emmett . . . the housekeeper," she said primly. "Your room is ready, Miss Winthrop; your colleague hasn't arrived yet, but we expect him by dinner. The professor will see both of you then." She grabbed the smaller suitcase and started back up the steps again, turning to glance at Zoë. "You can make an appointment to see the professor himself, concerning any outings," she said. "He is unable to see you now, but perhaps if you telephone this evening . . . ?"

"Aunt Zoë . . . ?" Thea said, balancing her back-pack and hefting the second suitcase with both hands.

"Don't worry, I'll be back tomorrow," Zoë said, reaching out with one hand to brush Thea's cheek.

"If you will follow me, Miss Winthrop . . ."

The housekeeper waited at the foot of a wide spiral staircase that curved around a central well ending in a high cupola ringed by windows. "This way," she said as Thea hesitated, looking around at the opulence of it all.

Thea brought her gaze back to the staircase. "Yes, thank you."

She was conducted to a room nearly four times the size of her own bedroom at home, with a canopied white bed against the far wall and a pair of French doors opening onto a tiny balcony with a wrought-iron balustrade. The doors were open, and a breeze stirred the filmy white drapes that framed them; beyond, Thea could see the city spread out below her.

"Wow," she said, dropping her suitcase by the door.

"The professor had this house built when he was first married. Every corner of it is special," Madeline said. "I've cleared the closet for you," she added, opening the closet doors for emphasis, "and there's a chest of drawers over there for your use. There's a laundry chute in the closet floor, and the bathroom is across the hall. For the duration of your stay, those facilities have been set aside for you and your colleague to share. He will have the room next door. I will leave you to settle in; dinner is at six."

She walked precisely through the spot where Thea could have sworn she had dropped her suitcase and left, closing the door behind her. Thea registered briefly, with a degree of surprise, that the suitcase in question was now tidily stowed on a luggage rack across the room—but her attention was not on the things she had brought with her. She stared at the open doors, transfixed by the view; there was something about the light outside that made her hands ache to bury themselves into it and weave a pattern that was rich and strange—twisted strands that encompassed breadth of space and light, and old magic, and power.

But first she wanted a computer, that step between worlds; she scrabbled in the smaller suitcase, which contained a laptop. Thea's parents had not been happy about letting her out of the house with her own computer, but she had pointed out that the things she could do with that computer were the main reason that she was being sent to Professor de los Reyes, and the Nexus might not be the best tool with which she could demonstrate those abilities to the professor. Her brother Ben had finally suggested that she borrow his laptop for the few weeks, and Paul and Ysabeau had agreed—though not without misgivings.

She had barely managed to pull the zipper all the way open before the suitcase appeared to take on a bizarre life of its own. Thea jumped back with a startled yelp as the closet doors sprang wide open and the contents of her suitcase began to unfold, piece by piece, levitating out of the suitcase and draping around hangers in the closet or tucking themselves tidily away onto the shelf beside the hanging rail. The underwear Thea had packed folded itself up neatly and then hovered expectantly in place just above the suitcase as though waiting for a place to be made for it. Thea glanced over to the chest of drawers, then crossed the room and carefully pulled the top drawer partway open. It immediately slid all the way out and the underwear settled into one corner.

Thea yanked on the zipper of the second suitcase, the bigger one, and watched, astonished and entertained, as that, too, emptied itself with swiftness and precision. A vanity bag, hairbrush, a handful of clips and barrettes, and Thea's favorite rose-perfumed shower gel were deposited in a tidy pile on top of the chest of drawers. Less than five minutes later both suitcases were empty, the smaller one nesting inside the larger one, the outer zipper of the larger suitcase zipping itself neatly closed. Thea's laptop and an assortment of things the unpacking spell didn't quite know what to do with were left sitting on the bed, awaiting manual disposition.

"Wow," Thea said again. "This is quite a place."

She thought better of messing with the computer for the time being, and decided to explore instead.

Hoping she wouldn't accidentally blunder into the professor's study, she opened the door to her room just a crack and peered up and down the corridor outside. It was empty. She scooped up her vanity bag and crossed the hall to where a door, left ajar, indicated the presence of the bathroom Madeline had said she was to share with Terry; she wondered whether the unpacking spell was in force there, too. She switched on the light, taking stock of the large room with its glassed-in shower and a double-sink built-in vanity, and placed the bag of her odds and ends beside one of the sinks, still closed. Before she had a chance to step back properly, the bag had been opened and its contents distributed—toothbrush and toothpaste in a rose-pink ceramic cup, lip gloss and deodorant in the mirrored cabinet above the sink together with her barrettes and elastic ponytail bands, hairbrush neatly on the counter beside the sink. Even the lint inside the bag was meticulously shaken out over the sink, and then the faucet came on briefly to sluice it all away.

"This will be quite a month," Thea muttered.

She left the bathroom to its ablutions and went to the spiral staircase that wound up toward another floor and swept down to the entrance hall where she

had come in. Thinking that the other floor, in someone else's house, would be better left alone, Thea
made her way down the stairs into the hallway, feeling rather like an old-time movie star making a
grand entrance.

The hallway was full of light, spilling down from
the skylight dome. It was paved in cool pale tiles,
and large tubs of some plant with huge pink flowers
flanked the curved ends of the stairs. Thea stood in
the midst of the hall, peering at half-open doors.
Through one, she could see wooden paneling, a
glimpse of a fireplace with a huge portrait of a
woman in an old-fashioned dress hanging above it,
books piled artfully on a side table. Through another
door, a set of heavy, high-backed carved wooden
chairs surrounded a massive table. A third room
looked more promising—a wash of sunlight spilling
over a burgundy rug on a warm hardwood floor, and
a chocolate-brown sofa peering out from underneath
a chenille throw that matched the rug on the floor.
On a side table along the wall there was a vase filled
with tall blue flowers.

Thea stuck her head around the door to peer in.
The room appeared to be a sitting room, with a double set of French doors opening out onto a patio

framed by rough-plastered brick walls half-covered with vine and a creeper with large, trumpet-shaped bright red flowers. A wrought-iron table and four matching chairs were set out on the brick paving, and beyond them a stretch of perfect lawn covered a gentle slope that led the eye straight out into yet another spectacular view of the city. The lawn was bordered by flowering shrubs, trees, and a flower bed riotous with color.

The French doors were unlocked, and Thea stepped out onto the patio, feeling the sun-warmed bricks beneath her sandaled feet. She thought about her own backyard, a patch of grass surrounded by natural cedar woods and a row of old rhododendrons, and couldn't help shaking her head, thinking of how much time and energy *this* garden's upkeep must take.

"Would you like me to show you around?"

An unfamiliar female voice made Thea spin around. She saw a slender girl with golden-blond hair held back from her face by a pair of combs; she wore a white T-shirt, jeans, and casual open-toed woven leather slides, yet she still managed to give out an air of being a queen about to hold court.

"You must be Galathea," the girl added, inclining

her head slightly by way of introduction. "I am Isabella de los Reyes."

Thea suddenly thought of Terry caught in that regal gaze, and fought a wild urge to giggle out loud—and then suddenly flushed.

"I'm sorry, I didn't mean to impose," she said. "I just got here, and since the room took care of the unpacking and my friend—the other student who's supposed to come here over the summer—isn't here yet, and the housekeeper said dinner isn't until six, and I . . ."

"As I said, would you like me to show you around?" Isabella said, smiling. "This house . . . can be a bit disconcerting to people who are new to it. I see you've been admiring the gardens."

"They're beautiful," Thea said sincerely. "You must have an army of gardeners."

"Not a one," Isabella said. "You know the Lawn-smooth spell?"

"The one that lets the grass grow only so high so the lawn never needs mowing? Sure. Our own lawn at home is just a postage-stamp-sized square compared to that, but my dad has the spell in place."

"No self-respecting mage is seen mowing his own lawn," Isabella said. "But my father created that spell, and holds the license to it. Even if he weren't wealthy before, he would be from the money *that* brings in. That and the Housetidy."

"You mean what hefted my suitcase from the floor to the rack?" Thea asked.

"Indeed. You don't drop things around this house and expect to find them where you left them. If you kick your shoes off at the door, you'll find them in your closet the next time you look. If you drop a half-finished novel on the table and forget about it for five minutes, it'll be back on the shelf. Sometimes with a bookmark in it . . . if the spell is working particularly well. The laundry chutes from every room collect dirty stuff and then it'll be delivered back to your closet the next day, washed and ironed."

"It would drive me crazy," Thea said without thinking, and then flushed again, biting her lip. "Sorry. But I'm not the world's tidiest person and I live in a house where six brothers came before me. My mother gave up a long time ago. We pick up our own messes . . . when we remember."

"This is the library," Isabella said, pushing open the door of the room with the portrait above the fireplace. Isabella pointed to the portrait. "That's Estella, Father's first wife, the one for whom this place was built. He has several . . . *photographs* of my mother in his study."

"Is your mother . . . ," Thea began carefully, but Isabella gave a short, sharp laugh that made Thea stop dead.

"My mother," Isabella said, "gave up too. She left this place a long time ago, when I was barely five, and left us to my father to raise."

"I'm . . . sorry," Thea said, feeling exceedingly lame.

Isabella turned and crossed the hall to the room where Thea had seen the huge old table. "That's where dinner will be," she said. "I'd better go and get ready. We dress for dinner in this house, just so you know."

"What am I supposed to wear?" Thea asked, astonished.

"If you get it wrong, he'll let you know," Isabella said. "Well, I'll see you at dinner, Galathea."

"It's *Thea*," said Thea.

Isabella shook her head. "Not in this house. Father doesn't hold with nicknames. You go by the name you are given by the Gods when you are born. You're Galathea, get used to it. Don't be late, by the way—Father hates it when dinner has to be held for latecomers."

She inclined her head at Thea by way of dismissal, and turned to waft her way up the spiral staircase. Thea wasn't sure what Isabella would be wearing for dinner, but she knew that she wouldn't be surprised at a tiara.

She went back to her room, where she discovered that someone had closed the French doors and tidied away the laptop onto a small desk. She wondered about plugging it in to recharge the battery, but quickly realized she would have to ask for instructions. What she had taken for an electrical outlet was no more than just a blank white socket-shaped plate set into the wall. She left that problem for later and opened up her closet instead, wondering if she had packed anything elegant enough for the professor's dinners. In the end she decided on a dark-red dress with a scooped neckline, dressed up with a belt made from old silver coins and a pair of dangly earrings. She was still standing before the mirror, wondering whether or not to add a draped silk scarf to the ensemble, when there was a knock on her door.

"Thea? You in there?"

She crossed the room in a couple of long strides and flung the door open. "Terry! I've never been so glad to see anyone in my life!"

"Well, thanks," he said with a grin. "What brought that on?"

"This place . . . is weird," she said. "I think we'd better pull a slipstream world fast, before you get into trouble. This place . . . is packed with magic."

"I know," he said. "I'd better not say anymore just yet. What's this dinner? That housekeeper woman told me to wear a tie." He suddenly realized what she was wearing and did a double take that made Thea suddenly blush almost the same shade as her dress. "Wow," Terry said, "you look pretty."

"Thank you!" she said, genuinely pleased. And then remembered something else. "But I am not even in the running," she added.

"There's a competition?" Terry asked.

"I've met your Isabella," Thea said.

It was Terry's turn to blush. "She isn't *my* Isabella," he muttered.

"Sorry," she said, contrite. "You'd better get ready. I am told the professor hates it when people are late. Which you are, by the way. What took you so long to get here? I thought you were supposed to be here before me."

"I was," Terry said, "but then they got another . . .

another . . . you know what. . . ."

Thea flung out a hand. "Stop! I need to plug in my computer before you can say anything about that . . . and there isn't a plug. Not that I can figure out."

"Yes there is. Watch."

Terry crossed over to the desk and crouched beside the blank plate in the wall.

"Where's your power cord?" he asked.

"In the case."

Terry dug around and came up with a power cord, grasping the business end with his right hand and pointing the prongs at the blank metal. For a moment nothing happened, and then the blankness acquired a translucent quality, like a soap bubble, and then vanished altogether, leaving behind a serviceable power socket in the wall. Terry clicked the prongs of the power cord into it, and gestured that Thea should plug the other end into the laptop. She booted up the computer, then pulled up the word processing program and typed up a couple of short sentences.

"Okay," she said, hitting ENTER. "We should be okay."

"We . . ." Terry began, but then something buzzed in the air around them, and then there was an audible snap, as though someone had broken a guitar string. The light in the room darkened for a moment, and then brightened again. Terry touched Thea's arm gently and pointed; the laptop's power cord dangled loose, the socket once again a blank plate in the wall.

Thea yelped in consternation. "What was that? I'd better not screw it up, my brother will have my head on a platter if I ruin his computer!"

Terry mimed writing, and Thea gave him a notebook and a silver ballpoint pen.

I think we need to find a way to make it compatible with this house, Terry scribbled on a blank page. *We'll talk later. But there was another you-know-what, just before I left. This time offering a diploma to whoever looked. Not specified in what, exactly, but I suspect it's in Jumping to Conclusions or perhaps Picking a Ripe Watermelon—but the problem was that the subroutine triggered something else entirely and the person who got the "diploma" was written up as graduated—and was therefore not eligible for a REAL diploma anymore. One of the kids at the Academy is going to have a hard time proving to someone that he's only sixteen and that he hasn't in fact graduated high school, let alone whatever that diploma says he's done.*

"Oops," Thea said softly. "But we'd better talk later. After dinner. I think your hand is going to be very sore if we don't get this computer thing figured out. I guess we'll have to talk to the professor about that."

"Well," Terry said, "that's what we're here for. To talk to the professor. Can you give me five minutes to get cleaned up? We can go down together."

"Sure," Thea said. "What do you think . . . scarf, or not?"

He looked back to where she was holding her scarf across the front of her dress, and rolled his eyes at her as he went out of the room.

He returned fifteen minutes later, dressed in a clean white shirt and a dark blue tie, his hair damp and slicked back.

"I guess I'm ready," he said dubiously.

They made their way down the spiral staircase, and then hesitated before the door of the dining room, hearing a murmur of conversation. Terry knocked softly.

"Come in," said a deep baritone, followed by the noise of a chair scraping on the floor. Thea and Terry stepped into the room, and were greeted by a tall, olive-skinned man with white hair slicked back from his forehead and a trim moustache and pointed salt-and-pepper beard framing a full-lipped mouth. The eyes on either side of a beaked aquiline nose were those of a raptor, dark and very bright. His hands were long and thin, with polished nails and a gold signet ring on the ring finger of his right hand.

Beside him, seated at the table, Isabella de los Reyes nodded at Thea. She wore a tight long-sleeved top made of layers of white lace, and pearls in her ears; her hair was piled on top of her head and held with a huge intricate antique Spanish comb.

Beside her, his elbows on the table, sat a lanky youth with glossy, slightly greasy-looking black hair curling around his collar, and a pair of gold wire-rim glasses perched slightly askew on a nose he had obviously inherited from his father.

"Welcome to my home," the white-haired man said, indicating the table set with gleaming crystal and silverware. "I am Sebastian de los Reyes. And these are my children—Isabella and Beltran."

To: Slender@goodbody.com
From: Bea Waif < director@goodbody.com >
Subject: Lose Weight Fast!

Have you tried everything, and found that the extra
pounds are still with you? We have the answer—no star-
vation diets, no exhausting exercise routines.
It's new, it's easy! Lose weight now!

* * * * *

To: YouR@gorgeous.com
From: Harry Ears < hirsute@wook.net >
Subject: Longer, thicker hair—instantly!

Haven't you always wanted it?

* * * * * *

To: drinkme@goodbody.com
From: Alice Hiand Lowe
< Deputy_Director@goodbody.com >
Subject: Control your height!

Have you ever dreamed that you could reach the top
shelf of your pantry? Have you ever dreamed that you
could walk past a chandelier without knocking into it?
Our preparation lets you control your height—no harm-
ful chemicals—no physical intervention—just easy
easy easy!

1.

DINNER PASSED IN a sort of formal daze. Everyone
sat around the magnificently set table asking very
politely for the salt or the basket of fresh-baked
bread. Isabella at least said thank you when she was

handed something, which was more than anyone got out of Beltran.

"Shop talk" of any sort seemed to be not considered suitable for dinner conversation. At the conclusion of the meal, Sebastian de los Reyes took his leave, reminding his new students that he would be seeing both of them in his study at nine sharp the next morning. Terry, suddenly made sharply aware of why he was in this house, looked as if he had just had a glass of cold water thrown into his face. Isabella and Beltran had smirked a little at the announcement, and it seemed obvious that it was a favorite ploy by the professor to keep his students on their toes.

Thea might have asked about it, if either of the de los Reyes siblings had showed any sign of being remotely friendly—but straight after the meal Beltran simply disappeared, and Isabella excused herself and floated up the stairs to her room, presumably to change. Terry watched spellbound and open-mouthed until Isabella, without even glancing back, had vanished around the curve of the stairs.

Thea elbowed Terry in the ribs.

"Unh?" he said, apparently having lost the power of coherent speech.

"Earth to Terry," Thea said.

He blinked, tore his eyes off the stairs, and looked down at her. "What?"

"We still have a problem," Thea reminded him. "That session tomorrow morning could turn out to be a very short one if we can't solve the computer question. If I can't slip us sideways into that other place where you are actually able to hold a coherent conversation. You want to try it again?"

"You want to risk your laptop?" Terry said. "If we get that kind of feedback energy again, it could fry its brains. Maybe we should ask someone. . . ."

His head angled upward again, almost instinctively, to the stairs where Isabella had vanished. Thea actually giggled.

"Not Isabella," she said.

"Well, Beltran didn't seem too friendly either," Terry muttered. "Perhaps we'd be better off just waiting for the professor's input tomorrow . . . even if you have to do all the talking initially. If he lets me at his Nexus . . ."

"Yes, well, we have to talk your way into that first," Thea said. "Principal Harris grabbed you because he needed you; the professor seems to be doing fine by himself."

"But that's why I'm here," Terry said obstinately. "To see how this other Nexus—" He shut his mouth abruptly, with a snap, looking a little wild.

"That was close," Thea said. "Don't say *anything* until we get this figured out."

"I miss Tess," Terry said.

"I miss *everybody*," Thea said morosely.

It felt a lot like school, but worse—all the weight of expectations, but without the support of being surrounded by friends. It certainly seemed as though Beltran and certainly Isabella were not the sort to go out of their way to actually befriend anyone whom their father's mentoring activities washed up on the shores of their world.

Terry gave Thea's shoulder a squeeze.

"We'll deal with the computer stuff tomorrow," he said. "I have a few ideas, but perhaps they're better saved for the professor. I'm going to go read for a bit, and then I suppose we'd better both get a good night's sleep. It looks like it's going to be quite a summer, one way or another."

They climbed the stairs together, and then waved at each other in a self-conscious way before disappearing into their own rooms. The house was apparently built out of soundproof materials, because once she shut the door to her bedroom, Thea could hear only silence—and, if she opened the doors to her little balcony, the sounds that drifted in from the outside, the passage of the occasional distant car, a cicada that seemed to have taken up residence somewhere very close by, the whisper of leaves in a light breeze. It should have been lulling, in its own way, but she could not seem to find that calm quiet place in which she could drift into sleep. She lay, instead, in the unfamiliar bed and stared with wide-open eyes up to the ceiling. Thoughts buzzed around her like angry bees, questions she could not answer, visions she could not quite understand. When she finally sighed and looked over at the clock, she realized that it was nearly half past two in the morning, that she was very wide awake and desperately thirsty.

The thought of padding around in her nightgown in the corridors of a strange house suddenly made Thea feel self-conscious. But the bathroom was just across the hall. She had not thought to bring a bathrobe, but she suddenly remembered that she had noticed one hanging in the closet when her suitcase had obeyed the unpacking spell. She switched on the bedside Tiffany lamp, with a stained-glass shade that sent a muted jewel-colored light across her bed-spread, and swung her legs out of bed. The bathrobe was where she remembered seeing it, a dark bur-gundy that looked almost black in the colored light—it was a shade too long, but she tied the sash securely around her waist and padded to the door in her bare feet.

The corridor was empty, lit by two sconce-lights that flanked the top of the stairs; a night-light spilled a faint green glow from the half-open door to the bathroom. The house was quiet. The thick carpet on the floor absorbed the sound of her footsteps. The only other thing she could hear was the distant sound of a haunting, plaintive melody being picked on a guitar.

The music became louder as she stepped across the hall. Disconcerted, she paused—and the music faded, becoming only a wraith of itself, a wisp of a tune that reminded her suddenly of another melody she had heard once, the flutelike tune that was an echo of the song that created the world, spilling from the mesas above Cheveyo's red desert. But this was not something old, it was something very new—a lure, not a memory. It swelled again as she took another step toward the bathroom. The faint green light that glowed beyond the half-open door suddenly took on a strange quality, a luminescence rather than a light, something dappled and living, like sunlight through thick foliage, filtered rich and green down to a forest floor; the music seemed to play that, too, a vision of old woods, the carpet beneath her feet suddenly ancient mulch deposited by centuries of fallen leaves and mixed with rich forest earth.

The door was not simply a door, it was a doorway.

To somewhere else.

Thea tensed, froze, knew that she should stop moving and run for the safety of the bedroom, close the door, and hope that the enchantment would be deterred. But her feet kept moving. The doorway called to her, reminded her of the portal she herself had once raised under the starlit skies of the First World.

This is stupid, she told herself even as she reached out to push the bathroom door wider.

As it swung open soundlessly at her touch, she glimpsed . . . something else, something *other*, certainly not the tidy, pretty guest bathroom where she had watched her toiletries arrange themselves neatly on the vanity cabinet.

She could not be sure of exactly what she saw, because at that precise moment Terry's door opened. Its quiet swish crashed like a discordant note against the guitar melody, which twanged into an errant chord and died very suddenly. The bathroom reasserted itself, awash in a green-glowing night-light; Thea saw her hairbrush on the vanity, and glimpsed herself in the mirror, a little wild-eyed, her fair hair loose around her face.

"Thea . . . ? What's going on?" Terry asked. He was barefoot, wearing a pair of bright red shorts and a faded T-shirt bearing the image of a monster with fangs dripping blood. "I thought I heard something."

"What did you hear?" Thea asked quietly.

"Music . . . ? I'm not sure. Maybe I dreamed it. What are you doing up? It's two in the morning!"

"I thought I heard something . . . too."

Terry stepped out into the corridor, looking left and right. "What?"

"There's nobody here."

But she knew she wasn't quite telling the truth. Because she *had* seen someone, just a blur, in the place that had not been a bathroom only moments before, a place she would have entered in another heartbeat and gone . . . who knew where. There had been a shimmer, beyond—a shimmer like green glass, and the mirrors had not been those of the guest bathroom in the house of Professor Sebastian de los Reyes. The face she had glimpsed in those mirrors from otherwhere had not been her own. She had not seen it for long enough to identify it with any degree of certainty, but she could definitely swear to a set of high aristocratic cheekbones, and dark eyes.

She knew she should tell Terry—but she shrank from it, from telling him how easily she had been lured, how little effort it had taken to bring her to the verge of stepping across to a place where she might have been worse than helpless.

"It's fine now," she said, turning away from the bathroom. "Go back to sleep. You have a big day tomorrow."

"So do you. Go back to sleep."

"I will. Good night."

"G'night," he slurred, turning back into his own room. "Who'd be playing music at this hour?" Thea heard him mutter as the door shut behind him.

The words froze her again, just for a moment. He *had* heard the same thing as she had heard, the guitar music, the ghost melody. It had been real, not just a dream or a figment of her imagination.

That "other" she had spoken to Magpie about, the one like herself, the one who was probably creating the spellspam magic—Thea had believed that he or she would have to be of the professor's household or have access to it, if what Terry had said about the second Nexus computer being used to send the stuff out was true. But it had been only a theory, until this moment. Until she stood at a portal of another world, and knew that she had been right.

Given the sudden unreliability of e-mail, Thea had been given a cell phone by her parents for the summer. But it seemed Professor de los Reyes's house did not like foreign electronics. The power sockets would obligingly appear when a plug was waved before them, but actually plugging anything in—especially things concerned with computers or communication devices—proved problematic. Thea's hair dryer performed just fine, but she didn't dare try her computer again before talking to her host, and her attempt to plug in her cell phone charger was no more successful. But that was academic, anyway, seeing as her cell phone appeared to be unable to connect to any kind of service from the house or the garden.

Breakfasts were apparently much less formal in this household than dinners were. After a frustrating early wander in the garden with the unresponsive cell phone, Thea came back into the house to be greeted with the delicious aromas of ham and eggs, maple syrup, and fresh-baked pastries.

The dining room appeared deserted when she peered inside, but breakfast was all set out, as were a small stack of white china plates and a neat rack of silverware. A shallow silver heating pan with a cover floated in midair over a small blue flame; upon investigation, it contained a ham omelet.

Thea suddenly felt ravenous.

She spooned out a serving onto a plate. A nearby toaster chose that moment to pop up with an English muffin toasted just the way Thea liked it. There was butter in a small round dish on the table, and four kinds of jelly in glass jars each covered with a differ-ent metal lid—one looked like a pile of grapes, one like half a strawberry, another like a raspberry or blackberry, and one like half a peach or an apricot. When Thea reached for the raspberry jam, the lid lifted off and a silver spoon dipped into the jelly pot, took out precisely the right amount, and dollopped it onto the two halves of her muffin.

Thea was sure that the people who lived in this house on a regular basis found all this very ordinary. But she spent the rest of her breakfast keeping a wary eye on the jam jars, just in case they decided to serve her again. Once or twice a lid trembled on the verge of popping open, as though Thea's thoughts were enough to trigger it, but she quickly looked away and things settled down again.

She was peeling herself a mandarin orange, after having polished off what was on her plate, when she realized that she had company.

Beltran de los Reyes was lounging in the doorway of the dining room when she looked up, arms crossed across his chest and one shoulder leaning against the doorjamb. He was dressed in jeans and a camouflage-print T-shirt, his narrow, aristocratic feet bare and possessed of toes almost long enough to be called Alphiri. As Thea looked up, he straightened and pushed his uncombed hair back behind his ears.

"Breakfast okay?" he asked.

"Yes, it's fine—I mean—it was here, I thought it was okay to just help myself. . . ." She flushed, but it was more with resentment at being caught off guard than with guilt. The flush deepened when Beltran laughed, stepping into the room.

"It's breakfast," he said. "That's what it's there for."

"But last night . . . ," Thea began, impelled despite her better judgment to try and explain herself, but Beltran waved a hand in her direction, sauntering off toward the omelet pan.

"Dinner is different," he said. "If we had to stand on ceremony for breakfast, we would all starve. Isabella rises at noon if we're lucky, and Father, like all insanely intelligent people who have too much stuffed into their brains, rises before dawn because otherwise the day isn't long enough."

"It's almost nine," Thea said, still holding her half-peeled mandarin. "What's *your* time?"

"If I can find something intelligent to do, then I'll get up early to do it," Beltran said laconically, spooning a huge quantity of something onto a plate. It had been an omelet when Thea had investigated the pan, but now it looked like it contained something entirely different, poached eggs maybe, accompanied by strips of roasted red pepper. This time the toaster yielded four pieces of sourdough toast. A pan Thea hadn't even noticed and could have sworn hadn't been there a moment ago produced a pile of hash browns with just the right amount of crispy crust baked on top. Almost as an afterthought, Beltran glanced over at the pastry plate and an apple Danish did a somersault from its resting place and landed neatly on the side of his own plate. He shot a sideways look at Thea as he came back to the table balancing all this, and caught her staring at the hash brown pan.

"What?" he said. "Would you like some hash browns? Help yourself."

"But it wasn't there," Thea said. "When I came in."

"You probably weren't thinking about it," Beltran said. "This is an Elemental house. It will come up with what's necessary."

Thea had heard the term, but it had been buried in adult conversation to which she had not been paying attention. She now filed it away under "Ask Aunt Zoë." In the meantime, she was aware that Beltran was staring at her.

She flushed again, and hated herself for it. She had never been particularly self-conscious about her appearance—she had grown up the only girl in a family of brothers, and she had never been primpy, self-obsessed, or vain. But now, in the house where

Isabella de los Reyes lived and under the scrutiny of Isabella's brother, she found herself suddenly wishing she were taller, or blonder, or somehow more worthy of notice on a purely physical level.

Which confused and annoyed her, because she had met this particular young man only the night before, had formed no special opinion of him other than perhaps a faint dislike, and the very idea that she had felt even the least need to appear agreeable to him made her feel suddenly crabby.

"What?" she said, more sharply that she had intended. "Have I got omelet on my nose or something?"

His thin lips stretched into a strange smile, and his eyes glittered behind his glasses. "Not at all," he said. "I was just . . . curious."

Thea bent over her mandarin, peeling it with studied attention, letting her hair fall forward to cover her face. "Anything I can help you with?" she said, aware that she was coming across as appallingly rude, but seemingly unable to help herself.

"I was just wondering what it was about you that made Wiley run," Beltran said conversationally.

"Who's Wiley?" Thea asked, looking up, bewildered.

"My tutor. Cary Wiley. He was supposed to be here all summer, and then we got notification that you and that other kid were coming. At the moment your name came up, all of a sudden, Wiley had business elsewhere . . . business that would last precisely the length of your stay here." He gave Thea a sharp look, but his voice was as light and unconcerned as though he were discussing the weather forecast. "Anyone would think he was running away."

"So what makes you think it was me?" Thea said. "Maybe it's Terry he's afraid of."

"That's just it; he isn't usually afraid of anyone," Beltran said, his tone still as lightly conversational. "But it was *your* name that did it. I was just curious. You don't look dangerous to me, but Wiley may know things from your dark past that even my father wasn't told. . . ."

"I don't have a dark past," said Thea, exasperated. "I don't have a clue why your tutor decided to leave."

"Double Seventh," Beltran murmured.

Thea stared at him. "Yeah, so?"

"So nothing," he said. "My father might be the authority on a lot of things, but odd magic is something that's right up his alley, having had me."

"Odd?" Thea said, frowning a little.

"Odd," Beltran said, shrugging his shoulders. "You know, *strange*. Weird. I've always been schooled by tutors, in this house—I've been known to . . . forget where I was, sometimes. I guess they just don't think I could be trusted to find my way home from, you know, an actual *school*, not without a nanny. Even if the rest of it didn't make the idea of sending me out into society a little scary."

"Why would it be scary?"

"Like I said," Beltran said, and crossed his eyes, sticking his tongue out. "I'm *strange*."

"We're all strange, when it comes to that," Thea said.

"Well, yeah," Beltran said, returning his face to its normal parameters. "I suspect that's the reason you washed up here."

Suddenly acutely self-conscious under his apprising gaze, Thea put the remnants of her mandarin on her plate and pushed her chair back with such force that she nearly overturned it.

"I have to go," she said in a high-pitched voice she barely recognized as her own. "The professor is expecting me at nine."

She picked up her plate and the dirty silverware,

looking around for somewhere obvious to put them. Beltran laughed softly, as though he had won some sort of a game.

"Just leave them there," he said. "The house will take care of it. And you don't want to keep Father waiting."

Thea all but threw the plate on the table and fled his uncomfortable presence, pursued by the sound of soft, mocking laughter as she made her way across the tiled floor of the entrance hall toward the professor's office.

2.

SHE AND TERRY, whom she discovered loitering self-consciously outside the closed double doors that led into the professor's inner sanctum, entered together. Sebastian de los Reyes held court in a room paneled in Spanish oak and redolent with the scent of leather-bound books and a whiff of wood polish. He greeted the two of them with a regal nod from behind a vast antique desk, inlaid with leather. A couple of neat manila folders and a red leather journal book lay in front of him, together with a bronze desk lamp with an antique patina and a green shade, a pewter cup containing a single fountain pen, a couple of small photographs in silver frames, and a brass egg-shaped ball on an elaborately carved pedestal with tiny dragon-claw feet at each corner.

"Come in," the professor said, "you are punctual and this is good. We will have a talk before we decide what needs to be done with the two of you this summer. Terry Dane, shall we start with you?"

"Sir," Thea said, her heart beating rather fast, seeing as she was basically derailing the professor's plans for the morning, "there's a problem that we need to fix first—before Terry is free to speak. . . ."

She quailed a little, as the professor's bright raptor eyes turned a sharp glance on her.

"Oh?" he said. The voice was a little cool, but not as forbidding as Thea had been expecting. She took a deep breath.

"You've probably been told that he cannot speak of . . . of anything magic," Thea said. "It's an allergy."

"An allergy. Yes." The professor steepled his fingers before his face, his elbows on the desk, the golden signet ring on his finger glinting.

"I can . . . fix it," Thea said, her throat dry. "I was able to, back at the Academy. But the problem is . . ."

"Yes?" the professor prompted.

Thea swallowed. "I need a computer to do it," she said. "I brought a laptop, but it needs to be plugged in to recharge the battery, and when Terry and I tried to do it, the thing just . . ."

"Ah," the professor said, one eyebrow rising.

"You ran afoul of the Elemental framework. My house does not permit devices capable of potential . . . damage . . . without my express permission, and without them being under my control."

"Sir, that's the reason they sent me here," Thea said bravely, lifting her chin. "What I do, I do with a computer. If not my own, then I need access to one that works in this house, with your permission."

"This isn't insurmountable, but it will take a little bit of time to deal with," the professor said. "In the meantime . . . Terry, too, was sent here because he is connected to the Academy Nexus."

Thea inadvertently glanced around for eavesdroppers; Terry, however, merely nodded.

"I have here letters of reference from a number of people, including your principal and at least two high-ranking Washington people," the professor said to Terry. "Your connection to this Nexus has already been approved. This is one of the hubs of known magic in this world, but I think that it has already been established not to cause you any of your usual . . . difficulties. We will deal with the laptop situation later—but under the circumstances . . ."
He frowned slightly, tapping one long finger on his desk, and then rose from it in one elegant fluid

motion. "I have had students staying here with me before, working on certain aspects of their chosen field where I could mentor and assist them—but neither of you is quite the store of student that I am accustomed to. I was hoping to spend some time getting to know the special circumstances that brought the two of you to me, and to postpone the Nexus itself until at least our next interview, but it seems that if we are to get anywhere today those plans need to change. Please do me the courtesy of staying silent and in your seats."

"Yes, sir," Thea said meekly.

The professor crossed the office to a wall completely covered with bookshelves. He stood before the shelves for a few moments, his hands clasped behind his back, looking for all the world as though he was scrutinizing the shelves for a particular volume. Then he casually let his hands fall away from each other and reached for a book with his right hand while his left rose in a tiny, arcane motion too fast for the eye to follow. As the book he had extracted fell into his hand, the bookshelves shimmered gently, as though a veil had been dropped between the wall and the professor, and then dissolved away altogether to reveal a wall bare of neither decoration nor any working parts, other than a small niche in the wall that contained a built-in desk barely large enough to contain a flat monitor, a slim keyboard, and a tiny cordless optical mouse. There was only just enough room left over for the professor to lay down the book he was still holding; he did so, and tapped something on the keyboard. The monitor blinked and came to life. The professor tapped some more and then turned his head marginally.

"Well," he said. "Bring a chair over, if you please, and let me see what it is that we are up against here."

"Thea," Terry murmured, rising slowly out of his chair.

"May I?" Thea said, getting up off her own chair and carrying it over to the keyboard. The professor made room for her, but hovered over her shoulder, still within arm's reach of the keyboard.

"Tell me what you are doing as you do it," he instructed.

"I'm just . . . writing it down," Thea said, settling down to type. "Nothing different—this room, you, us . . . but one sphere removed, a world where Terry's allergy doesn't exist."

"Fascinating," the professor murmured, bending

slightly at the waist in order to read over Thea's shoulder.

She hesitated for a moment when she was done, her hand hovering over the ENTER key. "Will your house . . . accept this?"

"I have no idea," the professor said. "The exact circumstances have never come up. However, I am present, and I am able to countermand any erroneous responses on the house's behalf."

"What *is* an Elemental house?" Thea asked.

"Now is hardly the time to discuss that particular issue," the professor said, with just a hint of rebuke. "Please proceed."

Thea flinched at the cool reprimand in his voice, and hunched over the keyboard. The wraith of Cheveyo stood at her elbow, shaking his head. *Questions, always questions with you, Catori . . .*

She closed her eyes when she hit ENTER, but nothing happened—beyond the now-familiar tiny shiver as the worlds she had shuffled settled back down around her, in the new and different conformation.

"Say 'spellspam,'" Thea said over her shoulder to Terry.

He cleared his throat. "Spellspam," he croaked. The professor looked up in professional curiosity, waiting to see if Terry would choke on his own words—but the house had apparently accepted Thea's instructions and was happy to allow the existence of the world-bubble Thea had created.

"Fascinating," the professor repeated. "I do believe you are something I had lost all hope of seeing before I die. Something genuinely new. I have never, in any aspect of my professional capacity, seen this done before. I have had a suspicion that maybe . . ." He had been about to say something, perhaps something confidential, but caught himself, breaking off in midsentence and striding back to his desk. "All right," he said, briskly businesslike once again. "I have the basic information in these folders, but it is clear to me already that they have told me nothing at all of what I really wish to know. So—we will talk. Start at the beginning, please, and tell me everything. Even the things you consider unimportant."

"I didn't really start—," Terry began.

"I was always—," Thea said at the same time.

The professor sighed and lifted a finger.

"One at a time," he said, "would be infinitely more useful."

"Yours," Terry said after a pause, turning to Thea. "I came in later. I'll pick up as we go."

"I . . . ," Thea said, and then dried up completely, skewered by both the professor's hawk eyes and Terry's own far more friendly gaze. She sat for a moment in her chair, hands folded in her lap, trying to corral her words. "Can't I just show you?" she asked at last, plaintively.

"I do believe you have done so," the professor murmured. "However, in my classroom I have often found it useful to have a student actually put into words something that had been merely action. As far as I know, you are unique right now amongst the known mages of this world. . . ."

"I may not be," Thea murmured.

The professor sat up. "What was that?"

"That would be my part of the story, sir," Terry said. "The things that I suspect. The origins of spell-spam."

"Yes," said the professor. "I've had a few of those . . . messages. And so have other members of this household. My son's tutor had to leave . . . quite suddenly. He pleaded family obligations, but I could not help noticing that he had raven feathers popping out in inconvenient places whenever he stopped pay-ing attention. I have a suspicion that he ran afoul of one of those . . . *spellspams* . . . of yours—why he didn't just say so and let me sort the problem out . . ."

Thea suddenly sat up, her eyes widening. Raven feathers . . . ? What was it that Beltran had called the absent tutor? Wiley . . . ? *Cary* Wiley?

Corey . . . ? In this house . . . ?

"There is at least one mage at government level who wants to believe that Thea was behind it," Terry said, oblivious to Thea's reaction. "Because, as you yourself have said, she is . . . unique. Or so we thought. But there must be at least one other person out there who is capable of manipulating magic through the computer. And it gets worse . . ."

"Go on," the professor said.

"I think it takes something like a Nexus to send the messages with working spells attached. It wasn't the Academy Nexus . . . and the only other one . . . is here," Terry said slowly, almost unwillingly. At the Academy, it had sounded perfectly feasible as just an idea; here, in this room, it sounded uncomfortably like an accusation.

And the professor certainly took it as one. His eyes flashed in anger, and he pushed back his chair from the immaculate desk with both hands. "You're telling me that *my* Nexus has been hacked?" he snapped. "Impossible. You have already discovered for yourselves what a formidable firewall this house is, by definition—over and above that, I have personally set up the security of this installation, and I have not observed any breaches in that security."

"Nevertheless," said Terry, going rather white but not giving ground. "I haven't been able to trace them back here, that is true. But I do believe that everything that we have believed about computers cannot be completely wrong—they are good storage devices, and they are good propagators . . . but I don't believe that some small-time hacker playing around with a basic home computer could have unleashed something like the spellspam epidemic. That needed power. A *lot* of power. The sort of power only this kind of computer has. So either it's your machine, or someone else has built a Nexus-type computer that isn't under our control. . . ."

The professor's eyes were still glittering dangerously, but he had his temper in check now. "I see," he said, after a long pause. "It looks like we are going to have a lot of work to do. You were sent here for me to help *you*, but it appears that you'll very much be returning that favor. You are telling me that you believe that the Nexus has been compromised without my knowledge?"

"Yes, sir," said Terry faintly.

"If it has, then it was done by a very subtle hand," the professor said softly. But then he collected himself. "All right," he said briskly. "We will proceed according to the original schedule, and then we will see where we can go from there. I still need to know everything that you know. For your part, Galathea, if you can tell me the *where* and the *why*, we can figure out the *how* and maybe that will give us the rest of the answers. As for the Nexus . . ."

"I've been pretty much running the one at the Academy for the last semester," Terry said.

"By which you are trying to tell me that those who entrusted you with that task believe you to be competent to carry it out," the professor said. "But if you are right, and the second Nexus has been hacked in a way that left me ignorant of the state of affairs, then we will need to proceed very carefully indeed." He smiled, and the smile was not a pleasant one. "You may know much—you are young, after all, and the cutting edge of knowledge always belongs to the next generation. But I think I may have things to teach you yet. . . ."

Thea looked away, because the glitter in the professor's eyes suddenly scared her. Humphrey May had said that he would be on her side, but it was with something not entirely unlike the sensation of stepping into a cold winter from a nice warm room that Thea realized that sometimes the line between adversary and ally could be a very fine one.

And with Corey in the game . . .

She shivered, letting her gaze skitter across neat bookshelves filled with rows of books, and then past them onto the picture window that opened behind the professor's armchair. It was only then that she saw that there was something resting against the chair, something that she had failed to notice before—the glowing polished wood of a Spanish guitar.

To: be_in@love.com
From: Justin Love< calling@cupid.com >
Subject: Falling in love is easy!

Never be alone again! Let us show you how to get that
vision you've been admiring from afar for so long into
your life!

1.

THE PROFESSOR KEPT them both in his study for almost another hour, but he spent most of that time talking to Terry. Thea could not seem to keep her mind focused. She kept glancing back at the guitar by the window, trying to remember what exactly she had seen and heard the night before, wishing that she could weave herself another sideslip world where she could go and investigate her misgivings without the danger of being caught in the act by the very person whom she was investigating.

Terry could not help but be aware of her discomfort, but he tried not to draw attention to her. The professor appeared oblivious—until, some time later, he turned to her.

"I will instruct the house to permit your laptop," he said to Thea. "You will please oblige me by not abusing that privilege and doing anything that the house might interpret as dangerous—by which I merely mean anything done without my knowledge.

I will support, and indeed encourage, exploration—
seeing as that could only help in the task that lies
ahead of us. But I do expect to know what you are
attempting to achieve, and how. We will begin
tomorrow. You may go now." It was a dismissal,
accompanied by the briefest of nods. "Terry, you
will stay for a little longer, if you please. I have a few
things I still need to understand about what you
think you learned through the other Nexus before I
can try tracking any illegitimate e-mails that may
have found their way through this machine. . . ."

Thea slipped off her chair, fought the impulse to
curtsy, and left the study as quietly as she could. All
of a sudden she felt very lonely.

She fished in her pocket for her cell phone, hoping
that the professor's fiat had stretched to *all* the electronics that she had been unable to use in this house,
but it still read *Searching for Service*. She pushed the
phone back into her pocket with a sigh. There was
suddenly a lot that she wanted to talk over with
Aunt Zoë.

Perhaps if she could find the housekeeper, she
could ask if she could use a phone to call Zoë's
hotel—but even as she hesitated, she heard a sound
that froze her in place outside the professor's study.

Guitar music.

Except . . . this was different from the night before. The sound quality was definitely more . . . normal, not as thin and otherworldly as the previous night's music had been. And it seemed to be coming from the sitting room from which she had gone into the garden, or perhaps from the patio just beyond.

Thea's mind flickered with a vivid vision of that green light she had seen coming out of the upstairs guest bathroom, growing like tendrils of vine, little tentacles of light snaking out into the corridor and changing the sense of time and place . . . and then she shook herself.

"Don't be a total idiot," she told herself squarely. "It's broad daylight. Someone's playing the guitar. Big deal."

The pep talk didn't really help, but it made her realize she could not lurk outside the professor's study door waiting for Terry. She needed to talk to him, but it would have to wait until the professor released him—and in the meantime, investigating the guitar music seemed as good an option as any.

Aware that she must look awfully suspicious herself to anyone who might have been observing *her*, Thea crept across the hallway and tried to peer unobtrusively around the half-closed door to the sitting room.

The room was empty, but the French doors to the patio were open, and she glimpsed someone sitting out there in one of the cast-iron chairs, a guitar laid casually across a bent knee.

It wasn't anybody she recognized, or had yet been introduced to in this house.

"Do come in," said this stranger suddenly, his voice deep and male and pleasantly courteous, as Thea hesitated at the door. "Or come out, as you please. I'm quite safe, I assure you."

He turned his head a fraction as he spoke, and Thea caught a glimpse of a profile every bit as aquiline and aristocratic as the professor's own. Whoever this was, he must be family.

Thea stepped out from behind the door. The man in the chair lifted his guitar out of his lap and laid it with an elegant little flourish against the table beside him, and then actually got to his feet as Thea entered the room, offering a little bow that seemed more in place in some old-fashioned movie than under the present circumstances. Thea had the distinct feeling that, had he been holding her hand at the time, he would have bent over it, as if he were some Spanish prince. As it was, she half turned around to see if there wasn't someone behind her to whom the bow had been directed. Isabella, perhaps; she would probably assume it was no more than her due.

But there was nobody in the room except herself, and she took a couple of steps into the room and hesitated.

"You were . . . ," Thea began, and then gestured toward the table. "I heard someone playing a guitar. . . ."

He glanced down at his instrument. "Everyone in this house plays the guitar," he said. "It's the equivalent of drumming one's fingers or doodling. One learns to pick it up whenever one is at a loose end."

"I didn't mean to intrude . . . ," Thea said, beginning to withdraw. *Everyone in this house plays the guitar. Then which one of you was it last night . . . ?*

"Nonsense," he said gallantly. "Allow me to introduce myself. I'm Larry."

The name fit his clothes, not his person. He wore neat but faded jeans and a blue T-shirt, with a bracelet woven from string and beads on his right wrist and a beat-up watch on his left. His feet were clad in a pair of high-top sneakers. A single gold hoop earring gleamed in one ear. The rest of him was an olive-skinned, dark-eyed vision of a hidalgo—one not in the first flush of youth, however. His long dark hair, which he wore loose and cascading down past his shoulders, was liberally threaded with gray, with one particularly vivid broad and almost snow-white streak falling over one temple.

He smiled at Thea's frank appraisal, and bowed again. "You're not convinced, are you . . . ? It works in most places, but why am I surprised that this house completely neutralizes that name? Anywhere else I'm Larry Starr, poet and troubadour. Here, I am Lorenzo de los Reyes, eldest and somewhat prodigal son."

Thea flushed. She seemed to have done nothing else since she had entered this house but be rude to the people she had met here.

"I'm Thea Winthrop," she said. "I'm . . . a student."

"Double Seventh," Larry said.

"I beg your pardon?" Thea said, startled.

"I may write poems for a living, but I was born into one of the oldest and most highly mage-gifted families around," Larry said. "We keep up with such things. My father might have harbored ambitions in that department, but he was not a seventh child.

What, if you don't mind me asking, are *you* doing in my father's house? Not that your being who you are doesn't answer that question, given the circumstances. . . ."

"What circumstances?" Thea said, torn between curiosity and suspicion. The man was utterly disarming, and yet he seemed to know far too much for comfort.

"Your early years were . . . somewhat less than what the media had been led to believe would happen," Larry said gently. "I remember the pictures in the newspapers. You, in your mother's arms . . ."

"*That* picture," Thea said, rolling her eyes slightly.

Larry grinned. "That's okay. You've changed a lot since then. So—what are you doing here, in my father's clutches? Are they letting him study you?"

"In a . . . manner of speaking," Thea said guardedly. "There have been . . . developments."

"Well, I had better warn you," Larry said. "He wasn't expecting me home right now. He always gets into a bit of a mood when I turn up, because he thinks I have failed him in some fundamental way—a gentleman must indeed be able to write poetry, but doing it for commercial gain should have been beneath me. So he always assumes I am here to ask for money."

"Are you?" Thea said, and then blushed again. It seemed an awfully personal question to pose to someone whom she had met moments ago, and of whose loyalties—*everyone in this house plays guitar!*—she was less than certain. But there was something engaging and open about Larry, and he fielded the question with humor and grace.

"Not *always*," he said, "and as it happens, not this time. There's a conference I'm on my way to, and I figured I would stop by and pay my respects. I thought Papa would be around—I didn't realize there would be students this summer." He tilted his head, looking at Thea with slightly narrowed eyes. "Or that the students who were here would be so young. And so important."

Thea, about to protest, decided against it. She hooked her thumbs into her pockets, a self-conscious little gesture, and brushed against her cell phone. She pulled it out a little way, and then pushed it back in with a small frown.

"Having trouble with the phone?" Larry said conversationally.

"It doesn't seem to work very well," Thea murmured.

"You brought it here with you from the outside?

226

No, it wouldn't. My father is defensive of his privacy, and this is . . ."

"Yes, an Elemental house," Thea said. "He told me it would be okay to plug in my laptop, later—but I was hoping that the phone would start working, too. . . ."

"If he didn't specifically sanction it, then it wouldn't have," Larry said. "It's a simple question of whatever isn't explicitly permitted being absolutely forbidden. Whom did you want to call?"

"My aunt is in town," Thea said. "She said to call if I had time."

"Oh, I'm not sure if Father would like his secrets talked about in the streets of the city," Larry said, and he sounded serious enough for Thea to look up in sudden panic—certain that he would go straight to the professor's study and denounce her as some sort of traitor. But Larry was actually smiling. He dug in his own pocket and produced a tiny, razor-thin cell phone. "Let's try this," he said. "What's your aunt's number?"

Larry had no trouble dialing the hotel; he wished the receptionist who answered the phone a pleasant good morning, and then offered the phone to Thea. "You shouldn't have any trouble now," he said. "I'll leave you to your phone call; when you're done, just leave the phone on the coffee table in the sitting room. The house will take care of returning it to me."

"Thank you! I mean—" She looked away, distracted. "Aunt Zoë? It's me—hang on a sec—" But when she looked up, Larry had disappeared, together with his guitar. "Can you come and get me? I need to talk to you—there's all kinds of things—this house is *weird*."

"Thea, weird follows you around. What's the matter with the house?"

"It's haunted," Thea said.

"It's an Elemental house, as I've heard," Zoë said. "It's possibly the *first* one that could really be called that, and it remains one of the most sophisticated ones ever built. It would definitely seem haunted if you didn't know—"

"Aunt Zoë," Thea said, "trust me, I can recognize a spell when I trip over one. But this was different. And if Terry hadn't turned up, I might not be talking to you right now."

Zoë hesitated. "You think there's some sort of danger?"

"I don't know. I need to tell you . . . I need to talk to you about this. . . ."

"I'll be there in half an hour," Zoë said.

"I'll be outside," Thea said.

Just leaving the phone on a table seemed a little churlish, but she was certain that the cell phone would be back in Larry's suitcase, or even pocket, before she left the room.

She practically ran Terry down in the hallway outside.

"I thought I heard you talking," he began, but Thea grabbed his hand and tugged him toward the front door, lifting her other hand to her lips to indicate silence. Terry followed her out onto the front steps. The door shut behind them with a firm click of a lock falling into place.

"How do you plan on getting back . . . ?" Terry began.

"We'll ring the doorbell," Thea said. "Shush. Not yet."

"What?" he said. "What do you think you're—"

"I'll tell you, when we get out of here," Thea said.

"*Out* of here?" Terry repeated, baffled.

"That was my aunt I was talking to, on the cell," Thea said.

"Oh, so you got it to—"

"No, not *my* cell."

"Whose, then?"

"*Later*, Terry!"

Terry rolled his eyes, but decided to hold his peace for the time being.

When Zoë's rental car rolled into the gravel driveway, Thea raced down the front steps and flung open the passenger door. She squeezed into the backseat, and beckoned to Terry, who had remained frozen at the top of the stairs.

"Come *on*!"

Terry came down the steps somewhat more slowly and climbed into the front next to Zoë.

"Terry, this is my Aunt Zoë. Aunt Zoë, this is Terry Dane. Go!"

"We met, I think," Zoë murmured, putting the car back into gear and pulling away as Terry slammed the door shut. "You were the second ghost in Paul's study."

"Yeah. Um, hi," Terry said. He fastened his seat belt, and then turned to Thea.

"Is now 'later' enough for you?" he asked plaintively.

"Where to?" Zoë asked in the same instant.

She and Terry glanced back at one another, and burst out laughing.

"Okay, Thea," Zoë said, still grinning, "I am enjoying the cloak and dagger, but I think I need to hear the rest of this. The Ghirardelli place down on the waterfront has a nice little café—what say we go out and grab a bite to eat?"

"You know how you thought that spellspam were sent through the second Nexus?" Thea said, curled up in the backseat.

"That's what I just spent nearly three hours talking to the man about," Terry said, sighing. "I was hoping that we could change the—"

"Have you ever considered," Thea said darkly, "that the professor himself might be behind it all?"

2.

ZOË'S FOOT SLAMMED on the brake, and the car bucked like a rabbit; someone behind them honked impatiently.

"*What?*" Terry said, aghast, turning around to face Thea. "What on earth are you talking about?"

"There's all kinds of strange things going on in that house," Thea said, sounding a little defensive. "And—well—he has the know-how. And he *controls* that place. I don't see how anything involving the Nexus could have happened without his knowledge, at the very least. But there's more than that. Corey's been inside that house."

"Corey?" Terry said blankly.

Zoë lifted her gaze for a moment to meet Thea's eyes in the rearview mirror. Her eyebrow was raised. "Corey? *Your* Corey? The trickster Corey? He's here? You've seen him?"

"No," Thea said grudgingly. "But I was talking to Beltran at breakfast . . . he said he's got this tutor, and the guy left the house as soon as he got wind that I'd be there this summer. Beltran called the man Wiley, *Cary* Wiley . . ."

"That's pretty thin . . . ," Zoë began, but Thea interrupted.

"Yes, but then the professor mentioned this tutor again, this morning," she said. "And something he said . . . he said that he thought this Wiley guy might have left because he acquired . . . what he thought might be spellspam problems. The professor said, remember, something about feathers popping up? Just nod . . ." Terry did, keeping his mouth shut. "And that's when it clicked—Cary, Corey, Wiley, trickster, it all fit, and the last time *I* saw him he was having trouble keeping the raven feathers from popping up where he didn't want them, and it . . . had nothing to do with spellspam. . . . It was probably my fault." She gulped, and then plowed on. "And the professor seemed awfully cavalier about that—a tutor with feathers on his face? Surely someone like Professor de los Reyes could have seen through a Corey disguise? And then there's the guitar music . . ."

"What guitar music?" Terry asked.

"Last night. When you came out of your room, you know, when you thought you heard something?"

"When I saw you in the hallway, yeah, what about it?"

"I had heard something, too," Thea said. "That was why I was there. And there was something . . . strange going on in the bathroom. Even for that house."

"Thea," Zoë said, "stop. I think I need a triple espresso before you start on any more of this. I need a caffeine buzz for any of it to make any sense whatsoever. Help me keep an eye out for parking spots . . ."

"We can't be anywhere near the place yet, and anyway, Aunt Zoë, what's with the car? Wouldn't it have been easier for you to 'port?"

Zoë was shaking her head. "Where's your sense of adventure?" she said. "I don't know the city, and if I just used 'ports to get from one place to another, how would I ever get to know it?"

"That *is* a one-way street, I think," Terry said diffidently as Zoë started to turn.

"Oops," she said, swerving back into the street she had been on. "Next one, I think."

"You just get *lost*," Thea said.

"I know," said Zoë, flashing her a quick grin in the rearview mirror. "It's fun. Sometimes the shortest road to a place is found when you take a wrong turn."

"You sound like *you* might have written that horrid 'go somewhere interesting' spellspam," Thea muttered.

"We can't *all* be doing it," Zoë protested.

"Are they still happening? I haven't been near a computer for a while," Thea said.

"Oh, yes," Zoë said. "Annoying stuff. The latest one's been going around like an epidemic—make your heart's desire fall in love with you. I've been told that it's hard to put your hand on a red rose these days, so many of them have been snatched up by poor bespelled lovelorn people trying to win their so-called true love's heart."

"Well, at least it's harmless enough," Thea murmured. "Getting a red rose is hardly like getting a pair of penguins or a Chinese magazine subscription."

"Don't you think we should change the subject, at least for a little while?" Zoë said, glancing at Terry. "It's rather rude to have a conversation that one of us can't take part in."

"I've done nothing but be rude ever since I got into that house," Thea said. "One way or another, I'm always doing or saying the wrong thing. I didn't even say thank you for the cell phone."

"What?" said Zoë.

"Well, *mine* doesn't work. That house doesn't like it," Thea said.

"But you called me."

"That was on Larry's cell."

"Who," Terry said plaintively, "is Larry?"

"The prodigal son," Zoë said. "Larry Starr, is it? He's back?"

"You know him?" Thea asked.

"Never met him, but in his own way he stirred up just as much drama in the community as you ever did," Zoë said. "His father practically disinherited him when he . . ."

"Parking spot," Terry said.

"You can't fit in there," Thea objected, surveying the tiny gap that Terry had spotted.

"Want to bet?" Zoë said, beginning to edge in.

"Without magic?" Thea said.

Zoë glared at her. "Just a smidge would do it," she said.

Thea smirked.

"Right," Zoë said, "now it's a challenge."

Terry clutched the dashboard as Zoë edged backward and forward for some minutes before wedging the car in between two other parked vehicles so closely that Thea, after scrambling out of the back of the thing and inspecting the car's position, found that their car's bumpers were actually touching those of the car in front.

"Okay," she said, "but getting out . . ."

"You never said anything about not using magic then," Zoë said. "Now come on. You can tell me the rest of what's been going on when I've got a cup of coffee in front of me and my strength back. Come on, Terry, let's go and talk about everything except the real reason you guys are here, for a little while at least, so you can join the conversation . . ."

Thea straightened from her bumper inspection and stuck out her tongue at her aunt. At least Terry was grinning again, she was glad to notice. She felt rather contrite about dragging him out at all—given his handicap and knowing that he couldn't take part in whatever she needed to talk over with Zoë.

And then she noticed a sign, and had a better idea.

"Hold up!" she called after Zoë and Terry, who had started walking away. They stopped and turned back; Thea was still standing a few steps away from the car, fishing in her pockets. "Aunt Zoë, do you happen to have a couple of bucks on you?"

"Um, sure . . . why?" Zoë said, and then shook her head sharply as she followed Thea's gaze to a swinging sign advertising a cybercafé and realized what her niece was thinking. "Thea, no," she said. "It's too dangerous."

"Why? All I need is access to one computer, for a very short time, and I can deal with . . ."

"But then what? You leave? And someone else turns up . . . ? It's a Terranet café, they sell time by the half-hour—and you remember what happened when you were doing this back in your father's study?"

"I should have gone to get my own laptop before we left," Thea said, casting a mutinous glance to the ground. "I didn't think."

"Well, I have a better idea," Zoë said. "Come on."

Thea fell into unwilling step behind her aunt. The walk took longer than Thea had anticipated, but once inside the Ghirardelli café they seemed to be in an alien world whose atmosphere was only barely enough oxygen and the rest nebulized chocolate. Zoë paused and scanned the patrons already seated at the tables. At least two people were sitting there with laptops open in front of them. One was a young man with a shock of unkempt hair, a pair of earphones in his ears, and a somewhat glazed expression on his face, his fingers beating a tattoo on the table next to his half-drunk cup of coffee.

"That one," Zoë said. "He smells just oblivious enough that he wouldn't notice if a meteor hit him."

"What are you doing?" Terry said, fascinated.

"Borrowing the laptop," Zoë said. "Thea, how much time do you need?"

"Only a few moments—enough to type in a couple of sentences—"

"Do you need to get back in to erase it, after?"

"Send it in an e-mail," Terry said. "I can check quickly to make sure that he doesn't keep copies."

"How much time?"

"Two minutes," Terry said, exchanging a glance with Thea.

Zoë nodded. "Okay. Give me a sec."

"What are you doing?" Thea whispered.

"Stealing two minutes for you," Zoë said. "I'll rig up a short-term time-lapse spell. All that anyone else will see is someone who went by his table and took his coffee cup—and people will see what they want to see, and assume that it was someone working here cleaning up. *He* won't remember anyone at all. When I say go, you have two minutes, max—get in, type, get out. Thea, set up entry *and* exit. We won't get another shot at this."

She turned away for a moment to concentrate on the spell, and then motioned Thea forward with a wave of her hand. "Let's go," she said abruptly.

Thea began to move and then hesitated as Zoë fell into step beside her. "Where are *you* going?"

"I want to see what it is exactly that you're doing," Zoë said. "I promise I won't interfere, I just want to look over your shoulder."

"But don't we need a lookout?" Thea said, glancing around.

Nobody seemed to be paying attention. In fact, most people seemed frozen in mid-motion, a precariously tilting cup halfway to their lips, forks about to spear something on a plate.

"I didn't realize just how dangerous everyday life looks from a different angle," Thea said, suddenly diverted by the spectacle.

"Your two minutes are running," Terry said.

Thea risked another glance around the room. "All right, then."

The young man whose laptop they were appropriating appeared equally frozen in time, perhaps in mid-blink, because his eyes were half-closed as his hands hovered above his keyboard. Thea pulled the laptop out toward herself.

"E-mail software already open," Zoë said, glancing at the screen.

"*No!*" Thea yelped, yanking the computer away. "You don't have the dreamcatcher filter, you don't know what he has in there . . ."

She wore her own dreamcatcher, the one that Grandmother Spider had sent her, on a thong around her neck; she fished it out with nervous fingers and peered at the e-mail open on the screen— and was rewarded with precisely what she had hoped not to see, an e-mail squirming with magical energy, now powerless to harm her but radiating its message out to anyone close enough to see it. It was one of those misdirected Cupid's-arrow e-mails that Zoë had mentioned earlier—*Falling in love is easy*, the subject head cajoled.

"If it's so easy, why do we need you?" Thea said, obliterating the e-mail and hoping that Zoë hadn't seen it for long enough to be affected, or else that she had already been exposed, and was immune. She called up a blank e-mail and typed in Terry's address, and then with another quick glance over the top of the laptop and around the room, typed in a few short sentences, paused as if she were done, suddenly smiled mischievously and added a few more words, and then hit the SEND button. "Okay, Terry," she said.

"Move," Terry said, reaching across her. She shuffled under his arm to give him access to the keyboard, and he made a few quick keystrokes of his own, his eyes darting quickly from side to side as he scanned the screen.

"Time," said Zoë warningly.

"Done," Terry said, pushing the laptop back into position.

They moved away briskly, making for an empty table across the room; the stasis bubble broke even as they reached it and pulled out chairs to collapse into.

"You should get one of those palmtop computers," Terry said. "Little ones, you know. You can slip them into a pocket. They won't do all that much, but at least you can tap a few words into it if you need to, like today, and some of them recognize handwriting with a stylus on the screen—and it's easier to carry around than a big laptop . . ."

Zoë laughed, a little unsteadily. "Young man," she said, "I don't think that's an entirely safe suggestion. I don't know that I'd like the idea of letting Thea loose in society with means to juggle reality as she chooses. Speaking of which, did it work?"

"Terry, say . . ."

"Spellspam," Terry said carefully, and then drew a deep breath. "There. Yes. Now start again. What possessed you to accuse the *professor* of sending out spellspam? What possible reason could he have to risk throwing away a lifetime of scholarship and reputation?"

"He sounded awfully ferocious about it in the study," Thea said. "And then there's the guitar . . . although Larry, or Lorenzo, or whatever his name is, did say that everyone in that house played the guitar. . . ."

"But that's just it, Thea, I don't think I heard the guitar, precisely," Terry objected.

"You heard something," Thea said. "Or at least you *said* you did, at the time. You must have heard something, or you'd never have come out there."

Terry scratched his head. "Maybe I was dreaming. Maybe we both were."

"Maybe it's Isabella," Thea said.

"No, it most certainly is not!" Terry said, sitting up in outrage.

"Why not? Tess said that she'd applied for an internship at the FBM, which means she's got the know-how . . ."

"She wouldn't do stupid stuff like that," Terry said sharply. "She's only just starting to build a reputation—why on earth would she gamble her future away on this kind of idiocy?"

"Guys," Zoë said gently, "while this is fascinating, I might point out that we have an audience."

Terry's head whipped around. "Where?"

"Third table over. Close to the wall there. I can smell him listening."

Thea, twisting in her seat, saw a man sitting at the table Zoë had indicated, his head down as he nursed a mug of something between gloved hands. He wore a sort of cowboy hat, pulled down over his forehead, and his feet, stuck out in front of him, were shod in snakeskin cowboy boots.

And, as he turned slightly toward them, apparently aware that he had been seen, those eyes.

"That's Corey," Thea said in a low voice.

Corey tipped his hat to them with a languid

motion, pushing his mug away with the other hand. Then he got up, pushing his chair back very slowly. Thea tensed for his approach . . .

. . . and a moment later found herself staring at an empty table, and a roomful of people who seemed to have only just restarted an interrupted movement or conversation.

"Where'd he go?" Thea said, her voice unnaturally shrill.

Zoë was scowling. "That slubberdegullion," she snapped. "He must have been watching us all along. That spell I did was pretty basic; it would certainly not have affected *him*—and he just up and used it against *me*. The exact same thing."

"But if he's here . . . ," Thea said, her eyes darting around nervously for any long-fingered, pointy-eared folk who might have been trying to pass as human. Where Corey was, she had instinctively grown to expect to find Alphiri . . . and if he was here, so were they, and the stakes had just gotten higher.

"I'd better take you back," Zoë said. "And perhaps we'd better not do any more excursions until I can call in the heavy artillery. I can handle a lot of things, but I don't know how I'd do in hand-to-hand combat with the Trickster himself, especially if he has reinforcements waiting."

"It's a long walk back to the car," Terry said grimly.

"We're not going to take the car," Zoë said. "We'll 'port back—there has to be a public 'port square within a block of here. I'm not sure where the closest one is to the professor's house, but we can figure that out when we get there. I'll come back for the car later. I won't risk the two of you any more than necessary . . . and whatever you might think about the professor right now, Thea, behind the walls of that Elemental house is probably where you're safest right now."

"But Corey was there . . . ," Thea began.

"He isn't there now," Zoë said, "and that's how it's going to stay. I'm going to go in and have a word with the professor, whatever that pompous house-keeper of his has to say about it."

"I wrote in something about the car when I sent my e-mail," Thea said mournfully as she was being shepherded toward the door of the establishment. "It would have been fun to have been there when you tried to get out of the parking spot."

"If any funny business happens when I go back for it, I'll try to forgive you," Zoë said. "Now hurry up."

The first public 'port they stumbled on had a substantial line already in place. Zoë eyed it with misgivings and shepherded Thea and Terry away.

"We don't want to be standing around there for too long," she muttered. "There's got to be another one just around the corner."

The 'ports were plentiful in the area, but they all seemed to be thronged, and it took them almost twenty minutes to find one that Zoë deemed acceptable, with only two couples ahead of them in the line. The other 'porters were efficient in their passage, and it was only a few minutes until it was their turn.

Zoë gave the professor's address and asked to be deposited at the nearest 'port location.

It turned out that a visitor 'port pad was on the landing of the steps leading to the professor's front door. This was unusual. Very few individual homes had private 'port facilities—they were expensive to maintain and could be tricky if allowed to get run down. However, as everyone kept saying, Professor de los Reyes's house was no ordinary home.

"Oh, good," said a voice as the three of them took a moment to blink and regroup, "at least you won't be late for dinner. Madeline was angry enough that I'd let you two go out at all without my father's signed permission."

"Aunt Zoë," Thea said, "*that*'s Larry."

"Ah, the aunt," Larry said, smiling. "Your hotel's receptionist has a lovely voice. Let me know if you need to use my communication devices again at any time, Miss Winthrop—"

"Excuse me," said a voice behind them, from the front door.

They instinctively parted like an enchanted sea to allow the passage of Isabella de los Reyes. She wore leather jeans that fitted her like a second skin and a bomber jacket of faded brown leather over a black turtleneck, with her hair loose and falling over her shoulders like a golden cloak.

"There you are," Larry said equably to Isabella. "I was starting to wonder. Well, if you will excuse us, I'm taking my little sister to dinner out on the town. Good luck, inside!"

He had been standing beside a great big gleaming beast of a motorcycle; he tossed a spare helmet to

Isabella as he spoke. Larry swung his long legs astride the motorcycle and kicked it into life. It roared as Isabella hoisted herself gracefully behind him.

"Later!" Larry said, saluting the trio on the stairs. Isabella didn't even turn her head as the motorcycle surged forward and roared down the driveway, spraying gravel.

"Out of the frying pan, into the fire," Thea muttered.

When she got no response, she glanced up at her two companions. Terry looked like he had a particularly bad case of concussion, his eyes glazed and fixed in the direction in which the motorcycle had disappeared—but that wasn't unexpected. Terry wasn't wholly rational where Isabella de los Reyes was concerned.

But Zoë was another matter. She was standing there with her hands at her sides, a silly grin on her face and her eyes unfocused.

"Aunt Zoë?" Thea said, tugging at her sleeve. "Are you okay?"

"You never told me he smelled like summer," Zoë said languidly, staring after the vanished motorcycle.

There was an awful silence. "The e-mail on the

laptop in the restaurant," Terry said.

"The spellspam?" Thea said faintly.

Terry nodded. "The one that was open when you grabbed it to write in your own. She saw it. I was too late."

To: Rich@beyonddreams.com
From: Jack Pott < jackpot@international_lottery.com >
Subject: You Won!

Your name has been pulled by our completely impartial
computer program from MILLIONS of people! You've just
won the ultimate Net Lottery! Your opening this e-mail
will notify us that you have received your prize!

1.

THE THREE ON the doorstep might have been distracted by Larry and Isabella, but either Isabella had conscientiously closed and locked the door behind her or the house had taken care of that detail. If Thea had hoped that they could simply slip inside unobserved, the locked door put an end to that idea, and Terry reluctantly lifted the large brass knocker on the front door and brought it down hard, three times.

They might have expected the door to be answered by the housekeeper, but it was Beltran who opened it and stood there staring at them in a manner at once vacant and disconcertingly knowing.

"About time," he said, leaning bonelessly on the doorjamb. "Father was a little disconcerted to discover that you had both done an unsanctioned flit."

Terry glanced at him with a raised eyebrow, looking back at Thea, but held his peace.

"The professor knew that my aunt was out here," Thea said as she followed her two companions into the house.

She was barely one step behind them, but she knew immediately that she had crossed an entirely different threshold. She should have tripped over Terry's heels, but there was nothing in front of her but empty space—nothing like the professor's elegant entrance hall, just a large room full of a diffuse greenish light with walls that appeared something rather like a cross between mist and mirror and shimmered deceptively just outside the corner of her eye.

A flamboyant guitar chord came drifting in from somewhere, disembodied, oddly triumphant, confirming her instinctive recognition of the place that she had stepped into. This was the world that had beckoned from the guest bathroom the other night, music and all, and this time . . . this time she had been distracted, and the doorway had been cleverly concealed from her until it was far too late.

She froze. Only her eyes moved, raking the insubstantial "walls" of this room, but there was nothing here to give her any kind of clue; she put out a careful hand behind her, feeling for the doorjamb that should have been there. And then froze, again, at the sound of soft laughter coming from somewhere behind and to the left of her.

"Gone," a voice said. "You're through it, and it's gone, that door. There was no further use for it."

"Where are the others?" Thea asked carefully.

"They're back at the house, of course. Only *you* are not."

"Okay," Thea said, exasperation overcoming caution, "where am I? And who are you?"

"I'm surprised you haven't figured that out already. After all, isn't this the sort of thing you do yourself? Make a world to your own specifications?"

Thea moved her head just a fraction, sweeping the formless green light that shifted and shimmered around her. "I usually do a better job than this," she said.

"Ooh, temper," said the voice, with an inflection of fake admonition. "They said you had that. That, and pride."

"Who said?"

"Well, Cary said that they said that."

"You're . . . Beltran, aren't you?" Thea said carefully.

That knowing laugh came again. "Hardly," the voice said dryly.

"You *are*," Thea said. "You just proved that. Beltran was the only one with a connection to Corey."

"Cary," the voice corrected.

"Then he didn't introduce himself properly," Thea snapped. "Where are you?"

"You're allowed to move," said the voice pleasantly. "It's all quite solid, I assure you—you won't fall through a hole into forever or anything like that."

Thea whirled, trying to catch a glimpse of the invisible person to whom the voice belonged. She had thought it was Beltran's, at first—but it sounded . . . oddly older, more worldly, more like Larry than like Beltran, except that this didn't feel Larryish either.

Whoever it was, she knew beyond a shadow of a doubt that she was talking to the other, the one like her, the one who had originated the spellspam. The idea that it might have been the professor himself was swiftly dismissed—the voice didn't sound *that* old, and the professor would have had no need . . . of this. Of the green light and the mirrors, and the drama of it all.

There was nobody behind her when she'd turned—not that she expected there to be—but that maddening, knowing laugh came again, from a different direction this time.

"Oh, come on," it said, needled, challenged her, dared her to forsake caution. "Explore, do. You know you want to."

"Oh, sure," she said. "And walk straight into some trap . . ."

"Something not unlike the one you're in now?" the voice inquired, dripping with fake concern.

Thea curled her hand, very gently, keeping the movement as hidden as possible; her fingers stretched into the green light . . . and *yes*, it caught, a ribbon of it floated into her palm.

I can weave this stuff. There is a way out of here. But I need time . . . time to figure this out. . . .

"Why did you bring me here?" she asked, still raking the concealing mists with her eyes, keeping him talking, keeping him focused somewhere else, somewhere other than on the hand that had now threaded three green ribbons between her fingers and was braiding them into a slim rope.

"Well, I figured we needed to talk," the voice said. "That's partly why they sent you here, you and

Terry—they want to figure it all out, and you're their only real hope for doing that. But—he can only come at it from the outside, and I built my fortress well. You . . . you could stumble in here. Without warning. Cary warned me about that. And I wouldn't want to be caught napping. So, I figured . . . we should talk."

"You're right," Thea said. She had a handspan of green light-braid now; she tugged at it experimentally, and it felt firm, attached to . . . something. "But not right now. I have . . . other things to do right now. Perhaps we'll meet again, now that I know where to look."

She wrapped the light-ribbon around her hand firmly, and *pulled*—and in her mind the Barefoot Road unfolded, the sickly green falling away from her as the reds and golds of the familiar mesas rose around her.

As soon as she felt her bare feet firm on ground that she recognized, she let go of the ribbon of green light, all but throwing it away from her, watching it tear and shred into nothingness, fading before it hit the Road. The light of Tawaha was warm on her neck and shoulders, but she shivered anyway, the memory of the green light touching her with icy fingers.

She was half-expecting to see Cheveyo waiting there again, but she was alone. The worlds she wove were her own now. She found herself missing him acutely for a moment, but then quashed the feeling, aware that it would probably bring him to her if she let it—and she couldn't stay here in the red mesas, not right now, not with the trouble brewing back at the professor's house.

She let her eyes drop back to the Road at her feet as she started walking, her hands briskly and urgently weaving the light and sounds of San Francisco around her.

It was Zoë she wove the absence of, Zoë whose shape she reached for as she found her way back to the professor's house, praying that she wasn't about to blunder through some (to her) incorporeal wall straight into the professor's study—but she emerged instead, somewhat disconcertingly, into her bedroom, with Zoë apparently asleep on Thea's bed. Zoë's bare feet, with their painted nails and one delicate silver toe ring, poked out from underneath a coverlet flung across her hips and shoulders, neatly curled up against each other like two sleeping cats.

The Tiffany bedside lamp was on; outside, it was pitch dark.

257

Thea swallowed. "Just how long was I gone . . . ?" she murmured to herself.

Zoë sighed and stirred under the coverlet and Thea hesitated, torn between waking her aunt to find out what happened and letting her sleep. She glanced around the room, noticing her laptop sitting where she had left it, with its power cord coiled help-lessly beside it and the power socket its usual blank square on the wall below.

The professor said he would fix it so that it would work—and now, more than ever, Thea needed access to the place where her power lived in this world. She decided she would let Zoë sleep, and hesitated, briefly, before picking up the power cord—but when she waved it in front of the blank wall panel the power socket obligingly presented itself. After a moment of holding her breath, Thea pushed the plug in and then reached out and switched the machine on. This time, things seemed to be working. The lap-top hummed into life, precisely as always, giving no indication that there had ever been any trouble with it at all. The Elemental house had apparently decided to be hospitable.

Thea waited impatiently for the machine to boot up, grabbing it off its perch and sliding down against the wall until she was sitting cross-legged on the floor with the computer across her lap. When it finally beeped its readiness, she called up her word processing program and typed furiously for a few moments, pausing every now and then to reword a phrase more precisely—who knew what would be important when the crunch came? Just as she was about to hit the ENTER key, a sleepy voice startled her.

"Thea . . . ? Is that you? What *happened*?"

Thea hit ENTER and took a moment to glance at the screen to make sure everything was well before putting the laptop down on the floor and scrambling to her feet. By the time she got to the bed, Zoë was sitting up, rubbing her eyes with the heels of her hands, her bare feet on the floor.

"How long have I been asleep?" she asked. "I feel tired enough to have slept for three days . . ."

"I was hoping *you* knew," Thea said.

Zoë woke up a little bit more. "It's been a madhouse here for the past . . . oh, for a while . . . I don't really remember much of it in the beginning, apparently I had to be de-programmed after the spellspam back at the café, but I do recall being coherent enough to have asked what had happened to you, and nobody would tell me, and then Larry came back, and then . . . I don't remember much more than that, other than weird dreams and waking up and seeing you. . . . What were you doing back there?"

"I got lucky," Thea said soberly. "I was just . . . making sure that I didn't get caught again, with the hole in the cage plugged up this time."

Zoë clutched at Thea's arm. "Are you sure you're okay?"

"Fine, now," Thea said. "Are you?"

Zoë nodded distractedly, kneading the back of her neck. "I feel so stiff, like someone broke bones and set them wrong," she said. "I think I need coffee, and you . . . I think you'd better talk to the professor. He was not happy, earlier—that much I *do* remember."

"Yeah, that makes me really look forward to seeing him," Thea murmured. "But I think I have it figured out—at least halfway."

"Just tell me again that you're really all right," Zoë said insistently. "I couldn't face your parents if something happened to you while I stood there like a mooncalf batting my eyelashes at a man . . ."

"You said he smelled like summer," Thea said, suddenly remembering the last thing she had heard Zoë say before she was dragged off into the green world.

"What?" Zoë said sharply.

"I guess you don't remember that," Thea said. "Are you still sweet on him?"

"Who? Lorenzo de los Reyes? I never *was*, Thea," Zoë said, a little defensively. "It was just the . . ."

"The spellspam, sure, but you *are* sounding rather like Terry does when he talks about Isabella, and he doesn't have the spellspam excuse."

Zoë snorted. "I am not a lovesick teenager."

"Yeah, *right*," Thea said, grinning. "Are you up to going in search of that coffee?"

"What time is it?"

"I have no idea," Thea said, realizing that she had managed to lose her watch. "Let me double check . . ."

She crossed back to the computer, hit the SAVE button, and glanced at the toolbar.

"It's almost eight o'clock," she said. "It's still early. Do you have any idea where Terry is?"

"Last I knew, with the professor, but that was hours ago," Zoë said. "Why do I suddenly feel as though I've just bitten into a not-quite-ripe orange? What is it that you're cooking up on that computer of yours?"

"The professor said I could, so long as I told him

about it, and this was important," Thea said. "I'm okay, Aunt Zoë, I promise . . . but I really would rather say this once, to everyone."

Zoë slipped off the bed, shaking off the coverlet. "Let's go, then—I'm starting to get really spooked here. I *knew* that the stuff was around; I should have been more careful. . . ."

"Perhaps Terry is right," Thea said as she walked toward the door, "I really should get one of those palmtop computers, something I could carry in my pocket. That way you'd never have had to poach someone else's."

"On the whole," Zoë said, falling into step beside her niece, "I would rather suffer the consequences than let *you* loose into the world with a computer in your hands."

"You don't trust *me*?" Thea said, a little taken aback.

"Thea . . . you *disappeared*. What is it now?"

Thea had come to a sudden stop at the top of the curved stairs into the main hall. "I thought I heard . . . music. . . ."

Zoë tilted her head to listen. "Sounds like a banjo to me."

Thea let out the breath she hadn't been aware she

was holding. "At least it isn't a guitar," she said, starting down the stairs. "*He* seems to have a liking for dramatic guitar."

"Who does?" Zoë said, following her closely, her eyes narrowed. And then, as Thea glanced around in eloquent silence, flung up a hand in a defensive gesture. "I know, I know, you only want to say it once. But are you still convinced that it's the professor who's doing the spellspam?"

"No," said Thea.

Zoë sighed and followed Thea the rest of the way down the stairs in martyred silence.

There was a muted wash of light coming from the sitting room. The French doors to the patio were open and there was a shadowy figure outside strumming on something that definitely looked and sounded like a banjo.

The music stopped as she and Zoë entered the room.

"Well," said a familiar voice, "I'm glad to see you came to no harm. Neither of you."

Thea, who had happened to glance at her aunt just as Larry spoke from the shadows outside, was a little astonished to see Zoë's cheeks flame into a violent blush—but she had no time to react to that, seeing as Larry had laid aside his instrument and stepped back into the room.

"I think my father would very much like a word with you, young lady," Larry said, smiling at Thea.

"I thought you played the guitar," Thea said, incongruously.

Larry glanced back to the outside table where he'd left his instrument. "I do. I also play the banjo. I rarely play it in this house. But this has been . . . an unusual day."

"Where is . . . the professor?" Zoë said faintly, sounding so unlike herself that Thea turned to look at her again. Zoë quelled her with a quick and violent look—*Not now!*

"Last I saw, cloistered in the study with young Terry. I will go and get him, if you like—or would you rather go seek him out there? The study is one of the most—how shall I put this—*secure* rooms in this house," Larry said.

"We'd better go there, then," Thea said.

"Very well. I'll go ahead, and warn them you're coming," Larry said.

"Thanks," Thea said, with visions of the Elemental house's defenses being turned on her if she tried entering the study without express permission.

Larry gave them a small bow and walked past them and into the hallway. Zoë turned to follow, but Thea grabbed her by the elbow.

"Something *is* still going on between you and Larry," she whispered. "Isn't it?"

Zoë shook herself free. "Don't be silly, Thea!" she said, and again the voice was completely unlike her—coy, almost arch. Her eyes slid away from Thea's as she started in Larry's wake. "Come on, we'd better keep up."

Thea, shaking her head, fell in behind.

2.

THEY WERE IN time to see Larry pause in front of the study door, with his head bowed, before the door was flung open by the professor himself. His eyes bored into his son, and Larry lifted his head without speaking, indicating Thea and Zoë with a nod.

The expression on Sebastian de los Reyes's face was a potent mixture of fury, frustration, fear, and—as he saw Thea—relief. He actually closed his eyes for an instant, as though a prayer of gratitude was passing through his mind. When he opened his eyes again he was his usual self—stern, aristocratic, commanding.

"You had better come inside," he said. "I think we are all owed an explanation."

"Thea?" Terry stood behind the professor, a barely respectful pace or two away, trying to peer past his shoulder into the hall. "Is that you? *Are you all right?*"

"She doesn't appear any worse for wear, from what I can tell," Larry murmured. "I did a scan, when she walked in. There's a . . . residue. But she is all right."

"I think I know who it is," Thea said faintly, standing in the hallway, everyone's eyes on her.

"Do you still think it is me?" the professor said, lifting one eyebrow. He glanced around as though his protected, secure, warded house harbored spies in every shadow. "You'd better come inside," he said, stepping away from the door and motioning them in. He lashed Larry with another sharp glance, and then let his eye stray briefly to the silent and still rosy-cheeked Zoë. "All of you."

Larry stepped into the room past his father, without looking at him. Thea followed him, brushing her hand against Terry's in passing. Behind her, Zoë brought up the rear and Thea heard the professor close the door.

"This would not have happened if you had not left the house without my permission," the professor said. "The house protects you. It is—"

"Not from within," Thea said, scraping up the courage to interrupt. "There are holes in your armor, even from outside, because otherwise I would never have been able to walk back in. But that doesn't matter, because it's already inside, the thing you want to protect against. It's inside your walls, and all the cannons face outward."

The professor folded his arms. "In case you failed to understand this, Galathea, I am responsible for you while you are in my care," he said icily. "What happens to you under my roof is mine to answer for. And you chose to slip out of that protective net and pursue your own suspicions . . . ? It was rash at best, and certainly foolish. You had better have a very good reason—"

"*I was scared!*" Thea blazed. "I could not use the only way I knew how to protect myself, because your house would not let me—but last night, before we came to see you, I was lured out of my room by guitar music, and then there was something very strange going on in your guest bathroom, across the hall from my room—there was a green light, and that music, and I knew that if I stepped inside I would not still be in this house at all. It was only Terry coming out of his room that snapped that spell, and stopped me—he thought he heard something too—"

"I'm not sure what I heard," Terry said, a little

lamely, when all eyes turned to him. "Honestly, I barely remember the whole thing. I think I might have heard that guitar she says she heard, but I might have just been dreaming . . ."

Thea was shaking her head. "No, something protected me. You might have been dreaming, but you were there when I needed you."

Terry smiled, almost bashful.

"And then, in the morning . . . I ran into Beltran at breakfast, and he said stuff that I didn't really connect at all—until I came into this study and *you*, Professor, talked about this tutor who had to disappear because you thought he had a spellspam problem—the feathers . . . ?"

"Cary Wiley," the professor said. "Yes."

"It wasn't spellspam. *I* gave him those feathers. And we saw him again, while we were out—following us, listening to us. I know who he really is, Professor, and it isn't who you think. When did he come to this house?"

"Oh . . . a few months ago. I . . ." The professor actually furrowed his brow. "Do you know, I am no longer sure. It seems very . . . hazy. My son has always been home-schooled, for reasons . . . we don't need to go into right now. But Cary is just the last in a long line of—"

"Not Cary. Corey. He is the Trickster himself, one of the ancient spirits of this land. He came for me, before—and I escaped before he could deliver me to the Alphiri. And now . . . he has come for Beltran."

Everyone stared at her. The professor went so far as to allow an expression of ludicrous astonishment to linger on his face for fully half a minute before he got his features under control.

"That's preposterous," he began, narrowing his eyes. "I would have known . . ."

"I *should* have known," Larry said suddenly. "I could smell it when I came into the house this time— but I couldn't resolve it, canid or corvid, and I didn't pursue it. But I could smell him. I could smell the shadows he had been hiding in."

"You're like my Aunt Zoë?" Thea said, briefly diverted. "You can smell someone's absence?"

"Larry's a felid," Zoë said faintly. "He's a cat-shifter."

Larry gave Thea a shrug and a quiet smile. "Sorry," he said. "It never came up. For the record . . ." He blurred briefly, and in the place where he had been, a serval cat stood with its tail twitching gently, turning its head to look at everyone in turn before it re-blurred and turned back into Larry.

"No *me desconcierte para fomentar, mijo*[11]," the professor murmured, without meeting Larry's eyes. The younger man kindled briefly as though in anger, but then quelled himself with a visible struggle.

"Professor . . . where is Beltran?"

It was Zoë who asked, careful not to look in Larry's direction, so careful that the effort was almost visible to Thea, a glass wall Zöe had raised between Larry and herself.

"He . . . ," the professor began, and then tailed off again, his mouth working in a expression of cha- grined self-reproach. "I was angry," he said, and he was speaking directly to Thea, which made her shiver a little. "And I was afraid. I should never allow my anger to rule my common sense . . . but there were too many things going on when you chose to return to this house. You and Terry had both disappeared without leaving word about your whereabouts, and then Isabella outright defied me, and Lorenzo admitted to knowing about the first incident and backed Isabella on the second . . . and

[11] *Do not embarrass me any more than necessary, son.*

then you returned just as I was dealing with *that* situation, and your aunt came into this house under an outside cantrip or charm, and we had to deal with that, and just as I cleared that up—with the necessity of keeping her away from the object of her bespelled affections for at least a day . . ."

"And then I came home and walked into the middle of this," Larry said, "and made things worse."

"And they had to put a sleeping spell on your aunt," Terry added. "Because that was the only way to keep them apart for long enough to . . ."

"I don't remember any of this," Zoë said, her cheeks scarlet again, keeping her eyes firmly on the professor's oriental carpet. "But where is Beltran now?"

"I remember seeing him just as we walked inside," Terry said. "And then I lost sight of him."

"I said something about going to his room," the professor said. "I do not recall precisely what, but something along those lines. And I assumed that this is where he went."

He hesitated for a moment, and then let his crossed arms drop to his sides. "I will find out . . ."

"I will go," Larry said quietly.

"Be careful," Zoë said as he opened the study door, quickly, almost unwillingly. For a moment he looked back, and this time they did manage to catch the other's eye.

"I'm always careful," he said, and slipped out of the door, closing it behind him.

"You'd better get back to where you were," the professor said to Thea. "Last night. The thing you saw in the corridor."

"Terry came out and broke it," she said, "and the spell, whatever it was, went away. It didn't come back that night, but then, when we came down here . . . I saw . . . that." She pointed to the guitar that still sat by the armchair in the window. "All I could think of was the music. And then you spoke of Corey as though you had no idea who he was . . . or didn't want to know. And then I thought—of all the people in this house—*you* control the computer, *you* had access to every-thing, *you* control this house . . . and then I came out of this room, and the first thing I heard when I left it was . . . someone playing the guitar."

"Larry," Zoë said quietly.

"Yes, but I didn't even know that he was here, or who he was; all I heard was the guitar, again . . . so I went to see, but there was no green light that time, and he seemed normal, but he did say that in this house *everyone* played the guitar, and all of a sudden

I didn't know if there was anyone I could actually trust. . . . I wanted to talk to you, Aunt Zoë, but my phone still didn't work—and his did—and he called you for me—and on the way out I grabbed Terry because I needed to talk to him, too—and the rest you know."

"*She* may," the professor said pointedly. "I was not there."

"Oh, okay, that's right—" Thea stopped, flustered.

"We went to a café," Terry said, "and we needed a computer . . . because Thea's hadn't worked, and I couldn't, you know, talk at all without that intervention—so she tried to talk us into letting us use a Terranet café on the way."

"That would have been appallingly reckless," the professor said.

"I thought so, too," Zoë said, "which is why I then cast a quick stasis spell so that we could, you know, borrow very briefly the computer of someone else who was already there—just long enough for Thea to do her thing—but then I wanted to see what she was doing, precisely, and there was an e-mail open on the screen . . ."

"Which was the one that caught you," the professor said.

"And then I smelled someone listening to us," Zoë said.

The professor frowned at her. *"Smelled . . . ?"*

"She does that," Thea said hurriedly. "She can smell things other people see, stuff like that. She told Terry and me that someone was listening to us, and I looked around and recognized him."

"Him?"

"Corey. Your Cary Wiley. The tutor. He heard everything we were talking about."

"And what, precisely, *were* you . . . ," the professor began, but the door of the study opened a crack and Larry slipped back inside.

"He isn't in his room," Larry said. "He isn't anywhere, as far as I can tell. Isabella is in *her* room, but she is sulking and won't talk to me—she said her brother wasn't in there with her. I tend to believe her; it would take someone hardier than Beltran to stay with Isabella in this mood. But he's gone, Father. He doesn't seem to be in this house at all. He did, apparently, leave you a message. . . ."

"Well, what is it?" the professor snapped, the tone of his voice belying the sudden devastation in his eyes.

"I printed it out—it was left on the screen of the

computer," Larry said, handing his father a sheet of paper.

"*The first one was fun,*" the professor read out loud, the paper shaking ever so gently in his hand. "*Remember the three days Isabella wouldn't come out of her room? She opened one of my mails, like I knew she would. She's always had a thing about her nose, it looks good on me but she thinks it wrecks her profile—so when I sent her an e-mail about 'making your nose smaller,' she opened it—I knew she would—and her face turned into a Persian cat's, she looked ridiculous—that's when I knew I could do it, this computer spell thing, and it was wonderful. Cary came soon after, once I'd sent a few out and watched them catch people, and said that THEY had noticed what I could do, and they could help—if I could do the things that they wanted . . . so I practiced. And it was easy, from here—I could send directly from the backbone . . .*" The professor's hand dropped and the piece of paper dangled from his fingers as he stared at the place where it had been. "You were right after all, Galathea," he said wearily. "It was me all along. I was using the Nexus . . . as the backbone, as my connection to Terranet, to the world, as it had to be, with the Nexus being what it is. I thought I had put up adequate firewalls for any outside attacks . . ."

"You had, sir," Terry said. "That, and this house . . ."

"Yes, but I was using it for my own family's Terranet connection," the professor said. "In hindsight, that seems as rash as anything I have accused you of doing today, Galathea, but it seemed like the obvious thing to do at the time—the Nexus was my family's entry to the 'net, and of course . . . Beltran could . . . use that."

"Have we established where *you* have been when you disappeared, Thea?" Larry said. "You may be our only lead to find Beltran."

"But he said . . . the voice said . . . that he was *not* Beltran," Thea said slowly.

The professor suddenly froze. "What was that?"

"When we all came back and I followed Terry and Aunt Zoë through the door . . . they came into this house, and I—went—somewhere else—that place with the green light that I'd caught a glimpse of back last night, upstairs. And I didn't see anything—anybody—I just heard a voice, and it sounded like Beltran, and then it didn't—I was pretty sure it was him but there was something—different—"

"This is all my fault," the professor said, and sat down very suddenly on the edge of his desk.

It was Larry who crossed the room in two long strides to support his father, and help him down into a chair. But then he stood back, crossing his arms in a manner disconcertingly like the professor at his imperious best, and his face set into harder lines.

"I wasn't enough, was I, and you tried to get what you wanted another way," Larry said.

"This is . . . a family matter," the professor said faintly.

"Not anymore, Father," Larry said. He looked up over his father's head at the other three. "He loved my mother," Larry said. "She was perfect in every way—beautiful and aristocratic, and gifted beyond measure in magic. He made this house for her, you know—his father and his grandfather both knew the last great Elemental mage personally, and it was his own imprint that this house was wrought in. But she gave him one child—me—and she bequeathed to me no more than the ability to become a serval cat, and a love for words and music. He wanted another child, someone more suited to what he wanted, and my mother loved him enough to try and give him that—and then died of it, her and the baby, both.

Complications at birth. I don't know all the details, I was barely twelve years old then."

Sebastian de los Reyes looked up, but Larry refused to meet his eyes.

"I was sixteen when he married Dorotea Rodriguez," Larry said, his voice dropping another notch, changing into something deeper, darker. "She was neither Spanish nor aristocratic—but this time he married a woman simply because he wanted her. But he still wanted those other things—the things that my mother could not give him. By the time Isabella was born, I was long out of this house—I had started writing music, and songs, and poetry, and I was living a life that was anathema to my father, failing in my duties to this family. And Isabella was pretty, and gifted, and the apple of his eye—and even I, when I came home infrequently, fell under her spell—but then, *then*, Dorotea was pregnant again, and this time it would be a son . . . except that it was not. It was two sons."

Zoë let out a small gasp, as though she knew what was coming; Thea reached for her aunt's hand, and Zoë's fingers wrapped themselves around Thea's tightly, almost painfully.

"You asked her to choose, didn't you?" Larry

said, turning to his father at last. "You only wanted one. But Dorotea . . . held an older magic than even you knew or could cope with. . . ."

"One twin was born," Zoë whispered. "And the other . . . was not."

"Was not *born*," Larry said. "But lived, nonetheless. And sometimes found a way to exist in the living brother's body. You were right, Thea. It wasn't Beltran . . . it was Diego."

"Lorenzo . . . ," the professor said, very quietly.

"You destroyed them both, my mother and Dorotea," Larry said. "And in the process . . . you got . . . oh, read the rest of that letter. It's a perfect ending."

Sebastian de los Reyes looked down at the paper he still held, but made no attempt to lift it and continue to read it. Larry reached over and plucked the letter from his father's nerveless fingers. His eyes scanned the page swiftly.

"Here," he said. "*I'm going to have some more fun now. With the other polities helping me out, I could do something really amusing. I'm playing around with a message telling people they've just won the lottery—everyone likes winning, don't they?—and I'll even make sure they get their loot—*

but it will be Faele silver, fairy gold, and all that they thought they had in their grasp when the sun goes down will disappear at dawn the next day—slipping, slipping, slipping through their fingers. . . ." Larry let the hand with the letter drop. "Just like you, Father," he said quietly. "What you thought you had—Beltran—it was Faele silver, fairy gold, and it's morning. And it's time to pay the price of your dream. You wanted a son who would be an Elemental, a great mage, someone to carry your name into posterity. Well . . . the name of de los Reyes will certainly be remembered now."

"We have to stop him," Terry said, sounding frightened. "If he does the kind of thing that Thea does—if he can exist in a world just enough like this one to influence ours—who knows what he will come up with next?"

"We have to find him first," Larry said quietly.

And looked straight at Thea.

To: Healthymind@healthybody.com
From: Dizzy Ease < doctor@healthybody.com >
Subject: Best Harmacy Online!

Do you suffer from any of these diseases:

Allergies	Jaundice	Scurvy
Borborygmi	Knock Knees	Tinnitus
Chicken Pox	Lycanthropy	Ulcers
Diarrhea	Morgellons	Vertigo
Eczema	Narcolepsy	Warts
Flatulence	Overweight	Xenophobia
German Measles	Phobias	Yawning
Halitosis	Queasiness	Zoonoses
Insomnia	Rheumatism	

1.

"**Y**OU CAN'T SEND her back there alone! She barely got out the first time!" Zoë said sharply, her words breaking the crackling silence that followed Larry's words. Zoë had appeared to have forgotten, in the heat of the moment, to whom she had responded, and she had roused up to her full height, eyes flashing, meeting Larry's eyes with fiery defiance.

"As to that," Larry said, "I must have been out of the room. Just exactly where is this *there* that we are talking about? And if it was something or somewhere designed to entrap, how *did* you get out?"

"It was thick with light," Thea said.

Zoë nodded. "You wove your way out of there?"

"Wove?" Larry echoed, puzzled.

"Long story," Terry said.

"Perhaps it is time that I heard all of it," the professor said with his old autocratic haughtiness.

"Right *now*?" Thea said, taken aback.

"As good a time as any," Larry murmured. "It isn't like we'll all go to sleep easily tonight."

Thea hesitated, and then turned to face Larry. "You knew who I was, when you first saw me," she said.

"Yes. Of course I did."

"You certainly knew all the things I *wasn't*," Thea said. "Everybody knew that. But the things that happened . . . in the last year or so . . . not many people knew of those."

"You weave light," the professor said, his voice a flat statement, his brow furrowed in a frown. "Yes. That was in your file. What does that have to do with the current circumstance?"

"That's only part of it. I just . . . weave. It started with light, and then it was . . . other things. That's how I came back—I wove a hole in the fabric of the world that only Aunt Zoë could fill, and then I let the world search until it found her to fill it—and then I was there, where she was. That's how I came back into this house, I returned to the room, upstairs, where she was."

"You came in together," Larry said, nodding. "I was wondering . . . But I don't understand—how did this get you . . . ?"

"She just told you. She weaves," Zoë said.

"She weaves worlds," Terry said. "We all did, at one point, all five of us back at school—Thea, me, my sister, and two friends of ours—we did it first because we all brought in something specific, a missing sense—our friend Ben can smell . . ."

He suddenly stopped, glanced back at Thea.

"It's okay," she said. "In this room I haven't set the safety to expire."

"What?" Larry said, swiveling his head from one to the other of them.

"I'm . . . allergic," Terry said carefully.

"Yes, I have a file on Terry Dane, too," the professor said. "Under normal circumstances, he can't say anything at all that has a magic overtone—he can't utter a magic-linked word or say a spell out loud, he cannot talk about magic at all without it shutting down his breathing. Classic allergic reaction. I am told that something similar afflicts his sister— Theresa Dane can't *taste* anything magic-made without swelling up and choking on it. That is why both of them were at the Wandless Academy—it was a safe, magic-free environment for them."

"Our friend Ben's father is a chemist mage who was dealing with Alphiri stuff, and Ben got infected by that—and now he can't *smell* anything magic without sneezing himself into a stupor," Terry added. " And Magpie, she's got the touch—a healer's touch . . ."

"I get the idea," Larry said. "But weaving?"

"That's what I do," Thea said. "That's what brought me here. They thought that Professor de los Reyes could . . . figure out what it is I do."

"What on earth would anybody think that Father would have to do with weaving? Weaving anything . . . let alone . . . light?" Larry shook his head, perplexed.

"She uses a computer," Terry said.

"To do . . . what?"

"To weave an alternate reality. A different world," Zoë said, finally stepping back into the conversation. "That was what we tried to do while we were out—help Thea weave a bubble where Terry could talk to us about everything. That's why I got the laptop . . . and saw that wretched spellspam." She blushed again and pressed her lips together in frustration.

"Perhaps it wasn't all spellspam," Larry murmured, tilting his head. "I haven't seen that particular incarnation of it, and I haven't been exactly . . ."

Zoë opened her mouth to protest, and Larry lifted a hand in a defensive gesture.

"However," he said firmly, "back to the problem on hand. So you can step from world to world as you like . . . ? Can Beltran?"

Thea shot him a startled look. "How would I know?"

"You were not in *this* house this afternoon," Larry said.

"That's true enough . . . I think he can, but I don't think he is doing it the way I am, and perhaps that's the only reason I was able to get out of there as I did—he didn't expect . . . perhaps he thought that he could trap me by not giving me anything familiar to lean on, by wrapping me in formlessness and mist and that weird light—but instead he gave me the very thing I needed . . ." She blinked, suddenly sleepy and worn out by the whole experience. "He said . . . we needed to talk."

"Then it might be easier than we think," Larry said.

"He said we needed to talk," Thea continued. "But that was when *he* brought me there—and he said that he didn't want me 'blundering in' where he didn't want me to be. He *has* to know that once I got back here, you would all know whatever I'd learned, and what makes you think he would even let me back in . . . ?"

"Let alone out again, now that he knows that you can do what you did," Larry murmured. "I see." He looked up as Thea suddenly smothered a yawn.

The professor appeared to take notice of the yawn, too.

"It's late," he said. "We can do nothing useful tonight. I suggest that the best plan of action is to figure it all out in the morning."

"But it was last night . . . that it all . . . that he . . ." Thea began, her heart suddenly thumping painfully.

"I'll stay with you," Zoë said. "I'll sleep on the floor if necessary. In fact, I probably should. Right there across your door. If you tried sleepwalking anywhere, I would know about it."

"I consider that an excellent idea," the professor said. "As for sleeping on the floor . . . that will not be required."

"All you have to do is ask for an extra bed in the

287

room," Larry said. "This is . . ."

"An Elemental house," Thea said, chorusing the words with him. "I'll make you a deal—I'll tell you about light weaving if *someone* please explains to me just exactly what an Elemental house is."

"I'll give you a textbook, if you like. There will be a test in the morning," Larry said.

Terry laughed, a little self-consciously, and then Thea giggled, and in a moment they were all laughing. Even the professor managed a watery sort of grin.

"Definitely time to head upstairs," Larry said. He turned to his father. "Do you . . . need any help?" he asked carefully.

"No," the professor said, standing up. And then, with a sideways look at his older son, "Not in the way you mean, anyway. But thank you."

"Do you want me to deal with battening the hatches?" Larry asked.

"That would . . . be good," the professor murmured. "I find myself rather tired, after all. And you know what measures need to be taken to safeguard this place from further incursions, at least for tonight."

"I will take care of it," Larry said.

The professor gave a faint nod. "Very well, then. I will . . . leave it in your hands. If you will all excuse me, I have some thinking to do. We will meet in the morning."

"Good night, sir," Terry said.

The professor inclined his head in acknowledgment, and then he was out of the study, walking slowly and carefully down the hallway, making his way to the great stairs in the entrance hall.

"Will he be all right?" Zoë said quietly.

"He took a blow tonight," Larry said. "Wounded pride can be a mortal wound, and with him, tonight . . . it's a deep one."

He bent his head and ran his long fingers through his hair in a gesture that was pure weariness.

"You should turn in, too," Zoë said.

"I still have . . . a few things to do," Larry said. "Make sure everything is secure for tonight."

"Can I do anything to help?" Terry asked. "I could deal with the Nexus aspect of it . . . if that's the backbone of what runs this place . . ."

"Not really," Larry said, and quirked another quicksilver grin in Thea's direction. "It's the Elemental thing. Go on, upstairs with all of you."

Zoë hesitated, but Thea suddenly smothered

another jaw-cracking yawn and it broke the moment. Larry politely but firmly herded everybody out of the study and closed the door behind them, letting them find their way to their rooms.

Thea wasn't sure if she could go to sleep. In the darkness of the bedroom, which had somehow already acquired an extra bed, Zoë murmured a few encouraging words and then appeared to go to sleep herself—rather quickly, Thea thought.

Thea, still awake, found herself remembering Larry's voice, his words all mixed up and jumbled in her head.

Dorotea was pregnant again, and this time it would be a son . . . except that it was not. It was two sons.

One twin was born . . . and the other . . . was not. But lived, nonetheless.

It wasn't Beltran . . . it was Diego.

Diego. Diego de los Reyes.

Thea mulled the name around in her mind. Beltran's lank hair and drooping disposition, the habit of draping himself on every surface as though he needed constant support to stay upright, kept intruding; Thea tried to invest that personality with the voice that had spoken to her out of the green mists of that other world, and could not make it fit. They might have been twins, but they were very different people, Beltran and his shadow-brother.

There had been, initially, that reaction that she had had—the sense that she wanted, *needed*, to be somehow better, prettier, more personable, to have more of whatever it took to be worthy of Beltran's notice—but that, in the end, had merely served to goad her into being annoyed with him. She had watched Beltran's sister, because of Terry's interest in her, and had wound up transposing quite a bit of Isabella's imperious arrogance onto a personality that might not have been a very good fit. If someone had asked her to describe Beltran, only a few short hours ago, the word "arrogant" would definitely have been part of the description—but now as she cast her mind back over their few encounters, Thea was hard-pressed to make that particular description stick . . . on every occasion except one.

Back at the front door.

And *that* might have been Beltran's body, even Beltran's body language, but it might not have been Beltran at all.

One twin was born . . . and the other was not.

"It must have been so lonely," Thea murmured to

herself, muffled into the safety of her pillow.

Diego. The shadow-twin.

He was not real—not alive—not sharing her physical world at all, unless one counted him using Beltran as his puppet . . . but he was like her. How they had both come to use the computer as a source or a conduit of magic, in a way that none other of their kind had apparently ever been able to do, was a moot question.

Thea felt a powerful affinity there, mixed with revulsion at what Diego de los Reyes had chosen to do in order to use his gift. And this, although it might not have been entirely unexpected, astonished her. He had done—he had the potential to do—so much harm . . . and she *empathized* with him?

Her mind alive with questions and apprehensions, Thea lay on her back, utterly convinced that she would not sleep at all that night—but in her next moment of awareness she found herself lying on her side with her cheek pillowed on her palm and realized that she must have nodded off after all. But something had woken her now. Something had changed in the room.

She lay very still for a moment and then hoisted herself quietly up on her elbows and peered across the room at the other bed.

"Aunt Zoë?" she whispered.

Thea had always had her own room at home, but a year spent as Magpie's roommate had sensitized her to the sounds, the mere presence, of another human being in the room at night—and those sounds were absent. Zoë's bed was empty. She was gone.

Thea sat up sharply, suddenly far more awake than she wanted to be. Zöe's bedclothes were pulled half-straight, relatively neatly, suggesting that its occupant had left the bed by her own choice rather than having been taken from it violently or involuntarily. It was also still warm, implying that such a departure had occurred not too long before.

Thea hesitated for a long moment. She very much didn't want to go in search of Zoë, or leave this room at all, and there was a deeply rational core of her that told her sharply that there had to be a sane explanation for it all, and that Zoë herself might return at any moment. But another part of her was hearing guitar music and that strange knowing laugh from out of the green mists, and was suddenly terrified of what her being alone in that room might really mean.

"I'll just look," she whispered to herself at last,

more for the value of hearing her own voice than for any actual need to say anything out loud to a room empty of anyone other than herself. She retrieved the bathrobe from the closet where the Elemental house had tidily stowed it, and reluctantly padded to the bedroom door in her bare feet.

The corridor outside her room was empty when she peered out, and the bathroom across the hallway seemed to be its normal self. But a faint murmur of low voices did reach Thea as she hesitated in the doorway of her bedroom, uncertain of what to do next, and her old eavesdropping instincts kicked in. She sidled along the wall of the corridor toward the main stairs, where the voices appeared to be coming from.

She craned her neck carefully around the curve of the wall, and snatched herself back very quickly when she realized that the acoustics of the place had been deceiving and the voices she had heard were coming from a couple of people sitting and talking quietly on the stairs not too far from where she was hiding.

Larry and Zoë.

2.

THEA COULD SEE them from the back—her aunt's hair mussed as though it had been finger-combed, a T-shirt pulled on over jeans; Larry's half-profile, turned toward Zoë, leaning back against the stairs behind him with both elbows.

". . . hate the idea," Zoë was saying. "It seems that we're always on her for taking things in her own hands, and when she doesn't, then we push her into doing stuff anyway. And the truth is, out there, she's still on her own. Whether or not we give our permission for her to go. It isn't as though, with our backing, she has . . . I don't know . . . backup. We don't know nearly enough about anything to even think about the logistics of that."

"But if she could take someone with her . . . would it matter?" Larry said softly.

"I have no idea. It could. It did once before,

apparently, when all her friends joined her in that other world she created, the place to where she lured the Nothing . . . but that was different . . . they all had a role there, somehow. Now, though . . . I'm not sure."

"Oh, Aunt *Zoë*," Thea muttered, barely out loud, rolling her eyes. *I can take care of myself, go talk to Humphrey May!* she thought.

She must have missed an exchange or two, because the next thing she heard was Larry's voice, and the words didn't make sense.

"I know. It's my house."

Thea blinked, and then realized that the voice had not come from the stairs at all . . . but from *behind her*.

She snapped her head around and could not suppress a startled yelp as this motion brought her face to face with a large cat sitting close enough for its paws to be practically on top of her feet. The cat's tail swished a couple of times, and then it morphed smoothly into Larry, crouching in his place, grinning at Thea.

She looked back to the stairs. Zoë was still there, but this time her face was turned back, toward the head of the stairs. There was still a Larry-like shape beside her, but that shredded even as Thea looked, proving to be a deft illusion.

"How did you know I was here?" Thea blurted.

"How come you're up?" Larry asked, ignoring her question. "Any strange serenades in the night?"

"No, I just woke up and Aunt Zoë wasn't there, and . . ."

"And you thought you'd go look?"

"I wasn't going to go far," Thea said rebelliously.

"Yes, well, you didn't need to," Larry said.

"Is everything okay? Thea? What are you doing here?" said Zoë.

"Fine," said Thea abruptly, feeling a little mutinous at having been snagged like a novice and not as though she had spent a lifetime practicing the art of eavesdropping. "I woke up and you weren't there, and I thought . . ."

"I'm sorry, sweetie. I couldn't sleep," Zoë said apologetically, sitting down on the stairs again in a slow graceful sideways motion. "I didn't mean to scare you. I just wanted to see if . . . everything was all right out here, and then I got talking to Larry . . ."

"Well, we aren't all likely to go meekly to our beds," Larry said. "What do you say I go and find us something to drink? It's too hot for cocoa, but how about pink lemonade?"

Zoë made a face. "I'd say it smelled like cheating," she said. "If you're going to conjure up lemonade, at least let it stay the color it was supposed to be."

"Done," Larry said, helping Thea up and shepherding them both in the direction of the stairs.

The lemonade, chilled to just the right temperature, was waiting for them on a tray in the sitting room by the time they came down the stairs, along with three glasses.

"I could get used to this," Thea said, accepting a glass that Larry poured for her. "Just think of something, and it's there . . ."

"Elemental houses," Larry said, chuckling. "I did promise you an account. This house wasn't so much built as . . . grown. It might look like brick and mortar and iron and tile and wood and glass—but all of it is Elemental, made of some aspect of Earth, Air, Water, or Fire. And Spirit, the Element that unites them all."

"You mean it's an illusion?" Thea said, looking around. "It *feels* very solid . . ."

"Nothing that Tesla did was illusion, although it might all have looked that way," Larry murmured.

"Tesla?"

"There are many kinds of Elemental mages," Larry said. "The Spirit dimension is always there, because that is the power behind this—but you can have One-Element mages, Two-Element mages, Three-Element mages . . . and it gets rarer and rarer as you go up that list. There was only one Four-Element mage in human history, and that was Nikola Tesla."

"We studied him," Thea said, sitting up. "At school—not the Academy, back when I was doing Ars Magica, in my other school—we had an entire paper we had to do on him."

"He was a phenomenon, indeed," Larry said. "Stronger in some Elements than others, to be sure—Water was not his favorite, and he understood Air but could be downright shaky on it sometimes— nonetheless, he had a degree of mastery over *all* the Elements, which none before or after him could command. My great-grandfather and grandfather knew him personally; my great-great-grandpa met him not long after he arrived up on our shores from the wilds of Eastern Europe."

"With no more than four cents in his pocket," Thea said, the long-ago school essay coming back to her. "I remember asking Dad to tell me what four cents would have bought, even then, and he couldn't even come up with a cup of coffee."

"Yes, but he had a talent that shone from him like a light," Larry said. "They stayed in touch, Nikola Tesla and my family, throughout the ups and downs of their lives. When Tesla's laboratory burned down, years later, it was my revered ancestor who helped tide Tesla over when nobody else would. And then, at his peak, when Tesla was getting ready to tie it all together and change our world, my grandfather was born, and they all thought he might be a nascent Elemental . . ."

"Was he?" Thea asked, sipping her lemonade.

"In point of fact, he might have been—but nothing like Tesla, maybe a One-Element mage, if that. He had a great facility with water. But it was Tesla who tested him, and Tesla who watched him grow and waited with his parents for something special to show."

Thea nodded in complete understanding. "I know how it feels," she said.

"He never quite made it to where they wanted him to be," Larry said. "And so things went on. My great-grandpa wasn't rich, but when the occasional disaster struck Tesla—and he was a disaster magnet, it would seem that a Four-Element mage is not at all suited to a practical existence in our world—it was he who handed out "loans," which both of them knew would never be repaid. But those were generally good years for all of them, anyway—Tesla *and* my family. Tesla was eighty when my father was born, but he gave him a birth-gift—a seed of a house, one of the few true Elementals, to be kept against his coming of age."

"This one . . . ?" Thea said, open-mouthed. "*This* house was . . . made by Tesla himself?"

Larry nodded. "It was kept as a great treasure," he said, "but after that . . . things went downhill fast. Tesla became obsessed with things even he could not achieve, he became more and more of a hermit, and soon not even the family 'loans' could help—he was living alone, penniless, and on credit—and he died without a single friend by his side, alone in a hotel room. The government seized all his books and papers after his death, but they couldn't find the important stuff, the real Elemental stuff, all that was kept in his head—but there are photographs of him holding fire in his hands and smiling through it . . ."

"I've seen them," Thea said. "In school. You *knew* him?"

"Well, not personally," Larry said, grinning.

"But this house . . . ?" Zoë prompted.

"The seed survived for decades," Larry said. "They gave it to my father when he came of age, and *he* kept it safely stowed away . . . until he met my mother, and there was nothing he would not do to make that relationship happen. And that was a bad time, because . . . the seed needed an Elemental mage to trigger it . . ."

"Is Professor de los Reyes really an Elemental?" Thea said, sitting up.

"Well . . ." Larry seemed suddenly reluctant. "Let's just say it took three tries to do it right," he said at last, reluctantly. "The first time he tried to open that seed capsule, it nearly self-destructed, taking him with it. You might think he controls this place and is brilliant and arrogant and everything that goes with it—and it's true, but it's all been hard-earned, toiled for and sweated for every step of the way, and even then . . . he might not have triggered *everything*. That's why he wanted an Elemental mage child."

"But you know how to deal with the house," Thea said. "Are *you* an Elemental . . . ?"

"There are certain aspects of it that can be taught,

by rote," Larry said. "Those, I have down pat. It's like learning a multiplication table. But the finesse . . . the finesse of it was always just a little bit beyond me. And when I chose to turn away from it and pursue my own path—my father saw that as a reaction to failure rather than the choice that it was, and he called me a coward and I called him worse, and it was years before we could be civil to each other again."

"Can either of the other two do it?" Thea said carefully, setting her glass down.

"Isabella . . ." Larry frowned, thinking, shaking his head a little. "She got Father's arrogance in full measure—but it was her mother's magic that she got, the earthier, simpler kind—she is talented and able, and more than competent in her own field, but she is not an Elemental. Beltran . . . I don't know. I never got to know him that well. He was always a bit of a loner—and while it is obvious that he is capable of functioning within an Elemental environment by the simple fact that he is able to live in this house and make it do his basic bidding, I am not sure that he is an Elemental mage in the sense that he might have been able to trigger the original seed without mishap, for instance."

"How about Diego?" Thea asked quietly, her hands clasped in her lap with fingers intertwined.

Larry looked at her in silence. "I honestly don't know," he said at last. "My God, I am still trying to grasp the idea that something like him . . . some*one* like him . . . is out there in the first place. A whole other world I never dreamed existed. Another brother," he said softly.

"How did you learn about the Elemental stuff?" Thea said.

"Father taught me what I needed to know when I was a boy," Larry said.

"And did he teach Isabella and Beltran?"

"I would guess, some," Larry said.

"And whatever Beltran knows, Diego knows . . . or can find out?"

"I can't be certain of that," Larry said. "I can't be certain of anything when it comes to this—all I have are the bare facts, but when it comes to magic, sometimes one wild or unexpected word can make a complete mockery of the facts. And I've been away too long. I don't know what the wild word is, or was, or if it has been uttered at all or is still merely hanging over all of us waiting to explode. Maybe your coming here, Thea, was precisely the thing that was necessary to tip the balance. We can't tell—nothing is linear in magic. Sometimes cause and effect can switch places without warning."

"What if . . . he can?" Thea said. "What if he can access the Elemental magic? I don't know what it is that I do, exactly, or how it measures up—but I'm not sure that I can do anything against something that . . ."

"Thea . . . you've already escaped him once," Zoë said gently. "And if I understood you correctly—when I woke up and you were there, at the computer—you were sort of . . . writing yourself an insurance policy, weren't you? Writing in an ability to sideslip out of whatever he might drag you into?"

"But that might not work, now," Thea said.

"It's like I said," Larry replied, "magic is its own rule. All we know right now that we can swear to is that Beltran is no longer in this house, that he had been getting some sort of lessons from an unexpected and what we might consider to be an unwholesome quarter, and that Diego is still at the spellspam business."

"He is?" Thea said quickly.

Larry grimaced. "I caught one just before I left the Nexus," he said. "The filters trapped it, and your friend Terry loaned me his dreamcatcher device—nifty things, those, any way *I* could get one of them . . . ?"

"Sorry, special issue," Thea said. "What was it this time?"

"It's just a list of diseases—from the mildly embarrassing and amusing to things that could be quite serious. I suspect there will be a lot of sick people in the world in the morning, although I've already sent out an e-mail to the FBM people in Washington, warning them. The thing is, they can't prevent it—it's too late for that. If I've seen it, it's already out and it is possible, indeed probable, that far too many other innocents have been snagged by it. The thing is, it is so *obvious*—the subject line is even misspelled in a heavily hinting way. 'The best harmacy in the world,' something like that. Pharm without the p turns into harm. I really don't see how we can get around it. It's up to you to find him. The rest of us wouldn't begin to know where to look."

Thea drew in a long breath, but said nothing.

"It's okay to be afraid," Larry said abruptly.

Thea lifted her head.

"Anybody would be," Larry said, his voice very gentle. "It's the reaction of sanity. Frankly, I would be far more worried if you were out there straining at the leash. With a touch of fear comes prudence, and I know that you won't do anything just to prove a point. I trust you on this. You and Diego are very different—but I also think that in a lot of ways you are alike. Both young, both loose in this new field of magic, tangled in computers and in the virtual world—and I think that works both in your favor and against you.

"There's a little of the Elemental in me," he added. "Maybe it's that . . . and maybe it's just that I've always been a good judge of character. But I think you've just proved to me that you're the one to do this, to follow Diego to wherever he is holed up. Only someone who knows to be afraid of a task like that is to be entrusted with doing it."

"Cheveyo said . . . that only gods and fools are completely unafraid. Those who know they cannot be hurt and those who don't believe they can be," Thea said. "He said the rest of us do well to know when it is good to be afraid."

"A wise man, this Cheveyo," Larry said. "Who is he?"

"Long story," Zoë said.

"Another one?" Larry said, smiling. Zoë blushed.

"Well, you owe me one, after tonight. What do you think," he said, turning to Thea, "do you feel ready to go back to your Elemental bedroom and try and get some sleep? Tomorrow . . . might be a long day."

"All right," Thea said. She got up, freeing her hand from Zoë's. "Are you coming up too, Aunt Zoë?"

"Oh, go on," Zoë said, finally laughing out loud. "I'll be up in a moment."

"Good night," Thea said, turning to go at last.

"Good *morning*," Larry said. "In theory, at least."

Thea turned once, at the door of the sitting room. "There's just one thing I don't understand," she said. "The Alphiri . . . were watching me all the time. They tried to *buy* me when I was little. They wanted what I could do. But . . . so can Beltran . . . I mean, Diego . . . how come they've been content just sending in Corey? Why haven't they got Diego already? And what if they *do* . . . ?"

1.

WHEN THEA WOKE the next morning, Zoë was gone from the room again—but there was a note laid on her bedside table, propped up against the Tiffany lamp.

I'm not far, come down to breakfast when you wake up. Think of whatever you'd like to have, and it'll be waiting for you by the time you get downstairs. It's . . .

". . . an Elemental house," Thea finished out loud, grinning, and extricating her bare feet from her covers. "Fine. I want a waffle, and I want fresh strawberries. And I mean *fresh*. Let's see how you deal with *that*, house."

The house maintained a dignified silence, and Thea dressed, stuffed her feet into a pair of scuffed

309

ballet flats, and opened her bedroom door.

The bathroom across the corridor appeared to be occupied, but the door wasn't closed, just pulled to and left slightly ajar. So was the door to Terry's room; Thea paused in the middle of the corridor.

"Terry?"

There was a sound of rinsing and spitting from the bathroom.

"Out in a sec," Terry said.

He emerged from the bathroom a moment or two later, his hair still standing up on end from being slept on.

"Any serenades in the night that I should know about?" he asked.

"No, I just had midnight lemonade with Larry and Aunt Zoë," Thea said, "and found out a few more things about this place. I'll tell you over breakfast. Wait for me, I won't be long."

Terry nodded and Thea slipped into the bathroom to brush her teeth, brush her hair, and run a washcloth over her face. She inspected her chin in the mirror, but the thing she had thought was turning into a magnificent zit turned out not to be life-threatening, and she decided to leave well enough alone. Terry was waiting in the corridor when she was done, running both hands through his own hair in an effort to make it sit flat.

"That's what they invented combs for," Thea said.

Terry stuck out his tongue at her in a manner that suddenly forcefully reminded Thea of Frankie. She wondered what her brothers were doing with their summer while she was dreaming up her favorite breakfast in the world's only original Elemental house and preparing to chase down cyber-ghosts. Her mood momentarily swirled into a potent mix of homesickness, smugness, and pure terror—and then she got distracted by remembering the waffles and the fresh strawberries that ought to be waiting downstairs for her. She thought she could see the smell of those strawberries, much like Zoë might have done—a faintly pink mist hanging in the air of the corridor and leading down the spiral staircase.

The breakfast room was deserted. Terry appeared not to have thought too hard about his own breakfast because he just got bland, generic fare—eggs over easy, hash browns—but Thea's strawberries proved every bit as fresh as she had specified, and she bit into them with gusto while they rehashed the previous day's events.

"*Find him*, they said," Thea said. "What if I do?

Do they send in the cavalry?"

"They didn't the last time," Terry said.

"You mean with the Nothing?"

"You figured that one out. You and Magpie and Ben."

"And you and Tess," Thea said. "We all shared that one. The idea, the execution."

"Yeah, the execution," Terry murmured. "And the responsibility. You have no idea how long, after, Ben moped about that whale. And we all knew that it was the right thing to do, then—that he even had the whale's blessing, that it was traditional, that it was the way things were always done."

They looked at each other, understanding the unspoken thoughts. *We killed something. Even with the built-in absolution of a willing sacrifice . . . we bear the guilt of it.*

We. If Thea went after Diego, she would have to go alone—or he might never let himself be found.

And if she found him, there would be choices. Choices that would be far, far more difficult than luring a mindless monster into the body of a willing sacrifice.

"That was different. That was not . . . real. It wasn't a *person*."

"We all heard it scream, in the end," Terry said. "If that last cry was anything to go by, it understood what was happening, which made it alive enough for any given definition of sentience. It *understood*."

"It may have grown into a set of senses, but I don't think it started with them," Thea said obstinately. "And it was a monster, in every way. Aunt Zoë said it smelled like carrion. We knew it was dangerous to our kind, that it killed. We lost people we knew to it."

"Twitterpat," Terry said.

"And others. Maybe they were strangers, but they were no less dead. We knew . . ."

"Well, it's the same thing here," Terry said. "Except that this time we have a monster who is like us, who has a face, who maybe has a motive we could understand."

"Diego hasn't killed anybody," Thea said stubbornly.

"But is that because he won't?" Terry said. "Or is it because he can't yet, because he hasn't figured out how? If he comes up with something that kills . . . well, he already knows how to send it. He's had enough practice runs. He's also had enough hits to know that it will work, that it could be devastating.

It could even change our world. Permanently. He'll be a ghost in the machine, but he could control everything from it."

"All we need to do is switch off the computers," Thea said, perking up. "Wouldn't that work?"

Terry snorted. "Right. Like you could turn off every computer in the world. At the same time. Think again. It's like trying to switch off electricity—it would be like going back to the Dark Ages. We already depend far too much on them—how would you get everyone to give up the convenience and the speed, the sense of *security* that they still mean to most people? And there are so many computers out there now, in so many homes, how do you police a shutdown? It would only take one twit who didn't shut down because he knew better . . ."

"Well, what am I supposed to do about any of it?" Thea said.

"They'll tell you what you need to do," Terry said after a pause.

"I know," Thea said bleakly. "That's partly what I'm afraid of."

She stabbed the last strawberry with her fork and filled her mouth with it so that she would not have to say anything more.

It was precisely at this moment that the breakfast room was graced by the presence of Sebastian de los Reyes himself.

"Good morning," the professor said. He looked tired, as though he hadn't slept much, but he was much more his usual self than the night before—autocratic, august, apparently in control.

Thea swallowed the last mouthful of her strawberry as Terry scrambled to his feet.

"Good morning, sir," Terry said.

"Was Lorenzo here when you came down, by any chance?" the professor inquired.

"No, sir—haven't seen him," Terry said. "But we haven't been here long . . ."

Zoë suddenly poked her head around the door. "I thought I heard voices," she said. "Good morning. You have a lovely garden, Professor de los Reyes."

"Thank you," said the professor.

"My mother used to like it," said Larry, following Zoë into the room. "And it's always been pleasant in the early mornings."

The professor chose not to pursue that remark. "I have coffee in my study, if everyone's done with their breakfast," he said. "We should finish our conversation from last night. There are decisions to be made."

He swept everyone with an imperious glance, and Thea slipped off her chair, pushing her plate away. Terry was already at the door.

"Professor de los Reyes," a voice called out in the hallway as the professor led the way out of the breakfast room, "may I have a word?"

"Yes, Mrs. Emmett, what can I do for you?" the professor said courteously.

"It's Sam, sir . . ."

Larry, who had poked his head around the door, ducked back into the breakfast room with the others.

"Don't look now, but it's Madeline with Convalescent Boy," Larry said quietly.

"Convalescent Boy?" Thea said. "What's wrong with him?"

"Sam is always ailing with something," Larry said. "She had him quite late in life, and every time he clears his throat, she calls an ambulance."

"He isn't at all well," Madeline was saying out in the corridor. "I'd like the morning off so I can get him to a doctor. He seems . . ."

"What are his symptoms, Mrs. Emmett?" Larry

said suddenly, stepping out from the breakfast nook.

Thea stared at Sam, who was huddled up against his mother, shivering. His face alternated between a ghastly, pallid, waxy look and a flushed feverishness, with a scattered rash across his cheeks and forehead; he hung on to his mother's arm as if the very act of standing upright made his head spin.

"I can't make sense of it," Madeline said. "That's why I want him to see a doctor. He's got a slight fever, a bit of a rash . . . he's complaining of being dizzy, and of being nauseous, and of a ringing in his ears, and he says he couldn't sleep a wink last night but I can't keep him awake this morning, he actually fell asleep with his face in his cereal . . ."

"I don't feel so good, Mom," Sam said in a thin, reedy voice.

"I think he's going to . . . ," Thea began urgently, but was swiftly overtaken by events. Sam's lips trembled, his throat worked a few times as though he was fighting a rising gorge, and then he lost the battle and threw up a thin, greenish stream of vomit—some of it pooled in evil-smelling puddles on the clean tile floor, but the bulk of it landed squarely on the professor's hand-tooled leather slippers.

The professor's face did not change from its

expression of courteous concern. He did not even look down at his feet, keeping his eyes on Sam—who stood with his head buried between his hunched shoulders, weaving slightly on his feet and looking thoroughly humiliated and miserable.

"Oh, I am *so* sorry," Madeline gasped. "Let me just . . . Sam, do you want to sit . . . I'll go get a mop . . . I'm so sorry, sir, I don't know *what* the matter is—it could just be a bad flu, or some sort of allergy . . . or an overindulgence in junk food . . ."

"Overindulgence, but not in junk food. Tell him to spend less time in front of the computer, or at least to be more careful with it," Larry said. "No doctor will help him. It's no wonder you can't pinpoint a disease—those symptoms cover half a dozen of the things listed in that spellspam e-mail last night. You'd better bring him into the breakfast room so he can sit down, and we can counter the spell. And count yourself lucky that he didn't catch something worse. He might have prowled the halls as a werewolf last night. Er . . . I think I can manage a cure, Father, if you want to go and . . . slip into something more comfortable on your feet before we continue our meeting."

"My son will do what can be done, Mrs. Emmett," the professor said. "Would the rest of you like to wait in the study?"

His self-control slipped just a little as he eased his feet out of the offending slippers, a fleeting grimace of distaste on his face as he took a step back, avoiding the noxious pools on the floor. He did not even look at the ruined slippers as he turned away, leaving them in the hallway for the house to clean up, and climbed the stairs in his stocking feet.

"Go," Larry said, shepherding Sam and his trembling mother into the breakfast room. "I won't be long."

"This is from *last night*," Terry said. "Any more . . . stuff . . . turn up? Have you checked the mail this morning?"

"There's at least two," Larry said. "We've got more crud to deal with in the short term, but if he's upping his output, maybe he'll run out of practical jokes faster than he can keep up with it."

"Or think of more and more dangerous ones," Zoë said darkly.

"I always leave the worst-case scenario for the last resort," Larry said.

"If you plan ahead for it, you might never have to deal with it," retorted Zoë.

Larry shrugged. "Then I'd be worried all the

time," he said, heading into the breakfast room.

The other three made their way slowly to the professor's study, but Zoë hesitated at the door, her hand hovering over the door handle and then dropping away. "I think we'd better wait for one of them to come back," she said. "Other people's studies always smell dangerous, like you ought to leave them unmolested, and in this house I wouldn't want to trip any alarms."

"I wouldn't worry," Larry said, coming up the hallway, close enough to have overheard the remark. "You *were* invited."

"You fix him?" Terry asked as they filed inside the study.

"Of course, all it took was a direct reversal, and that's easy to do if you know what you're up against. He's his usual healthy hypochondriac self, and after his mother got done being worried to death about him, she got good and mad—and he's now banned from using the computer. For three days."

"Like that's going to help," Thea said. "Unless the spellspam stops . . ."

"Actually, one of this morning's offerings gave me an idea," Larry said. "*Enhance your senses*, the thing said, and I have no doubt it will be driving people insane. Spectacles and hearing aids are fine for people who have a deficiency in those departments, but can you imagine people with perfectly good hearing suddenly being able to *hear everything*—someone walking in high heels across a tile floor would be enough to send you over the edge, not to mention the sound of a faucet dripping on a different floor of your house—and the voices in your head, if you can hear every word, every whisper, maybe every thought . . ."

"You didn't see that one, did you, Aunt Zoë?" Thea said, suddenly sobered. With her own exotic abilities, Zoë was already operating under a sensory overload which most ordinary people would have been hard-pressed to cope with.

"No, I was careful this time. Safety in computing." Zoë said.

Terry was actually wincing. "Imagine trying to butter a piece of toast," he said. The memory of the scrape of a knife on the rough surface of crisp toast suddenly made everyone shudder.

"Or touching *anything*," Thea said, unable to pull her mind away.

"Or smelling *everything*," Terry said. "Ow. Complete overload."

"But you said it gave you an idea, Larry," Zoë said, settling herself into the armchair by the window. The light fell over her face and hair like a blessing, making her faintly luminous, as though she were a visiting Woodling basking in her forest's sunshine. Thea saw the awareness of this wash over Larry's face before he spoke.

"Yes. An idea. About Thea."

2.

THEA'S SMILE WAS wiped off her face. "What?" she said, looking warily up at Larry.

"Well . . . when you go looking for Diego . . ."

"Wait a minute," Terry said, "is she really supposed to—"

"Uh," said Thea.

"Perhaps we'd better . . . ," Zoë began, getting up from her armchair.

The door of the study opened just as they all spoke at once.

"One at a time," said the professor, "usually works better if you are actually trying to communicate. Is everything all right with Sam Emmett?"

"Absolutely," Larry said. "Do you want some coffee?"

"Yes, thank you," the professor said, walking around the desk to claim his high-backed chair.

"There are going to be a lot of doctors with their hands full this morning, people don't know any better," Larry said, pouring out a mug of strong black coffee and taking it back to the desk. "And some people won't go at all because some of the stuff on that list isn't symptomatic of anything specific . . . and just how do you cure someone of xenophobia, anyway . . . ?"

"Someone had better call my uncle," Terry murmured carefully.

"I already let the FBM know. I'll update them later," Larry said.

"Now," said the professor, accepting a mug of steaming coffee from Larry's hands, "what was this about an idea?"

"Wait, first of all," Zoë said. She came to stand beside Thea, facing the desk. "What *exactly* do you think it will accomplish? Sending Thea out like a hunting hawk?"

"Usually hunting hawks bring back the prey they've been sent after," Larry said.

"But she can't, Larry. Not this time. You yourself said it. If you believe that it is Diego de los Reyes who is behind this . . . she cannot bring him back. He never existed, not in this world. She might come back towing some lifeless shell . . ."

Zoë broke off, suddenly realizing that she was speaking of painful matters to the father and the older brother of both entities she was talking about, Diego *and* Beltran.

"You're right, that isn't going to help us," Larry said, and for once he wasn't smiling. "There is more to it than this. Thea, this isn't a recon mission. It's going into battle. You need to figure out how we can stop Diego from continuing with this—before it gets worse. You know how bad a library gone feral can be—escaped spells wreaking havoc everywhere, wild magic roosting in the rafters. If Diego loses control of his playthings, the entire world becomes one huge feral library. And you of all people know first-hand about those—your own father used to work at taming and containing the ferals when they got out of hand. If magic really gets let loose and out of control . . . our entire social fabric could unravel."

"But what do you want me to do?" Thea whispered.

The professor sighed, putting his coffee down onto his desk.

"One way or another," he said, "Diego needs to be stopped. It will be your task to find him . . . and if you cannot stop him yourself, then lead us to him.

As I understand it . . . you've taken reinforcements with you before, when you *wove* that other world where your encounter took place."

"With the Nothing?" Thea said.

"She didn't take us," Terry said. "We came after her."

"She left the door open for that. I know that you have taken others with you into, or at least through, those worlds. Is there a possibility that you might take, for instance, me?"

"Father," Larry said sharply, his head snapping around. "You of all people can't face him. You couldn't find it in yourself to destroy him if that was necessary. And that's only natural—he is your *son*."

"And your brother," the professor said.

"Who, then? The kids again? Me? Maybe we should call for FBM reinforcements and send in Luana Lilley."

Both the Academy students actually recoiled at that name.

"I'm not taking that woman anywhere," Thea said rebelliously.

"Then call Humphrey," Zoë said obstinately. "You like *him*."

"None of the above," Larry said sharply, cutting

through the discussion. "Look, if you were our quarry, would you just fling open the gates of your fortress if someone like Thea came knocking with an army at her back? No, she needs to at least lure him out by herself. If she leaves a way for us to follow and send reinforcements, that's an advantage. But in that first instance . . ."

"You want me to go in alone," Thea said faintly.

"Yes, because if you don't you'll never find him, because he won't let himself be found. One thing we do know is that he's good at hiding."

"But what if I *do* find him?"

"Well, that brings me to the idea," Larry said. "This sense-enhancement e-mail that he's just sent out is calculated to be malicious and painful, and the sense 'enhancements' will drive the victim crazy in the shortest possible time. But what if I could figure out the spell and recast it, and give you enhanced senses of a different sort, something that will help you look for him? You said there was a green fog all around you last time, and you couldn't see—what if I could give you enhanced vision, something to pierce the mists with?"

"I can weave that," Thea said.

Larry blinked. "Weave what?"

"I don't need to 'see' through the green mist. Last time I was trapped, and I wanted out, and so I did. But if I'm supposed to be doing something else, I can find him. I can weave a world where I can find him."

"Even if it's his world?" Larry said. "Do you have the power to change someone else's vision? Would he then have the power to change yours? This is so dangerous . . ."

"*Now* you think about that," Zoë snapped.

"We need to know . . ." Larry began, but it was the professor who leaned forward, both elbows on his desk, steepling his fingers in a gesture of emphasis.

"Too many things are telling me that this goes deeper than we realized," he said. "There is the tutor, who has been unmasked as being the Trickster himself, an ancient spirit entity of this land. There is the nature of some of the spellspams that have been recorded so far, which seem to implicate at least a surface involvement of the Faele. There is the apparently unrelated issue that I found mentioned in one of the reports, where the witnesses to a specific spellspam started speaking in foreign languages . . . one of which was Alphiri. Both Beltran and the individual of whom we speak as my lost son, Diego . . . may just be tools, used by the nonhuman polities for their own ends. And we have no idea as to what the politics—the Alphiri or Faele—are trying to accomplish by unleashing this kind of chaos into the world."

"Grandmother Spider said . . . they were looking for dreams."

The professor looked at Thea in puzzlement. "What was that?"

Thea tried to cast her mind back. There were times when she felt as though Cheveyo walked beside her at the Academy, when Grandmother Spider visited her dreams and spun stories, when the Trickster sat eavesdropping on her conversation in a café . . . and there were times when all that remained were the things she had learned from them.

Like the truth about the Alphiri. And then, the fear.

She had not known, when she was younger, that she was afraid of the Alphiri. They were everywhere she looked—she had grown up with them, they were the Trader Polity, the Messenger Polity, they had always been a part of her world—but her point of view had changed after her visit to Grandmother Spider's house, and the very fact that one couldn't turn around without bumping into an Alphiri peddling something or hovering at a portal had acquired a far more ominous significance.

Especially after what she had seen last summer in the woods near her home, the three Alphiri whom she had known, beyond any doubt, to be waiting there for *her*.

Thea found her heart thumping as she let her thoughts touch on the Alphiri, and on what she might still be facing before this journey was over.

"They buy, they sell, they copy, and they polish until it shines . . . but they cannot create or dream," Thea said. "Grandmother Spider said that they are searching for a legacy they can leave behind—and they want magic, and they cannot hold it." She lifted her gaze. "They wanted me," she said. "Before I was born, they wanted me. But my father told them that I was not for sale, that humans don't sell their children."

"But who would they have gone to, to bargain for Diego?" Zoë murmured thoughtfully.

"He is my son," the professor said heavily.

"*Beltran* is your son," Zoë said. "Diego is a lost soul. He does not belong to anyone . . . except, perhaps, Beltran, to whom he is linked because they were twinned in the womb."

Larry had been chewing his lip for some time,

apparently holding back from saying something, but now he shook his head, and begun to pace the study.

"It's all speculation," he said. "Everything we are talking about, we're pulling out of thin air. *We need to find him.* Before things get worse . . . and trust me, they will."

"What do you want me to do?" Thea said at last.

"Go into the woods and leave me a trail of crumbs to follow," Larry said with a crooked smile. "He won't be found except by you alone—but maybe I . . . or someone else . . . can follow the trail you leave behind, and find you both. With a bit of luck, that's all you need to do."

"But what if he . . ." Zoë began, and swallowed hard. "I promised her parents that I would look after her," she added softly.

"It's okay, Aunt Zoë," Thea said. Her voice shook, but just a little. "I'll do what I can."

The false wall of the professor's study was still open; Sebastian de los Reyes saw Thea's eyes go to the Nexus terminal and, after a brief hesitation, nodded permission. Thea walked over to the keyboard and sat down in front of it, very still for a moment, and then toggled to a notepad screen and began typing.

She paused for a moment when she was done,

read over what she had written, and then said, without turning around, "Terry . . . watch my back."

And hit ENTER.

She could not use the Barefoot Road for this search—she could not weave an absence of a particular person and tell the Universe to take her to a time and place where that hole would be filled. There was nothing she could use to search. Putting in Beltran's image might have led her to Beltran himself—but all she knew about him at that point was that he was missing, and going after him might lead her into worse trouble than she knew. Diego might have been described as Beltran's twin, but Thea had no way of instructing her weave on how to tell the two of them apart.

She needed a void for this, something empty of form—because she was looking for a place, not a person, because a place was all she knew how to look for. The room of green mist and mirrors.

She remembered the quiet sky she had watched from Big Elk's back, and that was what she now floated in the midst of—a darkness flickering with thousands of diamond points of sharp light. Thea looked at them and wove into them the memory of the mist which had once surrounded her.

Green.

The strange, unnatural green glow that had spilled into the corridors of the professor's house that first night. The odd, glowing green mist that had surrounded her when she had first stepped into Diego de los Reyes's world. The green ribbon she had braided into a rope to take her home.

The stars began to bleed green—fading from bright white or flickering golden into points of green in the sky, like the eyes of a legion of malevolent cats, and then the greenness pouring from them, as though they were suddenly no more than holes in something holding back the greenness from her like an arched roof. And then the firmament became crazed with cracks, and the greenness oozed through the fissures, and then, as the black heavens crumbled away, pouring through like water, coming down all around Thea like curtains of light. The green smelled, somewhat incongruously, like the juniper bushes growing in the shadows of Cheveyo's desert.

"I know you're there," she said into the greenness after a moment, sensing that she was not alone.

There was a chuckle from behind her.

"Of course I am," the voice said, the same voice that had spoken before.

"This is childish," Thea said. "I already know what you look like. What do you think you're hiding?"

"Oh, you do?" the voice said, mocking gently. "Are you sure about that?"

"Of course I am. They said you're Beltran's twin. I know what Beltran looks like. And what did you do with him, anyway? His father . . ."

"His father never thought he fulfilled his potential," the voice said.

"I can understand that," Thea muttered. She had not meant to utter that out loud, but it slipped from her, the sentiment ingrained in her by the years of her own failures, by the still-bitter memory of her father's eyes every time those failures were confirmed.

"You think so?" The voice turned just a little savage, but its next words were sweet again. "As for Beltran, whatever makes you think that *I* have him? And whatever makes you think I look anything like him?"

"You're twins," Thea said.

"Not in this world," Diego said. "In this world, I am who I choose to be."

The green mists parted a little, fraying, and then withdrew to the edges of Thea's vision as though defining an arena. And in the midst of it, on a floor of mirrored black obsidian, stood a figure dressed in a white shirt open at the throat and tight-fitting black leather pants. A dagger with a jeweled hilt glittered from a scabbard hung from his belt, his right hand, with a heavy gold ring on the ring finger, resting on it in a deceptively casual manner. He was unexpectedly tall—Thea, who had calibrated her expectations to Beltran's size and build, found she had to revise her estimate of Diego's height by a couple of inches, lifting her chin to look him in the eye.

It was not until he laughed, his thin aristocratic face transformed by the sudden flash of white teeth, that she realized that she had been staring at him with her mouth slightly open.

"Oh dear, if only you could see your face," he said, chuckling.

"But you can't be Diego," Thea objected instinctively. "You're too old."

"You think I'm more like Lorenzo?"

Lorenzo—Larry—was indeed far more like this young Spanish aristocrat than poor Beltran had ever been . . . but Larry was real. Less of an idealized icon. Full of real-world laughter and pain.

"No," Thea said. "You're nothing like Larry."

Diego took his hand off the dagger hilt and waved it in a gesture of dismissal. "Doesn't matter," he said. "I am not like anyone. I am me. And this is my world. My sphere. I can do what I want and be what I want."

For a moment that sounded almost painfully wonderful. The much-younger Thea, the girl who had agonized over her inability to touch magic at all, would have given much to have had this kind of ability to escape.

"You can be who you want, too. You can choose." He stepped back, and behind him, on a wrought-iron stand, was a full-length mirror framed in a polished dark wood. "You want to see what you look like right now, to me? Come and look."

"I know what I look like. I know who I am," Thea said, but the certainty with which she had thought to utter those words was suddenly missing from her voice.

"Are you scared?" Diego asked.

Thea clenched both hands into fists, and then consciously relaxed them, finger by finger. "Of course not."

"Then come," he said. "See."

Refusing would have meant admitting cowardice—

but it was not that so much as an irresistible if unwilling curiosity that drew Thea the few steps she needed to take before she faced the mirror.

And then stood quite still, staring at her reflection in silence.

The image began as something almost humiliating—the child that she had once been, hair in two plump braids, a mutinous expression on her face and hands stuck rebelliously into the pockets of her jeans, her feet bare and none too clean. Then the mirror changed; the image flowed and reshaped, blurring as though someone had thrown a stone into water, and when the reflection was still again quite a different person stood there. Thea found herself gazing into the eyes of a young woman, wheat-gold hair falling loose around her shoulders. A golden filet bound what looked remarkably like a miniature version of one of Grandmother Spider's spun-glass dreamcatchers on her brow. Her face was thinner than she was used to, an image, perhaps, of what she would still become; she wore a dark-blue gown that reached to the floor, her waist cinched with silver, the off-the-shoulder neckline picked out with silver embroidery along the edges. Silver stars were scattered on the full skirt, making Thea look as though she were wearing the night sky.

"That's . . . not me," she said at last, still staring.

"It is," Diego said, his voice coming from quite close, and suddenly he was standing right beside her, reflected in the mirror by her side. "This is not a mirror that tells lies."

We look alike, Thea thought—an incongruous thought, because it was so obviously untrue. He was dark to her fair, male to her female, opposite in every obvious way—but there was something, something she could not quite put her finger on. Something in the eyes. Something that had to do with a power that had been sleeping . . . and which was now awake at last.

1.

THEY STOOD SIDE by side in silence for a moment, staring at the images in the mirror, and then Thea stirred.

"So why aren't they here yet?" she said.

"Who?" Diego said blankly.

Thea turned to look at him. "The Alphiri, of course. That's what's been bugging me all this time. They were after *me* from the cradle, just waiting in the wings, ready to snatch at whatever happened . . ."

"The famous Double Seventh," Diego said, a little sardonically.

"You know about that?"

"I may not live in your world, but that doesn't mean I'm ignorant of it," Diego said. "Of course I know about it. But the Alphiri didn't exactly make it public with you, did they? And anyway, they didn't *get* you."

"Not for lack of trying," Thea said. "And your precious tutor was already in line for a reward once, for trying to turn me in to them—so where is he now? And why hasn't he collected for delivering you?"

"Because he hasn't delivered anything," Diego said. "He never mentioned anything about Alphiri. It was never about that."

"Uh-huh," Thea said, unconvinced. "Just when did he show up? Did he come to teach you things, or did he come after you'd already figured stuff out, to sniff around and see if you could be the kind of pay dirt he couldn't hit with me? How on Earth did he find you, anyway?"

"I didn't have much of a life, before he turned up—we met in some empty sphere, and he figured out the real possibilities of my connection to Beltran," Diego said. "But that was . . . after the first e-mail. I'd already done that much on my own. The rest of it—the campaign—that was something we cooked up together. He said . . ."

"I have a good idea of what he said. He always says it—'Do I have a deal for you . . .'"

"Well, he delivered on his end," Diego said.

Thea glanced around her at the bare arena they were standing in—the polished floor surrounded by green light, and a single mirror in the midst of it.

"Yeah, sure. If you know so much about our world, you should have realized you were unique—with your connection between magic and computers—"

"But I wasn't," Diego said. "There's you."

"But you didn't know about me. Very few people knew about me."

"*Cary* did."

"Only because he was already in cahoots with the Alphiri, and then he tried to sell me to them. But if you were his next ticket to riches, you ought to be living in a far greater state of magnificence than this. It's what I would—"

She caught herself, chewing at her lip.

"What you would do?" Diego finished for her. He took his hand from the jeweled dagger and stuck both hands as far as they would go into the pockets of his tight-fitting pants. "That's why they wanted *you*. Because you can do it as you choose."

"So can you," Thea said, surprised. "You've proved that. Good grief, I *went* to that hellhole you made for Humphrey May. You can surely . . ."

"*I* didn't make that. *He* did."

"But you set the spell . . ."

"Sure. I set a general spell, and everyone who fell into that particular trap took it and ran with it. And created their own weird destination. Those are the best—you give them a push and watch them go running in every direction."

"You did some foul things," Thea said.

"I was just enjoying myself," said Diego, shrugging. "Besides . . . you may notice that nothing I've done has actually *lasted*—it's all like catching a cold, you get a few sniffles and a runny nose and then a week later you're fine again."

"You made people catch things a little worse than a cold, with that disease one," Thea said sharply. "I mean, *lycanthropy*?"

"That one was Cary's idea," Diego said, grinning broadly.

"The werewolf thing or the whole disease idea?" Thea asked, despite her better instincts. She knew there were better things she could be doing than chatting to the guy who had caused the biggest headache her world had known for a very long time—but there was a certain . . . professional curiosity.

"Most of the spam ideas were mine," Diego said, "inspired by Isabella's preening, some of them, and then a few that were just . . . wishful thinking. But the diseases one was Cary's, although I did come up with a few of the actual individual ones myself."

"Let me guess," Thea said, rolling her eyes. "Flatulence, halitosis, diarrhea?"

"Yeah," Diego said, scowling a little. "How did you know that?"

"I have six brothers." Thea said trenchantly, without offering further explanation.

Diego sniffed, offended.

"But speaking of Corey . . ." Thea said, after a pause.

"Cary. And were we?"

"Yeah, we were. He picked the mean ones, remember? Speaking of him . . . oh, how I suddenly understand Grandmother Spider not wanting to turn her back on him!"

"Who's Grandmother Spider?"

"We all have our friends," Thea said. "Mine warned me about yours. Where *is* he, anyway?"

"He said he'd be back, once he'd figured out the security situation back at the House," Diego said. "He wasn't entirely happy with me, before. I kind of . . . went over his head."

"You weren't supposed to try and lure me here without him, were you?" Thea said, suddenly apprehensive, casting glances at the green shadows around her. "He was supposed to have the cavalry here . . . why me? Why not you? You have far more access to a powerful computer than I ever did—"

"Because he needs a physical body to make that access work, of course," said a new voice.

Corey materialized out of the shadows, smiling . . . and he was not alone.

Behind him, three tall and unmistakably Alphiri figures came stepping delicately from the shadows. Two males, dressed in their usual weird idea of what constituted business attire—one wore knickerbocker trousers, his long-toed feet stuffed into knitted socks with every individual toe thrust into its own compartment, and the second one had pulled a straw Panama hat over both pointed ears, giving his face a strange, strained expression. The one woman wore a long gown of some sinuous flowing golden stuff that draped elegantly over shoulder and hip. Thea glimpsed bare feet and toes adorned with individual silver rings visible underneath.

Thea could not hold back a gasp. Diego's expression was more inscrutable, but there was a trace of surprise there, if not his own share of sudden apprehension.

"We meet again," said the woman in a melodious

voice, apparently speaking to Thea.

"In good time," said one of the men.

"As we knew we would," said the other.

Thea was suddenly forcibly reminded of her dreams, of the way they had spoken before—always in triads, as though everything they said had a magical significance.

"We come with an offer," the woman said, apparently a leader of some sort.

"As we did once before," her first echo said.

"By the power of the Trade Codex," said the second.

Corey cleared his throat. "As I said. Two of them, here together. According to the Trade Codex . . ."

"Be silent," said the woman.

"We are not done."

"The bargain is yet to be concluded."

"What bargain?" Thea said, her voice high with fear and desperation. She had set it up so that she could escape from this place—but that was without taking into account the presence of the Alphiri, and she was not entirely certain if her arrangements would hold up under the changed circumstances. She turned on Corey with furious resentment. "Where do you get off, meddling in our lives, anyway?

What did they give *you?*"

"Something I wanted," Corey said, with a wolfish grin.

"He doesn't speak for us," Thea said, turning back to the Alphiri, scrambling to remember what her father had told her about the polity and their trading ways. "Whatever bargain you struck with him, if it concerns me—me or Diego—it is worthless. Your own Trade Codex says you cannot steal."

"We do not steal," the woman said.

"He offered us hope," said the first man, and Thea's eyes widened just a little.

"He offered us access."

"Access to what?" Diego burst out at last, staring at the people in his little world.

"Perhaps you," the woman said, turning to him fractionally.

"Hope for a future."

"Power to create."

Diego glanced at Corey. "But you know I need Beltran," he said.

"That isn't going to be a problem," Corey said, smiling.

"*You* have him," Thea whispered.

"I don't waste resources. It became obvious that

he would be endangered if I left him where he was—he was blown as Diego's cover. So I made sure I had him safe, before I went to the Alphiri. I knew that they—the rest of the crew, back in the house—would send you out, Galathea. So I told the Alphiri I'd get you both."

"But you haven't got either of us," Thea said. "I am not yours to bargain away, and anything done here will be nixed at the Tribunal when this case is hauled before it—and it *will* be, you can believe that. And without Beltran, without access to the Nexus . . ."

She shut her mouth abruptly, aware of a concentrated and focused attention that all three of the Alphiri were paying to her every word.

"We don't need the Nexus," Corey said confidently. "There were lots of copycat spams . . ."

"Copied. Transmitted. Not created. Not what Diego can do," Thea said, unable to stop herself. She turned on the Alphiri. "Taken up and passed off for someone else's work. Just like you do with the golden and glittery things you dangle before the other worlds. None of them your own."

"That is why we are here," the woman said.

"For the future," said the first man.

"For the dreams," said the second.

"Well, you can't have ours!" Thea said. There was a part of her that trembled with pure terror and was more than ready to turn and flee, if she knew there were a place to flee *to* in this insubstantial world of Diego's.

"So it's the Nexus, is it?" Corey said suddenly. "But there is more than one way to access the Nexus . . ."

Thea had thought of the same thing, in the same instant. Isabella. Lorenzo.

"Oh no, you don't!" she muttered, turning just as Corey began to step back into a shadow. She whipped out a hand and closed it around his wrist, and then willed herself back, as she always did from an alternate reality she had woven for herself, back to where the computer was. Back to the office.

For a moment she struggled, almost feeling as if she would fail this time, stuck somewhere in between worlds, in unraveled strands that she could not re-weave. It was not the first time she had traveled with a companion in tow, but this was no ordinarily companion: it was Corey, the Trickster, and although taken by surprise, he was quick-thinking enough to realize that wherever she was taking him would not be a good place for him to be. But although it felt like swimming through molasses, Thea was suddenly aware that she was back in Professor de los Reyes's office, her hand still clutching Corey's wrist.

She felt hot and sweaty; her hair, damply irritating, was sticking to the back of her neck as though she had just run a race, and her shirt clung to her in miserable discomfort. But if she was feeling bad, Corey obviously felt a whole lot worse. He let out a startled yelp as they materialized in the study, his bony wrist jerking in her grip; it suddenly changed into a coyote's angular paw, and then, as she instinctively tightened her grip on it, into the wingtip of a raven, which pulled itself out of her scrabbling fingers as the bird tore free and began to circle the room right up underneath the ceiling, uttering raucous cries.

"Someone got spellspammed?" Larry said, staring up with an astonished expression.

"No," Sebastian de los Reyes said, his own eyes on the raven, "if I am not mistaken that bird used to be my son's tutor, Cary Wiley."

"Are you all *right*?" Zoë said to Thea, who was breathing in short gasps.

"Professor . . . the Nexus . . . you said you've been

using it as your family's Terranet backbone . . . You need to shut *that* down, now. Nobody gets access to Terranet through the Nexus except you, and then only when you have to . . . the Nexus is the reason that Diego was able to start sending out the spellspams, through Beltran . . ."

"That I have already done," the professor said, glancing at the computer console.

"But Beltran's disappeared," Terry said.

"*He* has him somewhere," Thea said, pointing to the raven, which had now perched on top of a high shelf and was eyeing everyone resentfully. "And he brought the Alphiri to Diego's world. He's been acting as a go-between all along, and now he's figured out that he needs access to the Nexus, and if he can't have Beltran, he'll take someone else. Someone with access. Family. Isabella, maybe."

Terry made an instinctive jerk toward the computer, as though he wanted to rip it out of the wall, before Isabella could come to any harm from it.

"But I thought it was the connection between the twins that was the important thing here," Larry said.

"He can change shapes," Thea said, settling into a chair and gulping down a glass of cold lemonade that had appeared unasked for on the table next to her elbow, provided by the Elemental house. "He can manipulate what he needs. He has Beltran; he can *change* him into Isabella or even you, Larry— someone with access, and knowledge. The computer . . . the computer needs to be shut off from *all* of you . . ."

"I've already taken care of that," the professor said quietly, standing over Thea with his hands clasped behind his back. "I have already regretted that rash act, and right now the only access password to the Nexus is mine. And I'm not about to divulge that. Now, tell me what you learned about my son."

"I don't know where Beltran is, sir," Thea said.

"No," the professor said heavily. "Diego."

"The Alphiri," Larry said suddenly, dragging his eyes from the bird on the shelf. "You said there were Alphiri. What did they want?"

"I think . . . the same thing they wanted from me, when I was little," Thea whispered. "They want a source of magic. One *they* can use. They couldn't tap into human magic, not as it was, not as they were— but if there is a way to use the computers, then they can use . . . someone like me. That was what they were hoping to buy when they came to my father,

351

when I was maybe three years old. And he told them that I wasn't for sale."

"Your father spoke for you," Larry said. "But Diego . . ."

"Diego is *my* son. I should be the one to step between him and the Alphiri," the professor said.

"Only . . . in theory, Professor," said Zoë slowly. "The Tribunal might have trouble with that. And if the Alphiri Trade Codex should be taken to apply . . . Diego doesn't 'belong' to anyone in the same way that Thea was claimed by her father. He was fathered by you . . . *but he was never born*, and if he belongs to anyone, it is to his twin brother, who is the other half of his spirit . . . and who's missing. Diego, in practical terms, can lay claim to himself— or so the Alphiri can argue."

"You mean they can still get what they want? Access to magic? They can *buy* Diego?"

The raven screamed, and launched itself off the shelf, straight at the people in a huddled knot in the midst of the room. Almost too fast for the eye to see, Larry had blurred into the serval cat and was in mid-leap before any of them had a chance to react, knocking the bird off-balance with one powerful paw. The raven squawked, ricocheted off a protruding corner of a bookshelf, and tumbled into an ungraceful heap onto the professor's desk. As it untangled wing from tail, the cat was upon it again, tail lashing, a paw pinning down each wing.

It was Zoë who ran up to grab one of the wings as Larry transformed again, the other wing in his own hand, just as the raven transformed back into the now somewhat disheveled man whom Thea knew as Corey.

"You will tell me where my brother is," Larry said, his face still in a very catlike snarl.

"Lorenzo . . . ," the professor began, and then paused. "*Larry*. I need to take urgent measures concerning this Alphiri threat. It is Diego who needs me now. May I leave Beltran in your hands?"

"Not his. Mine," said Thea.

2.

EVERYONE TURNED TO look at her again.

"I will take Corey," she said. "He will tell where Beltran is. I will take him back to the ancient light; let the sun judge him, if he has transgressed."

"She can do it," Zoë said, hanging on to one of Corey's wrists.

"Wait a minute," Corey began. "Wait just a minute . . ."

"If you have not broken the law, then you will not be found guilty of it," Thea said.

"Do you need help?" Larry asked.

"Both of you, come. I can't hold onto him and weave at the same time. Professor, the computer . . . ?"

"It's off the grid, right now," Sebastian de los Reyes said, rather grimly. "But if you don't need Terranet, you may use it."

"No. Just a keyboard and a screen," Thea murmured, setting her lemonade glass aside and getting up, a little unsteadily, to cross over to the computer console. "Bring him over, and make sure you hang onto him when we get across. I don't want him escaping into the Road."

"Whatever you say," Larry said, making sure his grip on Corey's right wrist was locked. "This way, if you please."

Corey turned his head toward the professor as he was being frog-marched to the computer console. "No, wait—I'll give you what the Alphiri gave . . ."

"Now, Aunt Zoë," Thea said, lifting her hands off the keyboard. She touched Zoë's free hand with one of her own, and then they were . . . no longer in the study. Red mesas rose around them as they stood on the Barefoot Road. Thea's feet were bare upon it; everyone else remained shod.

"Stay still," Thea instructed. "Don't move, and don't let *him* move."

"You'd better sit down," Larry said to Corey, giving a firm tug on Corey's bony wrist.

Resigned, Corey subsided into a cross-legged position on the ground.

Thea took a few steps on the Road, peering into the scrub and tumbled rocks by the roadside.

"You have need of me?" said a voice, very close by, and where nothing had been a moment ago, Cheveyo stood leaning on his familiar staff.

"I think I will always need you," Thea said.

Cheveyo inclined his head. "I see you bring company," he remarked, glancing to the trio on the Road behind her.

"He's Corey," Thea said.

"I know him," Cheveyo said.

"He holds knowledge that we need. More than that, he broke the law, and I bring him back here, to where his kind may hold him accountable."

"Some might say he is his own law," Cheveyo said. "He is the Trickster; to plot and to deceive is just his way; it is the reason for his being."

"But betrayal is not," Thea said. "And he betrayed more than one kindred."

"We cannot punish him," said a new voice, and Grandmother Spider stepped out from behind Cheveyo. "This is not a court that can hand down a sentence and enforce it with imprisonment or the lash."

Behind her, the sunlight thickened into the tawny shape of Tawaha.

"He is what he is," Tawaha said, in that voice that was liquid gold. "We are the Eldest, but he is part of the Elder Kin, too. We cannot punish him—but we can judge him, and we can reprimand. That carries its own weight."

Grandmother Spider raised a hand, and Thea turned her head to where Larry and Zoë crouched beside Corey, still holding on to him. Zoë's face was luminous with joy, which seemed strange under the circumstances until Thea remembered how her aunt had once described the "voice" of the sun to her. Hearing Tawaha speak was once more a vindication of Zoë's curious world, and she was glowing with it.

"Let him go," Grandmother Spider called, and Zoë and Larry let go of Corey's wrists. He staggered to his feet, making something of a production of dusting himself off. Then he glanced at the Road, at his own booted feet.

"The Road is not mine today," he said. "If I move, it will vanish."

"Leap," Cheveyo said serenely. "You didn't come here by a straight road anyway."

Corey eyed the gap between himself and the edge of the Road, and then shrugged, bunched his leg muscles, and launched himself into the scree. Larry and Zoë stayed where they were, keeping very still. The Road shivered, but held. Corey appeared to consider shifting into his coyote form and bolting for the hills, but under the stern gaze of both Grandmother Spider and Tawaha, thought better of it. He sighed, hung his head, and walked over to them, dragging his heels.

"I have seen, in the dreamcatchers," Grandmother Spider said. "There are no secrets that you can keep from me, not for long. I have found the boy you were holding, asleep in the dark, and I have sent Tawaha to wake him. He is free."

She made a gesture, and Beltran stood, weaving a little, in the shadow of a nearby boulder. Larry's shoulders tensed; Zoë reached out and laid a light hand on his arm, but he had already remembered where he was, and made his muscles relax. Thea stared at Beltran's face, trying to catch his eye, to communicate, but there was nothing in his expression, nothing except an almost unearthly blankness that made her hackles rise.

Corey's golden eyes flashed defiance. "She lies," he said, flinging out an arm at Thea. "I have my own laws. I have broken nothing."

"You are right," Tawaha said, looking down at Corey with both authority and compassion. "You are a shadow between light and darkness. You are choice. You were created by the needs of the folk who made you, and you were granted dispensation from many laws because of that, a very long time ago. But there are limits to what you are permitted to do—putting a rock into the bed of a stream to make a rapid or to make it choose to run in a different streambed is permitted to you, and doing so may be considered the reason for your very existence. The kindred of the many worlds need to be tested, and it is the obstacles the Trickster throws in their path that are the trials through which their mettle is proved. But putting a stone into a streambed is different from damming the stream to create a lake. And while you are permitted to play with the manner in which a stream finds its way to the great sea, you are *not* permitted to change its nature." He lifted his head to gaze at Thea for a moment, and then beyond her at her companions. "He will not cross your paths again for a while," Tawaha said. "We cannot undo what the Trickster does, but we can and we will keep a closer eye on him." He lifted a hand, limned in a golden glow. "Walk in the light," he said, and it was a blessing.

And then they were gone, the three of them, the Elder ones—the splendor of Tawaha, the grace of Grandmother Spider, the barely restrained defiant audacity, even in this tight corner, of Corey the Trickster.

In the absence of something that he could lean on or drape himself over, Beltran de los Reyes appeared to be practically ready to drop in a heap where he stood. Cheveyo, glancing back at him, shook his head a little.

"That one looks like he needs caring for," he said, "and it is too long a tale that you have to tell, as I understand, to do it justice now. One day you might favor me by coming to my hearth to share it. Until then." He raised his free hand in farewell, turned to give a small courtly bow to the two waiting on the Road, and then turned and walked away with a measured stride.

"Who," Larry said, "was *that*?"

"Anasazi shaman," Zoë said.

Larry's eyes flicked to her. "Funny."

"True," she said. "Ask Thea about it sometime."

"And the other two? The ones who took our trickster friend?"

"They made our world, once," Thea said, and could not help a grin at the sight of Larry's expression, fluctuating between purest awe and complete disbelief. "He is Tawaha. The Sun."

Larry instinctively glanced up to the cloudless desert sky where the sun hung in molten fury. "That?"

"Yeah, that," Thea said.

"There was a time before Thea could do this thing that she does, the computer magic," Zoë said.

"Or *anything*," Thea muttered. "The Double Seventh who couldn't—remember?"

"Yes, but—then you wound up at that school and they—"

"*Before* the school," Thea said, "they sent me here. And whatever the magic was that I had, Cheveyo helped wake it. Cheveyo, and Grandmother Spider." She reached out—blue from the sky, red from the dust at the Road's side, dark strands from the shadows under the mesas—and began weaving the strands between her fingers, smiling. "And I could suddenly do *this*," she said, dropping a patch of braided light into Larry's hand. "And after that, I could do . . . other things. Like make talking about magic safe for Terry back in our world, or go looking for Diego—weaving other places, other worlds, a different reality . . ."

"So let me get this straight," Larry said. "You have to use a computer, the cutting edge of modern technology, to let you reach back and touch the power of the elder days?"

"Well . . . when you put it like that, yeah," Thea said.

Larry shook his head. "The mystery of the world and all its wonders," he said. "I will *never* understand this. What's going to happen to this Corey guy?"

"That's out of our hands," Zoë said. "Right now, I think you'd better get Beltran, and we should go home—there's still all kinds of chaos waiting for us there . . ."

"Right," Larry said, snapping out of his mood and taking a step toward Beltran . . . and the Road shimmered once underneath their feet, and promptly vanished. They stood in the midst of scrubland and red dust, with no indication that anything other than that had ever been there.

"Oops," said Larry, who froze the moment he sensed something strange going on, but not fast enough to prevent it from happening. He looked around at Thea, somewhat sheepishly. "Did you need that to get us home . . . ?"

Zoë rolled her eyes. "Just get Beltran," she said. "Thea . . . ?"

"Under ordinary circumstances, I might have

wanted it—but I brought us straight here from the computer and I can yank us straight back—is everyone accounted for?"

"Yeah," said Larry, stooping to gather up Beltran into his arms, and then paused, peering at something at Beltran's feet. "Looks like he was retrieved complete with baggage," he added.

"I'll grab that," Zoë said, stepping up to pick up a battered leather satchel from the ground. She hefted it experimentally—the bag wasn't heavy, but it was full of something sharp and angled, its contents sticking points out. "Seems he travels light . . ."

Before she had finished speaking, the red mesas faded into the familiar shelves of Professor de los Reyes's study, which, in their absence, had become filled to capacity by people, all of whom seemed to be talking at once. It was a big room, but it was packed—and the sudden arrival of four more physical bodies did not improve matters at all.

"Thea!" It was Tess, Terry's twin—but before she had a chance to confirm Tess's improbable presence in this room, another all-too-familiar presence cut into her line of vision.

"There! Look! What did I tell you?" The voice

was close to a screech. Thea closed her eyes for a moment.

"Oh, great," she muttered. "*She*'s here."

"Luana, that will be enough," said another voice, firm and in control. Its owner turned out to be a woman in her late forties, ash-blond hair cut into a chic, swingy bob. "Thea, I'm Nancy Dane, Terry's mother. I've heard a lot about you." She glanced at Larry, in whose arms Beltran appeared to have passed out. "Do you need medical assistance?"

"It wouldn't hurt," Larry said. "I'm Lar . . . Lorenzo de los Reyes, this is my brother Beltran. Is my father here?"

"He and my brother have gone directly to the Alphiri," Nancy said. "Clear the way there. Let them through. Sandy, Alan, get the paramedics."

Larry glanced around. "Zoë . . ."

"I'll come and fill you in later. Go," she said.

He glanced down at his brother, took a deep breath, and shouldered his way past the throng and out of the study.

"What's going on?" Thea asked in a small voice.

"We were hoping someone would tell us," Nancy said. "There's been a veritable epidemic of those spellspam messages in the last twenty-four hours, and it doesn't show any signs of stopping; the Bureau was advised of what was happening here, but that was *before* the spellspam explosion."

"But that shouldn't have happened," Thea said. "If Beltran wasn't here . . . and Diego wasn't doing it . . . and this computer had been taken off the Terranet . . ."

"I think they're all queued," said Terry, elbowing his way to the front of the pack. "I don't think anyone's in control of it just now. I can't find the cache, otherwise I'd delete it all—but it's in there somewhere. Maybe when the professor comes back he'll be able to deal with it—he knows his systems, and may be able to ferret it out."

"I am perfectly capable of doing that," snapped Luana.

Nancy glanced at her. "We will wait," she said, with authority.

Luana tossed her dreadlocks. "I *will* file a report," she said.

"Luana, we are in a private residence," Nancy said firmly. "The computer in question may be the Nexus supercomputer and thus directly under our jurisdiction, but we appointed a caretaker for it who is currently not present, and therefore we will wait before we proceed with anything further."

"You are letting the boy fiddle with it," Luana said.

Terry bristled.

"My son has been working under Professor de los Reyes's supervision and has his express permission to access the machine," said Nancy.

"Hey, Thea," said another familiar voice into the silence. "When I suggested sending you here, I had no idea what kind of a hornet's nest you'd stir up. Do you want to tell us which universe you've just popped in from?"

"Hi, Mr. May," Thea said, smiling with relief, peering through a gap between Luana and Nancy to where Humphrey May sat perched on the professor's office chair.

But then Zoë stirred, and Luana Lilley caught sight of the satchel slung over her shoulder.

"What have you got there?" Luana said sharply.

"I have absolutely no idea," Zoë said, slipping the satchel off her shoulder. "When we got Beltran de los Reyes, this was left alongside him, so we just brought it along."

"Let me . . . ," Luana began, reaching for it, but before she could grab it, Humphrey hoisted himself off his chair, slipped sideways past her, and intercepted the satchel.

"No, let *me*," he insisted. "Let's not be too eager, Luana—remember what happened the *last* time you just flung things open without looking . . . ?"

Luana shot him a poisonous look, but he already had the bag in hand. He laid it on the professor's desk, undid the worn clasp, and gently shook out its contents on the desk.

They all stared at the handful of old-fashioned tapes used to store data in early computers, and one small white cube, no more than a handspan wide. The cube appeared featureless and blank at first, but they could see the ghost of a suggestion of patterns on its faces—the one currently facing the ceiling consisted of two wavy lines stacked one on top of the other—almost too faint to make out.

"What is it?" Thea asked.

"Those tapes . . . I'm not even sure if we can read them anymore," Humphrey murmured, stroking his chin. "We'll have to go into the basement and dust off some *really* old machines . . . if we've still got them."

"*Beltran* had these?" Nancy said, glancing up at Zoë. "The boy was barely born when these tapes were the cutting edge of our technology. If he was born at all. The last computer I remember that used those has to be twenty years old!"

"Whoever had Beltran had them," Thea said.

"What would our friend the Trickster be doing with these?" Zoë said in honest bewilderment.

"Well, assuming they aren't corrupted through improper storage or tampering, the answers are on the tapes," Humphrey said. "*There's* something you can make yourself useful on, Luana. Take these straight back to the Bureau and get started on them. The sooner we figure them out, the sooner we'll be able to solve this. And I have every confidence that you will get those answers ASAP."

"But what's *that?*" Terry said, poking a finger at the white cube. It rolled over at his touch, like a die; the wavy lines strengthened marginally as Terry's hand brushed it, and then they were gone as the cube turned over and showed, on a new face, a pair of bold upright lines rather like a Roman numeral II.

"That?" Humphrey said softly, staring at the cube with a curious expression on his face. "I've never seen one before, but I think that is an Elemental cube."

"Like this house?" Thea said, glancing around at the walls of Sebastian de los Reyes's study.

"Something like that," Humphrey said.

"But what does it do?" Tess asked, fascinated.

"As to that"—Humphrey raised his pale blue eyes from the mysterious object on the desk—"I have absolutely no idea."

To: occupant@yourmailbox.com
From: Ima Spye < spy@iknowall.com >
Subject: I know what you did last summer . . .

But who will I tell . . . ?

1.

THE ELEMENTAL HOUSE remained chaotic for some time. Luana and another agent were quickly gone, much to everyone else's apparent relief, taking the white cube and the mysterious, antiquated computer tapes back to the Bureau for analysis—but that left five Bureau agents still on site—Nancy Dane, Humphrey May, two paramedics, and one dour security type who slouched around muttering orders to a bevy of annoying implike winged creatures with red eyes and tiny barbed whipping tails.

Isabella was not in evidence. Larry had whisked Beltran away to a safe place somewhere, and then seemed to have vanished himself. Zoë, after reassuring herself that Thea was all right, appeared to have taken herself elsewhere, too. The professor and the twins' uncle Kevin, the head of the FBM, were still out on their errand to the Alphiri, and apparently incommunicado.

That left Thea, Terry, and Tess pretty much to their

own devices, and the three of them spent a couple of hours catching up in Terry's room until Thea finally growled something and flipped open her laptop.

"What are you doing?" Tess asked.

"I'm calling in reinforcements," Thea said, typing furiously.

"Don't you think there are quite enough people in this house?" Terry asked.

"Oh, we don't need any of *them*," Thea said, typing a period with a flourish. "Ready?"

"You're going to do that *thing*, aren't you? Off we go, 'round the mulberry bush," Tess said.

"Something like that," Thea said, and hit ENTER. And then the three of them were suddenly standing on the Barefoot Road again, Cheveyo's country, the place that Thea had only recently left behind.

Terry and Tess, in their own world, had visited the American Southwest. They recognized its geography, but for a moment neither of them connected it to a time rather than a place, despite Thea having spoken to them of her summer with the Anasazi. Then things suddenly became weird, fast. The sky above their heads darkened like glass into two increasingly transparent windows, and familiar if rather astonished faces peered through: Magpie and Ben.

"Where *are* you?" Magpie asked, and her voice sounded loud, like thunder, coming from straight above them. "You look like you're in a snow globe . . ."

Ben laughed. "Some snow globe."

"Want to join us?" Thea said, looking up with complete unconcern, as though she were talking to people hanging out of a second-story window and not out of a hot, washed-out summer sky.

"Sure," Magpie said.

Thea stretched a hand out to her. "Grab my hand," she said. Magpie appeared puzzled by this request, in much the same way that Thea had once been puzzled by an invitation to enter a spider's home, and Thea, remembering the occasion, grinned. "Just close your eyes and stick a hand out," she said.

Magpie's eyebrows rose a fraction, but she obeyed; her hand came out of the sky like a giant's, but somehow from the moment it emerged out of the blue to the moment her fingers touched Thea's it had shrunk to its normal size and Thea clasped it and simply pulled. In the next moment, Magpie stood beside them on the Road, her hand still clasped in Thea's.

"Wild!" she yelped, her eyes flying open.

"Ben?" Thea said, holding out her other hand.

"Are you sure about this?" Ben asked carefully. "It looks an awful long way down . . ."

"I'm here, silly, it's perfectly all right," Magpie said, staring around her. "It's so beautiful . . ."

"All right, then, if you think it's okay," Ben said. His hand came snaking down much as Magpie's had done, and Thea grasped it, and pulled him down.

"And then we were five again," Terry said. "Okay, now what? And I think you should have told somebody . . ."

"Who was there to tell? They were all too busy chasing their *own* tails to worry about where ours are. And we will be back before they know we're gone, I promise you that."

"But what can we possibly do in such a short time . . . ?" Ben began, but Magpie looked at him reproachfully.

"Time is as time does," she said. "It's obvious. Here, as much time or as little as you want can go by, and it will have absolutely nothing to do with how much time is passing on Thea's computer . . . right?"

Thea nodded. "I've fixed it so that we'll return less than a full minute after we left," she said. "They won't even know we've been gone. And it beats sitting around in that room waiting."

"The house will know," Terry said.

"Yeah but they won't be asking the house," Thea retorted. "Besides, I was invited . . . and I'm inviting you."

"Invited by whom?" Ben said, gazing at the apparently empty country around them.

"By me," said a voice behind them, and they turned to find Cheveyo looking at them with what might almost have qualified as a smile. "I was not expecting you back so soon, Catori, but my hearth has long been hungry for a good story. You and your friends are welcome."

He inclined his head a fraction, indicating a direction, and then turned and walked away.

"I think he wants us to follow him," Ben whispered, staring owl-eyed at Cheveyo's retreating back.

"Okay, then," Terry said, squaring his shoulders. "This should be interesting."

Magpie fell into step beside Thea. "This is what you were telling me about, isn't it? The Elder Days?"

"Uh-huh," Thea said.

"Do you think . . . that Grandmother Spider might show up . . . ?"

"We left the Elders with their hands full when we brought Corey back to them," Thea said. Magpie's face fell a little. "But you said it yourself—time can do strange things out here. You never know."

Magpie nodded. Thea reached out and squeezed her hand, and then lengthened her step to catch up with Cheveyo, who was poling himself along at his usual pace and simply assumed that everybody would all end up at the same place together sooner or later.

"I brought them here because there are things we need to learn from one another," Thea said quietly as she reached him. "It's a war council, if you want to call it that. And you said you wanted a story—I figured this would be as good a time as any to tell you one."

"As I told you, Catori," Cheveyo said without breaking the rhythm of his stride, "you are all welcome here."

"Even if we ask lots of questions?" Thea asked, unable to hold back.

Cheveyo bent his head a little, perhaps to hide a smile. "Even then," he said. "After all, I have made no undertaking to answer any."

"But I would be grateful for any advice you might

give us, after you've heard it all," Thea said.

"What you ask for, I will give," Cheveyo said gravely. "You honor me by coming to me."

Thea bent her head to acknowledge his consent and fell back again to join the other four. Ben, who was bringing up the rear, was limping.

"What happened?" Thea asked.

"I think I have a stone in my shoe," he said.

Thea's mouth quirked a little. "I had the same stone in my shoe when I first came here," she said. "The ghost pebble. Don't tell Cheveyo about it, he doesn't believe in them."

"How far are we going?" Ben asked.

"Not far." Thea pointed a little way up the slope, where the path rose abruptly onto a near-vertical mesa face. A switchback path meandered once or twice as the gradient increased and then appeared to end smack against the cliff.

Ben looked up the mesa. "We're climbing *that*?"

"There's smoke coming out from under that overhang," Terry said. "I don't think we'll be climbing."

"That's Cheveyo's house," Thea said.

"Wow," Magpie breathed, her face full of wonder.

"I can't see anything," Ben said, peering in the direction indicated. "Is there a village or something?

Where? Are we going to have to, uh, I don't know . . .
smoke a peace pipe or something?"

"Oh, for heaven's sake," Magpie snapped impatiently. "He's a shaman, not Sitting Bull."

Ben lapsed into a wounded silence.

Cheveyo had pulled ahead a little. By the time the
rest of them had staggered up the final switchback to
the stone house at the foot of the mesa, their host
had already lit a fire on the outside hearth and was
waiting beside it.

"Be welcome at my hearth," he said. "Catori tells
me that she has summoned her friends for a council.
Speak freely here of the things you came to talk
about. Catori has asked for such advice as I can
offer, so I will remain in your circle so that I may
learn what is needful for me to know."

It was Thea who first moved, gave Cheveyo a
small bow, and stepped up to the fireside to sit cross-
legged on one of the skins, facing the fire. Magpie
immediately did the same, and then the twins, and
finally, warily, as though he was still not entirely certain as to what to expect, Ben.

After glancing at Terry, Thea delivered a con-
densed version of the events of the previous few days
to Ben and Magpie. Ben listened in silence, sitting

with his arms wrapped about his shins and his chin on his knees, frowning as she spoke. Magpie, quick-silver as always, interrupted with questions when-ever they occurred to her.

But it was Ben who asked the question that stopped Thea.

"The Alphiri? Again?" he said. "Or is it more like, still? I get the feeling that it was only a matter of time before they showed up."

"You were awfully skittish about the Alphiri when you first got to the Academy," Magpie said.

"That obvious?"

"Not *obvious*. But just the way you reacted to stuff."

"Yes, when we first got into Signe's class," Tess said.

"But how did *your* learning how to do cybermagic suddenly get the Alphiri into this?" Ben asked.

"It wasn't even the cybermagic. Not in the begin-ning. That first time, when we all went back to the Hoh forest through the computer—you were all there with me. I had no idea what was going on, any more than you guys did. That was before we figured it all out."

"But you said that Corey wanted to hand you over

like a trussed Thanksgiving turkey way before that," Tess said. "You were still here, which was way before the Academy. So why then, already?"

"Because I was Double Seventh, and the Alphiri had been watching, and *something* woke out here." Thea reached out and snagged a thread of orange from the fire, a strand of charcoal gray from a shadow, a thin filament of blue from the pale sky above them—and in her fingers, the ribbons of colored light twined into a braided rope. "There was this. And there was the portal that I had made, back in Grandmother Spider's world. And Corey must have figured out or overheard what Grandmother Spider said to me—that the reason I didn't do magic in my own world was not because I couldn't do any, but because I chose not to do it. And the reason I chose not to do it had something to do with the Alphiri wanting me to do it. They already tried to buy me once, from my parents."

"You *could* suddenly do magic, and they sent you to the Wandless Academy . . . ?" Ben said. "After this?"

"I didn't tell anyone . . . not then. I thought that the best place to hide would be in the last place anyone who had any suspicions about me would think of looking, and that was the place where no magic was permitted, by decree."

Terry snorted. "And little did you know that you were at the source," he said. "Because of the Nexus."

"Maybe that's why we broke through at the Academy," Tess said thoughtfully. "None of us knew about the Nexus then. But it might have been what gave us the push into the virtual world."

"I guess that's how Diego de los Reyes fell into it," Thea said, nodding. "Without the pure chance of something like him being in precisely the right place to . . ."

"*Before* we get to Diego de los Reyes," Ben said. "This Alphiri thing."

"What about it?"

"Well, I don't get it," Ben said. "I don't know what the fuss is with this Diego guy, either. I mean, all that they might really have wanted was not so much to buy *you* as buy whatever it is that you could *do*. And as far as Diego is concerned—he isn't even really alive, is he? How can they possibly hurt him?"

"You think we should just let the Alphiri have him?" Tess said.

Ben shrugged. "It might even help matters," he

muttered. "At least he wouldn't be our responsibility anymore. And why do we care what happens to him, anyway? He's just a *ghost*. And one that seems more than capable of taking care of itself."

"I wouldn't wish the Alphiri on anyone, not even somebody like Diego. Especially not someone like Diego," Thea said passionately. "*We* might have choices; what are his?"

Ben gave her a smoldering look. "You might find out if you stop trying to make them for him," he said.

"I guess it would depend on what the Alphiri wanted the magic for," Magpie said, stirring.

"They sent the Nothing," Thea said grimly.

Ben stared at her. "Are we certain about that?" he said at last.

"Yeah, was it actually proved?" Tess said. "I know there was lots of speculation, but I don't know if I ever saw it stated outright anywhere."

"They sent it. Big Elk told me that much."

"Big Elk?"

"That's a story for another time," Thea said. "But the Alphiri want to assimilate the magic, not just use it. This time the trade they have in mind is far more fundamental than their usual bargain—they don't

just want access to a tool, they want to become it—
they want the magic. For themselves. They want to
be magic, not *do* magic. Doing this for them, on
their behalf, it would not be a job—it would be—"
She shuddered once, briefly, calling to mind the avid
gaze of the Alphiri who had been waiting for her in
the woods behind her home last summer, who would
have spirited her away if she had deviated an iota
from the trade agreement that they had already
entered into.

"The people you call the Alphiri are a long-lived
race, and they existed long before your kindred
emerged," Cheveyo said unexpectedly. "Their cul-
ture has endured for a span of time that would seem
fabulous to you. They look upon humans as
mayflies, ephemeral things, here one moment and
gone the next. But humankind has spun a cocoon of
dreams and magic for itself, and even when they
vanish, as all things do in their time, that will remain
behind, a memory of magic. When the Alphiri go . . .
they will leave nothing. It is as if a cold wind will
have swept in the wake of their passing, erasing the
tracks they have left in the sand. They have been
seeking magic for hundreds of years. Thousands.
One thing after another, one failure after another.

They may see a twilight approaching, and that could mean . . . that they are getting a little more desperate to find the spark that will let their memory endure after they are gone. They are running out of time. Your race, my children, is the closest they have come to finding something that they could take into themselves, call their own."

That was the longest speech that Thea had ever heard Cheveyo make. And yet it was not enough, because his final words left behind . . . a question.

"Why?" she asked.

"In too many ways," Cheveyo said, "your kind and theirs are far too alike. It was too long ago to be certain—perhaps Grandmother Spider might know. But it would not surprise me to learn that in the distant past they were gifted with magic, too, and that it is the memory of having once possessed it that drives them—and that they might serve as a warning as to what your people might become if you squander the gifts that you have been given."

"So you didn't say anything to anybody," Ben said, staring at Thea. "Nobody? What if the Alphiri *did* come to the school and try and snatch you away?"

"No portals," Magpie said, "and if any of them had wandered onto campus, just like that, someone would have noticed, stopped them, asked questions . . ."

"So—you hid," Ben said, ignoring the interruption, focused completely on Thea. "Fine—but then, what made you tip your hand? I remember when the Nothing came—people said that magic fed it, not stopped it—and yet there you were, plotting to defeat it with magic . . ."

"But nobody knew that kind of magic existed," Thea said. "And they didn't know *how* to stop it. Maybe that was just the desperation of the Alphiri taking form—but that might have let them succeed, in our world. If we couldn't stop the Nothing, which the Alphiri made from sucking out our magic, who knows what we would have been left with? It was Cheveyo who told me, when I was here, that the one thing I took with me from this place is knowing what battles to fight, being able to choose the place to make a stand—and I did that. And it worked."

"And now the Alphiri knew that you were awake," Magpie said slowly. "The Double Seventh thing, I mean. They were waiting for it, trying to trigger it, so that they could somehow claim it, but you stepped in their way, and now they knew you could do things."

"But you didn't *tell* anyone," Ben objected again. "How come the Alphiri knew and nobody else did?"

"Corey did. And there is still a bit of a mystery as to whether or not I actually had a bunch of gift-bearing Faele at my birth or not—apparently my father forbade it, but my mother kind of winked at it, and if *they* knew, then the celestial sphere would have been ringing with it. The Faele are not what you might consider to be trustworthy with something you might want kept a secret."

"That's not fair, they're tricksters but that kindred has their own sense of honor," Magpie objected. "Look at the Woodlings—they're a Faele kind—and Signe did something that breached that honor sufficiently for her to be exiled for it."

"But Corey meant to get something for the knowledge," Tess said. "The king of tricksters, and honor wasn't any part of that. Do you know what they offered him?"

"We probably never will," Thea said. "Although that cube we brought back when we got Beltran might have something to do with it."

"Cube?" Magpie said blankly, and Ben looked lost again.

Thea sighed. "Later."

"Did the principal know about you?" Ben asked suddenly, clinging to his own agenda with stubborn tenacity. "About what you could do?"

"Um, we had to tell him. I had to tell my parents. After the Nothing, I went home and had to come clean. And then when I showed them the ability to step between worlds . . . through a *computer* . . . that changed everything, again. It was kind of agreed that the Academy was the safest place for me, for the time being," Thea said carefully.

"Right there with the Nexus," Terry said.

"And then the spellspam started," Tess said suddenly. "And they all knew you could do magic stuff with computers. And when the Washington mages came in . . . that's why Luana had a bee in her bonnet that the whole thing was you."

"How did *they* find out?" Ben said. "Did you guys tell your uncle?" That to the twins, whose uncle was, after all, the head of the Federal Bureau of Magic.

"No, my father sent them in," Thea said. "Nobody counted on Luana being such a jerk about it, and then she made it worse. And then the spellspam began to come thick and fast. Humphrey May had the idea that Professor de los Reyes might be the best person to find out more about my gift."

"It was a good idea, at least in theory," Terry said. "He is one of the best mages we've got, and he also happens to know a great deal about computers."

"But *he* never showed any signs of being able to trigger anything magical with a computer," Ben said.

"Well, no—but as it turned out, it was his lapse of judgment with the Nexus that *did* trigger the rest of it."

"*Now* we come to Diego," Thea murmured, staring into the fire.

"I don't really know what happened there," Terry said. "Maybe this is where you get to fill the rest of us in . . . and then I'll tell you guys what I think is going on with the spellspam."

2.

THEA GAVE THEM an abbreviated account of the eventful few days at the Elemental house. She was aware that she was leaving things out—details that might have been important—but somehow she was not quite ready to share the vision of herself and Diego in that mirror, the feeling of the two of them being somehow alike, a spark of recognition, even an astonished sense of the first stirrings of a warmth that shaded from sympathy into friendship. She just gave them the bones of the story, as Larry had given it back at the house—the details of Beltran's birth, of Diego . . . was it Aunt Zoë who had called him a lost soul?

"I'm not sure how Corey found him," Thea finished, "but he must have been looking for an alternative to me—and Diego shines out there like a star. So far as I can tell there *are* only the two of us . . ."

"But it's different," Magpie said. "Diego exists only in that twilight place of green light and shadows. He can't change worlds like you do. Would the Alphiri want that?"

"He could manipulate magic," Thea said, "and *they* can manipulate computers. They didn't have to go searching anymore for arbitrary magic, which may or may not have served their purposes. If they could find someone who could channel it into a computer, then they could use that in any way they wanted to—and it would be cheap for the price."

"But then why didn't they grab Diego a long time ago?"

"They had no clue, just as we didn't," Thea said. "There *was* no Diego—just Beltran . . ."

"Diego was in the perfect position—he had a living twin through whom he could manipulate our world, and he had access to the second Nexus," Terry agreed. "But without that living link—it would be impossible . . ."

"But that isn't right," Ben said. "The spellspams came from all over the place, after they first began; there had to be other people doing this, too, and not through a Nexus supercomputer . . ."

"Copying, and sending on, much as the Alphiri

might have wanted," Terry said. "All the original stuff came from one source—Diego. And the early ones were really weak. The first person who saw one got the full brunt of the spell, and then it was spent. It was like lighting a firecracker. Almost exactly like it, in fact—I kept on stumbling across the empty shells of them, after, when I was doing clean-up."

"How did you know they weren't just your garden-variety spam?" asked Magpie, diverted. "I mean, there's thousands and thousands of those, so in the aftermath, weren't they just the same thing?"

"Spent fireworks smell," Terry said with a quick grin. "It wasn't hard to tell. But he got better, and quickly—they got more and more sophisticated."

"But they were all practical jokes, to one degree or another," Thea said. Diego's voice came back to haunt her—*I was only having fun*. He was completely alone, adrift in an empty universe, and depended on Beltran even for the outlet for his frustrated and pent-up intelligence. No wonder, when Corey found him, that he lapped up the attention . . .

She became aware that Terry was speaking, and shook herself out of her reverie.

". . . that's what I meant."

"Sorry," Thea said. "Run that by me again?"

Terry shrugged. "When you went to look for Diego and then the Alphiri showed up—he's lost his connection, with Beltran being out of the picture, but there's been more spellspam coming in, even *after* his connection to the computer was apparently shut off. He must have stockpiled them in the memory, and set a trigger, so if he got cut off, things would go on without him, at least for a while. That, and I have my suspicions . . ."

"About what?" Thea asked.

"It's just . . . he might have left a trail for himself, somehow, a back door," Terry said. "And also . . . things might be getting worse, in a hurry. He has no reason to play anymore—he knows he can do this, and get things done by doing it. What if he starts sending out stuff that isn't just practical jokes anymore?"

"The last one Mom told me about," Tess said. "It had something to do with shapeshifting, or something like that. Apparently those who got nabbed by it tended to . . . well . . . you know, change into the most inconvenient possible thing at the worst possible moment, like turning into a goat or a mushroom just as you're about to go on a date, or have to go and take some important exam . . ."

"That's still a practical joke, "Thea said. "It doesn't do lasting damage."

"You're still defending him," Ben said.

Magpie gave him a strange look. "You make it sound as though she's on his side," she said.

"Well, she sounds like it," Ben said. "His, against . . . against us."

"You sound as though you're *jealous* of him," Magpie said.

"But the spellspams *are* getting pretty nasty, and who knows how long one *stays* in the shape of that goat or that mushroom—or what it will do to you," Terry said. "And besides, that's just one of maybe half a dozen that came up in the last twenty-four hours. It's out of hand. I'm not sure, right now, what I fear more—that he's set himself up so that he can go back into the computer and take control of this thing, or that he has permanently shut himself out of it and *we* have to clean up a mess we barely understand."

"Where is this person you speak of, right now?" Cheveyo said quietly.

They had almost forgotten he was there.

"That's just it," Thea said. "We don't know."

"You left him in his place, though, didn't you? . . .

Him and the Alphiri?" Ben said. There was an odd sharpness in his tone as he spoke, as though he resented having to mention Diego at all.

"I came straight back," Thea said. "With Corey."

"*You* left him alone with the Alphiri," Ben said.

Thea's heart did a funny little lurch at that. "Yes," she said in a thin voice. "I did. I had to get back to the house, before Corey got loose again."

"He might have chosen to go with them, then?" Cheveyo asked.

"That's what the professor and Uncle Kevin have gone to find out," Tess said.

"A bargain is a bargain," Cheveyo said. "If the Alphiri can show that they have made one, it might be hard to undo it. And if you don't, you stand in grave danger from what the Alphiri will be able to do next."

"You think there might still be a chance to turn it?" Thea said.

Cheveyo considered this for a moment. "It all depends on the timing, and you don't know how long ago *any* of this really was, Catori, because you've been on the Road a lot in the past couple of days, and time . . . time tends to run differently there. If you can find this other mage you speak of, this boy you call Diego, and talk to him before the Alphiri have a chance to make their case, it might still be possible to change the course of events."

"But how on earth are you going to find him?" Magpie said, turning to Thea. "You basically vanished from his sight, taking someone he *did* trust at some point—are you going to be able to wander back in there at will? And you're going to have to do it at precisely the moment you left, if it's going to do any good. You *have* to be there before the Alphiri have a chance to seal any bargains."

"I know how to get his attention," Terry said.

"We're listening," Tess said.

"He made it his thing to send out this spam," Terry said. "What if *we* send one?"

"Tell me you're joking," Tess said, flushing a hectic red. "Mom and Uncle Kevin will flay you. Besides, you said you didn't know how exactly he did . . ."

"I didn't, in the beginning—but now I have a pretty good idea—and there's at least one Nexus computer where I don't need Professor de los Reyes's permission to access what I need. I can do the basic logistics, don't worry—but it would need you, Thea, to set it. You are the only one who has met him. *You* know what will bring him out."

And betray him, all over again . . .

"You asked for advice," said Cheveyo suddenly, getting to his feet. He made a single imperious gesture when they all began to scramble to follow him and everyone subsided back onto their skins. "It would seem to me that your quarry is a spirit who is searching for a place to stand on true ground, and I think that it would be well for you to choose that ground. He might not have realized until now just how important this thing that he does really is. He may have started doing it simply because it made him feel more real. The Alphiri have negotiated harder bargains than this. They have had thousands of years of practice. If you can get back this lost child of your race, you should do it—and if you cannot . . ." He looked at each of them in turn, a piercing glance from those luminous dark eyes. "If you cannot, then it may be your task to make sure the Alphiri do not own him," he said, and his voice was low and level. "And you will have to do whatever achieving that task may ask you to do."

He bowed his head lightly in farewell, and took one sweeping step away . . . perhaps behind a boulder, perhaps into thin air. He was gone.

"What does that *mean*?" Ben said.

Thea realized to her horror that she was about to cry. "He means we may need to destroy Diego," she whispered. "That . . . *I* . . . may have to . . ."

Magpie reached over and took her hand, squeezing her fingers. She said nothing. Ben kept his own eyes down, staring at the laced fingers of his hands.

"You heard him," Terry said, after a pause. "What we need to do, we need to do *now*. And you need to come up with a good lure."

"Even if he's gone with the Alphiri?"

"Especially then," Tess said gently.

"Will they let you back into the school?" Ben asked out of nowhere, suddenly lifting his eyes and skewering Thea with a challenging look.

"What?" she said, blindsided by the question.

"Well, more and more people actually *know* about you now," Ben said. "And that school was built upon the no-magic rule. What if they don't take you back next semester?"

"Not *now*, Ben," Magpie murmured. "Thea . . . they're right. We need to figure out what to do—if it's nothing, then it's nothing. But if you hang back . . . then the Whale Hunt might be worthless, and Twitterpat and all those others died for no reason at all, and we've lost a war we didn't even know we were fighting."

"*I know what you did last summer*," Thea whispered.

"What?" Terry said, staring.

"That," Thea said. "Send that. Make it look like a spellspam, fudge the addresses and all that . . . but make sure it's really aimed at him alone, at Diego. We all know how to target a spell."

"In theory," Tess said.

"Can you do that?" Magpie asked, turning to Terry.

"It will bring him?" he asked, speaking directly to Thea across the flames.

"It will," she said.

"Then I can do it," he said, hoisting himself to his feet. "Let's go."

To: unseen@hidden.com
From: Reddy O'Nott < hidden@unseen.com >
Subject: invisible

Nobody will ever see you again . . .

1.

IT DID NOT take Diego de los Reyes long to respond to the spellspam message. Terry's suspicions that Diego had somehow left himself with a back door onto the Terranet through the Nexus gateways seemed to be well-founded—even with the Nexus in Professor de los Reyes's study offline, a "you've got mail" ping on her laptop got Thea's attention less than an hour after she and the twins returned to Terry's room, after restoring Ben and Magpie to the places from which they had been plucked for the visit to Cheveyo.

"It's him," she said in a low voice.

"That isn't possible, not that fast, not without a connection," Terry muttered. "Gimme that computer."

Thea passed the laptop over without a word. Terry scanned the screen, first with the aid of Grandmother Spider's dreamcatcher and then without; he frowned, pressed a few keys, things shifted

398

quickly from one piece of software to another. "Where is it?" Terry asked finally, more fascinated than frustrated. "I can't find it. It isn't in your inbox, and I can't even get at the server to see what's on that, *we aren't online*—where is it?"

Thea retrieved the laptop, poked at a few keys herself. The screen blinked, and went an odd shade of gray-green, with two lines of bold black letters in the middle of it.

"Right there," she said.

"What?" Terry said, sounding mystified, turning the computer to face him again and staring at it in blank incomprehension. "Where?"

Thea sat back on her heels, staring at Terry over the top of the screen. "You can't even see it, can you?" she said. "It's for me. *Just* for me. To everyone else, it's not even there . . ."

Terry and Thea stared at each other, holding the computer sitting balanced between them with one hand each. "Well . . . ?" Tess asked. "What does it *say*?"

Thea turned the computer toward herself again and read the message out loud that only she could see. *"It isn't what I have done. It is what I will still do."*

"It sounds as though he's planning to go with

the Alphiri," Tess said.

"It sounds as though he's already gone with the Alphiri," Terry said grimly. "Are we too late, Thea?"

"Maybe not," Thea said. "Terry, can you trace where this thing is . . . You can't even see it. How are you to trace it? But that's where he is, where he sent this thing to me from. I need to—*yikes!*"

She reached out as she spoke to touch the screen of the laptop with an outstretched finger, and the yelp came when her finger simply sank into the screen rather than coming into physical contact with its solid surface. She snatched her hand back.

"What was *that*?" Terry said, staring.

But Thea was far away, remembering, standing once again with Grandmother Spider before a portal she had raised with her own hands, woven from starlight and memory and a haunting piece of music. The portal had shown her a way to go home, which she had used to spring a trap, pushing Corey the Trickster into the arms of the Alphiri, who had been lying in wait for her.

But Diego de los Reyes didn't know about that portal.

Corey did, of course. Corey was the only one who could have told Diego about it; if Diego was anything like Thea herself, the rest would have come naturally, like water gushing when an obstacle to its passage was suddenly removed.

But if this had the stamp of Corey's involvement, was it to be trusted?

What choice do I have?

Thea stirred. "It's a way in. A way straight to him. That's what we wanted, wasn't it?"

Terry and Tess exchanged frightened looks. Thea knew she sounded distant, detached, almost completely dispassionate—this was the goal they had been working toward, after all, and here was a means to achieve it. And all of a sudden there was no way forward except through that screen—and she recognized the color now; she had seen it before. It was a slightly corrupted shade of the green with which Diego veiled his abode.

Thea drew the laptop back toward herself, and for a moment Terry tightened his grip on it, but then he released it with an explosive little sigh. Thea laid it on the ground before her, very carefully, and then laid both hands lightly on the sides of the screen.

"I can see it reflected on your face," Tess said suddenly. "There's a light . . ."

"But there was nothing on *screen*," said Terry

obstinately. "Nothing that I could point to—"

"It's okay," Thea said. "It's what we wanted, it's a path, and I'm taking it."

"Thea, no—"

"We need to—"

The twins both spoke at once, both reaching for the computer, but Thea had already slipped her hands down and onto the screen—*into* the screen.

"Tell them I'll try," she said, and let the portal pull her through, arms sinking in to the elbows, then the shoulders, and then she shut her eyes as the light dimmed and greened around her. A single word echoed behind her, following her—*Wait . . .*

But then it was gone. And she stood back in the obsidian and green space where she had been before, Diego's place, stark in its painful simplicity. It was something he seemed to cling to, reluctant to exchange it for anything more complex, anything that he could not control, that wasn't familiar. For some reason that gave Thea an odd pang of something almost like hope—could a creature like Diego be useful to the Alphiri in the way that they wanted—without leaving this cocoon? And what if he wouldn't do it? *What if he couldn't do it?*

"Where are you?" she said, standing very still in

the midst of the obsidian floor. She had to force her-self to speak in a natural voice, not to whisper.

"Right here, of course. Where you expected me to be," said Diego's voice.

Thea had recognized this place instantly as she had stepped through into it, but there had also been something subtly different about it. She could not have said precisely what had triggered that instinct, but now it was Diego's voice that brought it into focus—as Diego himself stepped out of the shadows, matching action to words. He appeared to do so in a dozen fractured frames at once, as though coming at Thea from every angle and every direction.

Mirrors. The place was full of mirrors. Mirrors opposite one another, mirrors at an angle, like a car-nival funhouse, and a black-breeched, white-shirted, dark-eyed Diego in all of them at once, smiling.

"What are you hiding from?" Thea said, looking into one mirror after another, trying to figure out where the original was standing and which of the myriad of Diegos were just shadow and reflection.

"Hiding? I don't need to hide," Diego said. "Your message was irrelevant—everybody already knows what I have done this summer. And they're the ones who are afraid, not me."

"If you weren't, you would not need the mirrors," Thea said. "Or do you just like what you see so much that you can't get enough of yourself?"

It was a deliberate barb, and it worked, after a fashion. Diego snorted in disdain and somehow stepped out of his mirror maze, standing so that only two mirrors now reflected him, one from behind, one in profile. But he, himself, now stood solid, real enough for the ghost that he was, staring at Thea in challenge.

"I could have had company," Diego said. "In fact, I did, such as it was."

"You count Corey as company?"

"Well, he was here, wasn't he?" Diego said. "And he's far more entertaining that you appear to give him credit for."

"It isn't his entertainment value that I was questioning," Thea said.

"Yeah, well. Trust is relative. But that wasn't what I was talking about—I had the whole world to play with, didn't I? Until you interfered, that is. But—always excepting my tutor—that world stayed out *there*. For the most part . . . there's nobody here, in this place, *to* look at except me. Shadows are empty things, and silent. A guy could get awfully tired just being by himself."

"But you found out that you could communicate," Thea said. "And once you discovered that . . . why not something other than your games? Once you got into the computer, found your voice, learned how to make yourself heard through the wires—why didn't you make yourself known to them? You made the whole world dance to your tune, and you couldn't reach out to your own family?"

Diego's hands clenched suddenly. "They never wanted me. My father never cared," he lashed out. And then, turning a darkly malicious gaze on Thea, added silkily, "I didn't have the benefit of your family background. I was not an eagerly expected prodigy to be groomed for greatness. I never existed, remember?"

Thea suddenly remembered her own brothers—the complicated mess of *family*, from Anthony's superior putdowns to Frankie's disastrous attempts to measure up to the family standards—the bickering and the scuffles and the teasing, but also the way she knew that she could have counted on any of them to help if she ever needed them. She might sometimes chafe at the rough edges of her own little spot in the universe, but she had one, connected to those she loved and who loved her with a thousand delicate strands. Woven—she was woven into her world, into all of her worlds, a part of its fabric.

Diego saw her smile, and misinterpreted it.

"I thought that we were alike, when I first crossed your path," he said tightly, through clenched teeth. "But they've got you bound up tight; you're daddy's girl after all, trying to do well, taking it back home for the *family* to take pride in, to give you a reward when you've learned to perform some trick like a well-trained performing seal . . ."

"And all you see is the reward?" Thea said, her voice sharp. It had been a while, but she had not forgotten, could not forget, the barren years, the carefully hidden despair that once coiled at the heart of her family like a serpent. "You think being alone is a heavy burden? There were times I would have rather been an orphan than bring home yet another failure to lay at my father's feet. You have *never* felt the weight of disappointed love or of failing to live up to expectations. The only thing you've ever been is lonely by yourself—you have no idea how desperate it is to be lonely in the midst of people who love you, and whom you would have done *anything* to make happy . . ."

"I have always been free," said Diego softly.

The mirror behind him suddenly changed, and instead of reflecting a human shape, it was showing blue sky flecked with white clouds, and an eagle that wheeled with its magnificent wings outspread, screaming its defiance.

Thea responded with pure instinct. She reached out and did something . . . and the second mirror swiftly changed to respond—and the image was the same eagle, wings furled, head bent and covered with a leather hood that rendered it blind and docile, jesses attached to its legs, sitting on the gloved forearm while another hand, ungloved, stroked the back of the bird's furled wings with a possessive gesture of long, pale Alphiri fingers.

Diego's own mirror blinked into dimness; the bird in the Alphiri hand suddenly roused.

"You don't know what they offered me!" he cried out, as the hooded bird on the Alphiri's hand opened its beak and screamed.

The other hand in the image had disappeared as the bird stirred; now Thea brought it back into the picture, holding a piece of bloody meat, which it held out to the hooded eagle, just out of reach.

"That," Thea said. "Only that. Bait, lures. *They*

remain the hunters, the ones who are in control. And your prey would be us."

Other mirrors woke into light, a confusion of images—eagles, a glimpse of crystal spires, echoes of the laughter of human children as though the mirrors could transmit sound as well as visual images; Thea suddenly realized why it was nagging at her, why it was so familiar.

She had done this before. Images from her mind, a childhood memory, coming to life in a mirror . . .

"It's like a true dreamcatcher," she whispered, staring at Diego's mirror. "Like one of Grandmother Spider's dreamcatchers. You can turn it in or out, send or see, that's how you got to me even without the computer . . . but if you had this . . . why did you risk Beltran . . . why bother using the Nexus?" And then she put the pieces together, and her blood ran cold at the thought. "The Alphiri," she whispered. "You've already made that bargain, haven't you? *They* gave you this . . . They . . . but they had no true dreamcatchers . . . Grandmother Spider said she never sold them the real secret . . . they . . . *Corey stole it* . . ."

"I don't need you, any of you, not anymore," Diego said, and he had stepped back into the mirror maze, which reflected back a frightening mix of young man and raptor, human limbs and eagle eyes, a bird's foot with razor-sharp talons reaching out to draw a glove off a human hand. "I have all I need now. And all I ever needed was me."

"You're wrong," Thea said, desperate. She had spoken of her own burdens, but now, in the face of the mirrored world, they were the anchors that held her to her own existence, her own sense of reality. They were part of her, part of what made her alive . . . "None of it is real, Diego. None of it can ever be real—you have never known the reality, not directly, you don't have the memories—all of it's been stolen, or made up—none of it is *true* . . ."

But even as she spoke, she realized that something else was happening, that a part of her was still attuned to the dreamcatcher, she had touched one long before Diego had. There suddenly seemed to be more and more mirrors, and it seemed that some of them were from her own mind. Diego seemed to be receding from her, into a welter of color and shape that started to blur, shifting and changing like a kaleidoscope.

Too much, too fast, too powerful—she was being bombarded by a sensory overload, an avalanche of sight and sound and memory. Words wove themselves into her consciousness like she wove light on Cheveyo's mesas—*sometimes there's nobody here to look at except me*—mirrors . . . reflections . . . the catchers of dreams . . .

For a moment Thea was seven years old again, shrieking with delight, seated on a painted carousel pony with a tiny crown between its ears and bright jewel-like crystals set in its bridle. Everything else was a blur, except that too-sharp vision of the bright pony and its sparkling gems—and the flash and shimmer of mirrors on the central column of the merry-go-round as she rode past them, again and again, round and round. She found herself adding mirrors, more each time, reflecting the reflections of reflections, until the world was a vivid jewel of flame.

There's nobody to look at except me.

The mirrors. They gave Diego the illusion of not being alone—always, but only the illusion of it. He had sold his gift and his potential for a lie, a fantasy, a thing of mist and shadows that would have dissolved sooner or later, or possibly as soon as he had performed whatever service the Alphiri had had in mind. Thea focused on the thought that Diego had been lonely enough to accept that as a substitute for real companionship—and seemed to be willing to do that indefinitely. That he had considered this a fair trade.

But a bargain was a bargain—and the Alphiri could hold all of the human polity to ransom . . .

No.

Zoë had said it. Diego belonged to nobody. Nobody could bargain for him except himself. Nobody else could be held responsible for this bargain.

Mirrors.

Mirrors were a way out. They were also a prison. With enough mirrors, there would be only illusion—only and ever illusion—but never a road out to reality. But they had to face *within*. . . .

Thea recoiled even as the thought came to her. She could turn the mirrors. Turn them into a trap. Take the very thing that Diego had sold his soul to get—that illusion of not being alone—and use it to seal him into a living tomb where the illusion would be all he had, all he would ever have. These mirrors were real magic—a true dreamcatcher of the First World, the kind Grandmother Spider used to weave the threads of fortune for all the other worlds that spilled out in the First World's shadow. As long as Diego believed in what he wanted to see, he would continue to see it, vividly, brightly, unfaded as the days slipped by—but what he saw would still be just illusion. And in time . . . in the merciless passing of years and decades and maybe centuries . . . the mind would tire, and the focus would weaken, and the world of illusion would grow dark. Sealed within would be that thing that Aunt Zoë had called a lost soul, forever sundered from any true companionship with his own kind.

He had been given an illusion, and he seemed perfectly happy with it—but the more he had of it, the less human he would actually be.

The road had come to a fork, and Thea was the only one standing there. The responsibility was hers, and if she chose the wrong road, or even just the easy road, what lay at the end of it might be no less than extinction for her kind.

But she could stop Diego. She had to stop him. There was nobody else.

It was too great a burden.

The carousel continued on its endless journey, round and round and round, the carnival music still driving the painted pony onward, but Thea was no longer the innocent child that she had once been. It was herself—not the enchantress Diego had shown her the first time she had come here, but the reality of what she actually was, a long-legged, fair-haired girl with sad eyes who was going to imprison the bright and dangerous spirit that was Diego de los Reyes forever.

She watched the central column of the merry-go-round begin to turn dim as she began turning inward the bright mirrors with which it had been tiled, facing inside, facing that place where Diego was—giving him what he needed, a reflection of what he thought of as true. And then the column began to change shape, its smooth cylinder bulging out, swelling into an ovoid, then a sphere—a dull-surfaced sphere pocked with scars and scuffs and scratches, with a single beam of coruscating, multi-colored light like a shaft coming out from the top, dancing out into the void, the only light in the world.

The sparkling lights of the carousel winked out one by one as the music began to fade; only a memory of the shape of the painted pony remained underneath Thea as she clung to the pole that had once anchored it. She found herself crying, softly, quietly, as the last of the mirrors came flying through the shadows—a butterfly, shiny-winged, veined with dreamcatcher strands and tendrils, floating gently near the shaft of light that rose from the sphere that now contained Diego's spirit . . . then beside it . . . then pushing a wing into it like a blade, the light going into eclipse, darkening by slivers and notches as the wind crept across ever so slowly until it was finally hovering right on top as though the light was what was holding it up. Then it settled, gently, folding its wings down over the light. For a moment a ray or two of it still escaped—gold or amethyst or neon blue—and then, soundlessly, the wings came down. The light went out. The sounds faded away.

There was nothing except darkness. Thea found herself drifting, beginning to forget, the shape of the pony under her hands losing any meaning at all, just a piece of darkness more solid than the rest.

Quiet . . . empty . . . alone . . . alone . . .

She never knew just what it was that brought her back. She remembered falling, and then being hurled back through the improbable portal of the laptop screen as though rejected by that other world—and at the time she even knew why. The guilt she carried within her would not be silenced; she had to return to face her choices in this world, the real world—the world for which she had traded Diego de los Reyes, and all that he might have been. The pain was real, and violent, and she found herself on the floor of Terry's room in the Elemental house, curled up into a ball. She had the dim impression of Tess crouching beside her with a frightened expression on her face, but beyond that there was nothing except the formlessness and the dark, and the sense of being left adrift and alone. For all she knew, she might have simply passed out, and the whole thing might have been no more than a dream . . . except for a tiny charm of a painted carousel horse tightly clutched in her hand.

Humphrey May had to run a restorative spell on Thea twice before he pronounced himself satisfied that she should be left to rest; it was only after the second time that Thea could gather enough strength and concentration to rasp out a question.

"Professor . . . Diego . . . Alphiri . . . are they back . . . ?"

"They're back. We'll talk after you've had a

couple of hours' sleep. Trust me."

Thea did trust him. She thought she saw her aunt's worried face hovering on the edges of her field of vision, but she was too tired to do more than smile wanly and then close her eyes.

2.

SHE WOKE SEVENTEEN hours later.

The house was almost back to normal. Most of the Bureau personnel had left; Beltran, apparently rendered almost comatose by the loss of what had been his other half, had been taken to a hospital for observation, and the paramedics had been dispatched back to base, together with the security person and his imps. Nancy Dane had left with Tess—the summer internship that had brought Terry to this house was, by mutual consent, postponed to a more auspicious time, but he had asked to stick around at the house until Thea herself was ready to leave. The only people left were Isabella, who was not much in evidence, Larry, Zoë, the professor, Terry, Thea herself, and Humphrey May.

Humphrey took Thea out into the garden in the late afternoon on the following day. As the sun's low golden rays dipped down toward the western horizon, he asked her to cast her mind back and tell him what had happened between her and Diego de los Reyes.

"I honestly don't know," Thea had said. "All I can give you is the visions."

"That might help," Humphrey said.

"He was . . . a little like me," Thea said, looking away. "But he never had the sheltering harbor that I had, not ever. He spent his entire existence by himself. And when he realized that he could reach out . . ."

"He was a child, in so many ways," Humphrey said. "He was just learning to play. If we'd gotten to him sooner, maybe we'd have had a chance—but the Alphiri got there first, and when we did get there, it was too little, too late."

"What happened? What did they say? Did they talk to the professor?"

"Professor de los Reyes and Kevin MacAllister spent a *very* long time cooling their heels in the antechambers of the Alphiri Queen's throne room," Humphrey said, "and then they were told, without ever being admitted, that the situation they had come to discuss was no longer valid and to return when they were prepared to present a case that better matched the current state of affairs. They came back frustrated and furious, I can tell you—in fact, Kevin went straight to the capital to talk to the president. And then Terry was screaming up here that you were in trouble and we found you, practically a shell of yourself, and by the look in your eyes, whatever you've brought back with you is still haunting you. Did you dream, while you slept?"

"No," Thea said. "Not that I remember."

"That's good, I tried to specify a dreamless sleep when I gave you that restorative spell," Humphrey said. "But you still might dream. Traumas come back to stalk us, and whatever happened to you, it was traumatic. Meanwhile, it seems we haven't found the right coach for you yet. But for now, is there anything at all you can tell me?"

"I don't even know where to begin," Thea said helplessly. "Diego had somehow found a way to reach out to the 'net *without* the benefit of a computer, Nexus or no, and he could access that cyberworld that he and I could somehow weave and manipulate in a way that transcended having the basic tools that *I* need for the job."

"That much we gathered," Humphrey said.

"There was more spellspam, after the 'net access was cut off, when Beltran was taken away . . ."

Thea was shaking her head. "No, Terry explained that—some of those were queued messages he had left in the computer, and without him to send them out one by one, a whole heap tumbled out at once—that was different—but the way I got into his world this time . . ." She paused, remembering the frustration on Terry's face as they tussled over the laptop, the message that he couldn't see. "Back when I first visited the Anasazi time," Thea said, "I made . . . a portal, I guess. A gate between one world and another. *He* did the same thing, upstairs, yesterday. Diego. He made the computer into a portal. I stepped through my own laptop's screen to get to him."

"Oh, my," Humphrey said softly.

"And when I got there, there were the mirrors. Hundreds of mirrors. And they were the kind that showed . . . what you wanted to see, what you put into them. And he had an eagle in his, flying free, and then I tied the eagle down in hood and jesses and made it sit on an Alphiri hand, and he told me I would never understand him." She was crying now, openly, and Humphrey fished in his pocket and came up with a fine linen handkerchief. "The thing is, I do understand him. I know how lonely I could be, sometimes, and I have people surrounding me all the time, whenever I want someone, I can touch them, even my wretched brothers . . ."

Humphrey laughed, and Thea managed a small watery smile. She wiped at her eyes ineffectually with the back of her hand.

"I could have liked having him around, as a friend, if things had been different," she said.

"I can understand that," Humphrey said.

Thea shook her head violently. "No, you don't! I *liked* him . . . despite everything . . . I would have been a friend . . . but I betrayed him, *I* locked him into those mirrors . . . I made a sphere, and the last thing I can really remember is closing it. He's inside it now, the sphere of mirrors, and everything he thinks and does is reflected back at him. He may not even realize yet that he is trapped in there, but he will, sooner or later, he will—and he is a bright and vivid spirit, and it *will* drive him mad eventually. And I did that. *I* did it to him."

"Thea," said Humphrey with a strange little smile, "do you know what the last recorded spellspam was?"

"What?" she asked, looking up.

"The subject line was *invisible*," Humphrey said. "The message was, *Nobody will ever see you again*."

Thea let out a small whimper. "*I* did that," she said. "I made him invisible. Nobody will ever see him again. I don't even know if I would have the first clue, myself, how to ever even find him again—let alone how to free him . . ."

"That might be just as well," Humphrey said, "if you're right about what will eventually happen inside that sphere you locked him into. Even arguably sane, Diego de los Reyes was something to be reckoned with. If ever he lost his reason, it's just as well that he is locked away from us permanently. You did well, under difficult circumstances."

"I killed him," Thea said bleakly.

"He was never *alive,* Thea. Not in the sense that a life can be taken away. He existed, certainly—but by our definitions of life, he was no more than a spirit, a ghost, a speaker from the shadows."

"But *real*," Thea said. "For all that."

"Yes," Humphrey said, and there was a world of compassion and understanding in his voice. "Real enough . . . to the few who could reach out and touch him. Like you. But all you did was close the mirror wall—he himself built that. Right now his existence is still undimmed—he exists in that sphere just as he has always done, he's alive in there, alive and surrounded with his illusions . . ."

"And he might as well be dead," Thea said. "I feel . . . like I need to wash myself clean of it. Every time I look down at my hands, the shadows still cling to them."

"That's twice you've taken those shadows on," Humphrey said. "You're making me look bad. It's people like me who should be stepping up to save the world, not kids still in high school . . . and now that I think of it . . . if you need a job after you graduate, come knock on my door. There's always a berth at the FBM for you."

Thea shot him a black look. "And work with Luana Lilley?"

Humphrey threw his head back and actually laughed. "We could make sure that wherever she's stationed, you were posted to the opposite corner of the country," he said. "But I'm afraid you'd have to get in line, as it were. For a talented mage, that girl sure has a knack for annoying people."

"Have they figured out that stuff we brought back yet? The tapes? That cube?"

"The tapes are awfully corrupted; they're trying to

restore them manually—you don't have to worry about running across Luana for a while, she's in charge of that project and she's got her hands full with it. The cube . . . the cube is my problem, and I have a few ideas on that score, but it's premature to talk about that." He got to his feet. "The sun's set, the house should have dinner ready, and you and your aunt are going home tomorrow. You need a rest, and the professor needs to figure out how he is going to reconfigure the Nexus so that this sort of thing doesn't ever happen again."

"What happened to having the professor figure *me* out?" Thea said.

"I think you figured *him* out," Humphrey said, grinning. "I know you feel very much alone. I realize that Diego's very existence was kind of electrifying. None of us thought the cybermagic you do could ever happen again—that you were a fluke. But we did find out otherwise. I talked to the professor about all of this, after he returned from the Alphiri court, and he thinks . . . and I agree . . ." Humphrey took a deep breath. "Thea, it was Diego who was the fluke. He was the wild card, the thing we never looked for, never expected. You . . ."

"Nobody expected me, either," Thea said.

"But we should have," Humphrey said. "That is the way things have always worked. Magic grows, finds new channels, blossoms in new and unexpected places. We should have realized that the neutrality to magic that we so relied on in computers was only a temporary thing. It was just . . . too new. We hadn't become used to it yet. But I think we are beginning to do that—and you are the living proof of it. For what it's worth, Thea, it's looking very much like you aren't the *only* one with the cybermagic gift. Just the first."

Thea stared at him. "You mean, you think there will be others?"

"Perhaps there already are, in their own way—your friends from the Academy have, at the very least, been able to follow the paths that you have blazed, if not make their own. I think we are going to grow into cybermagic, make it as much our own as we once did with spells and cantrips and magic potions."

"So if we had left Diego alone . . . if the Alphiri *did* take all our magic away . . . it would only have been the magic we have right now," Thea said. "We would have found another place to go, another thing to be . . ."

Humphrey was shaking his head. "Our primary

gift of enchantment is that ability to make new things out of old, to reshape, to transfigure, to hope, to dream, to learn. If the Alphiri had taken our gift, that would have gone, too. And without that we would never have survived."

"That still leaves me . . . alone," Thea said.

"Oh, no. never that. You will never be alone," Humphrey said. "We are all with you. Every step of the way."

Thea knew he was right. She was surrounded by family and friends; all she had to do was reach out and touch them, in this world or in some other that she could weave for herself to be happy in. But that still left a small dark place inside of her. She had had no real idea about how much the very idea of the existence of Diego de los Reyes had mattered to her until it was far too late.

THE HOSPITAL COULD find nothing physically wrong with Beltran, and sent him home after twenty-four hours.

"I should go and see him," Thea said to Terry as the two of them sat out on the patio the day after Beltran had come home. "I feel . . . responsible."

"You hardly know the guy," Terry objected.

"Not true," Thea said. "I met . . . the other half of him. I know that much of him. And I can't help thinking . . . wondering . . . how much of Beltran was in Diego?"

"You mean how much of Diego was in Beltran," Terry said. "Sometimes . . . you sound as though Diego was the one that was real and Beltran was the one that was the shadow."

"Maybe you're right," Thea said.

Terry gave her a strange look. "You can be very weird."

Thea slipped off her chair. "I think I'll stop in and at least say hello," she said.

"You mean good-bye," Terry said. "We're more or less on our way out of here. Assuming they are letting him have visitors, anyway."

"You coming?" Thea said, pausing at the French doors.

Terry sighed, slipping off his own chair. "I suppose you're right," he said. "He sure did get a raw deal."

The door to Beltran's room was ajar, and Terry and Thea slowed down in the corridor as they heard voices coming from within. A woman's voice. There was something about it that was familiar, something else about it that made that familiarity seem . . . strange.

A softness. A gentleness. Almost the kind of tone that a mother would use to a sick child.

"Madeline . . . ?" Terry hissed to Thea as they hesitated outside the door.

"Isabella," Thea whispered back, even as the voice inside the room fell silent.

Terry knocked softly.

"Who's there?" The imperious voice belonged to Isabella de los Reyes.

Thea stook a step into the room, poking her head past the door.

"It's Terry and me," she said. "We just thought . . . we'd come by and see how Beltran is doing."

Terry followed Thea into the room and now they both took in the sight of Isabella, her hair pulled back into a simple ponytail and wearing a faded T-shirt and ratty jeans, sitting cross-legged on the bed where her brother sat propped up with several plump cushions. There was a book in her lap. Apparently she had been reading to him.

Isabella's usually alabaster skin was suffused with an unaccustomed blush, as though she had been caught doing something illegal.

"Beltran is fine," Isabella said, with a hint of frost. "He needs rest . . ."

"It's all right," Beltran said suddenly, his voice oddly husky. "I *want* to talk to her."

Isabella glanced down at him, and then she uncoiled from the bed, laid the book down on the bedside cabinet, and skewered the visitors with a diamond-hard, haughty stare.

"Do not," she said, "tire him out."

She walked out without giving them another look, her cheeks still flushed. She had looked embarrassed. Caught out in a weak moment, showing tenderness.

When Thea turned back toward the convalescent's bed, Beltran was looking at her, a very faint smile curling his lip as though he knew what she was thinking. It was almost a Diego face: knowing, sardonic. But at the same time, it was not. There was a pain there, a sense of deep loss, of emptiness.

Thea stared back at him in mute silence, trying to find the words with which to address Beltran, dismissing those that she would have used to Diego, suddenly aware there were tears in her eyes.

"I know," Beltran said suddenly, breaking the silence between them. "I *know* what you're thinking. And it isn't true."

"But he is gone," Thea said helplessly.

"Yes," Beltran said, dropping his eyes. "He is gone. I remain. Half of me remains, maybe."

"Don't say that," Thea said, her heart giving a queer lurch.

He shrugged. "What's left?" he said. "I was apparently just the puppet for a shadow show. Isabella told me some of what happened—how stupid is that, being told what happened by someone

else, when you've been part of it all along? I was the
one with access to a computer, I was the one with the
hands to type what Diego wanted . . . but I typed
what Diego wanted, and I have no memory of doing
any of it."

"God," Terry said, his professional curiosity
aroused now. "How do you mean? How *did* he . . .
you . . . get past the failsafes and the security firewalls? I've seen the safeguards and filters the professor has in place, and yet you and Diego just slipped
under it all like a shadow. You said *you* were the one
who typed it in, who dealt with the Nexus—can you
remember any of that? Anything of what you did?"

"So you can stop me from doing it again?" Beltran
said with a wan smile.

"That's not what I . . ." Terry said, abashed.

"But that's what I'm saying. I don't remember, any
of it. None of it is me. I don't really know Diego—I
don't remember being him—but from what everybody tells me, he was special, and intelligent, and
unique . . . maybe even an Elemental . . . and now all
that's left is me. And I'm empty."

An echo of a thought came back to haunt Thea.
She had been thinking of Diego when she had
thought, *We are alike.* But she recognized what

Beltran was saying, too. This twin, too, was like her. Like she had once been, before the unexpected gift had made itself known. Beltran, like Thea, was part of special circumstances—and Beltran, like Thea, found himself locked into a pattern of being the One Who Couldn't.

Impulsively, she crossed over to the bed and hugged Beltran, who pulled back a little.

"It wasn't your gift," she said, letting go and sitting at the edge of his bed. "It wasn't *your* world. It was his world, his place in the world, and you were forced to live it. But now he's not here anymore, and the only world that's left is yours, and it's going to be what *you* make of it."

"And what if it's nothing?" Beltran said

"You know how you throw a stone into a pool, and it makes circles in the water . . ." Thea said, half-smiling, remembering her own conversation with Grandmother Spider.

Beltran gave her a strange look. "What has throwing rocks into pools got to do with it?"

"If you think of it like . . ." Thea began, but someone cleared their throat at the door of the room and she stopped, turning. Isabella stood there imperiously, arms crossed, one eyebrow lifted.

"I thought I told you not to tire him out," she said.

"We're just talking," Thea said, glancing back at Beltran, and then realized that Isabella was right, that Beltran's eyelids were drooping and that he had let his head sink back against the cushions. She slipped off the edge of the bed. "Okay. We'll let you rest. Can I . . . is it okay if I write to you?"

"I'd like that," Beltran said, very softly, and let his eyes close.

Thea and Terry sidled past Isabella as though guilty of a transgression, refraining from speaking until they reached the grand staircase.

Thea caught sight of Terry's expression and finally couldn't hold it back any longer.

"Who knew she had it in her?" she murmured, just loud enough for Terry to hear. "Who knew Isabella de los Reyes had a heart after all . . . ?"

The summer internship had ended early, and Thea had gone home. It had been a relief to have a home-coming, this time, where she could spill everything for her parents and not hold back and try to work things out on her own, as when she had returned from Cheveyo's last summer.

"But, Thea," her father said to her, "let's get one thing straight. You really can't go running off on adventures on your own—please, you *have* to understand that. After you graduate high school, we will see what we can do next. Maybe even Amford."

"Anthony will have a fit," Thea said, unable to suppress a small gloat. Anthony, the eldest, had been the star of the family for too long not to put up some sort of fight if it looked like Thea might be on the way to upstaging him. Rubbing his nose in it, just a little, was something that Thea was rather looking forward to.

"*Thea*," Ysabeau said reproachfully, but not without an answering grin.

"Look at it this way," said Zoë. "Maybe he can finally score a date with Isabella. He can always say he's *your* brother . . ."

And then the rest of the summer slipped by without anybody really paying attention, and September came in with its first sprinkling of gold in the crowns of the trees, shorter days, and cooler nights.

Thea's bags were already packed, ready for an early-morning departure for school on the following day. Another season, another year spinning into its close. Another year coming up full of Mr. Siffer's moody mathematics and Signe's trips into field and forest and Magpie's wounded creatures squawking or whimpering or chirping in a box in her closet.

The first traces of a chill that spoke of fall were in the air in a park near her home as Thea leaned on the parapet of an arched stone bridge spanning a ravine and facing a rushing waterfall. It had rained in the past few days, and the falls tumbled into a chaos of foam and sparkling water, spilling into the brittle autumn sunshine—not yet the torrent they would become in the aftermath of the harder rains of late autumn, nor the wild white water that tumbled over the rocks in the wake of spring snowmelt, but a bigger presence, nonetheless, than the barely-there veil of water which was the falls' normal state in the hotter, drier summer months. The scent of fall tangled into the rush and roar of the water; the trees sighed and whispered in the silence as the first touch of fall color began to touch the maples and the alders. Thea liked to come to the falls just after it had rained, when the creek was cold and the trails muddy and empty of crowds. This was a place where she could think, where she felt close to the pure magic of water and stone and tree and sky.

A late-season jogger came trotting past on the

bridge and paused as she came abreast of Thea.

"Excuse me, would you know the time?" the jogger asked politely.

"September," Thea said with a little smile, in the finest Aunt Zoë tradition.

The jogger gave her a cross sideways look and turned away, the expression on her face leaving no doubt of her opinion of today's rude teenage generation. But Thea had already forgotten her—this time she was not here just to say good-bye to her waterfall for the season. This time she had come for more than that.

The fingers of her left hand had been playing compulsively with something in the pocket of her anorak; now she finally brought it out into the sunshine and held it in the palm of her hand—a small painted charm of a carousel pony. She had hung onto that, in the wake of what she had done that summer, a symbol, a potent reminder of all the things she had fought not to allow to overwhelm her. She had brought it here, to the falls, to the place where she had always found peace—and here she would leave it, and hope that some of the sting would be drawn from it.

She closed her hand into a fist over the charm,

hesitated for a moment, and then flung the tiny painted carousel pony and all its memories with all her strength into the roaring falls. For a moment it caught the sun and glittered with an improbable jewel-like sparkle—and then it was gone, vanished into the white foam.

"Not alone," she murmured. "Just the first."

ACKNOWLEDGMENTS

I am indebted to Ben Crowell, Piret Loone,
Helen Hall, Irina Rempt, Phil Tourigny,
RK Bose, and Ari Nordström—and
their various secondary sources—for their
help with Chapter 5.

My heartfelt appreciation to Ruth and
to Jill, for all that they do.

And, as always,
my thanks to Deck for everything.